THE QUIET SOLDIER: PHUONG'S STORY

Creina Mansfield

University Press of North Georgia
University of North Georgia
Dahlonega, GA

Copyright 2014, Creina Mansfield

All rights reserved. No part of this book may be reproduced in whole or in part without written permission from the publisher, except by reviewers who may quote brief excerpts in connections with a review in newspaper, magazine, or electronic publications; nor may any part of this book be reproduced, stored in a retrieval system, or transmitted in any form or by any means electronic, mechanical, photocopying, recording, or other, without written permission from the publisher.

Published by:
The University Press of North Georgia
Dahlonega, Georgia

Printing Support by:
Booklogix Publishing Services, Inc.
Alpharetta, Georgia

ISBN: 978-1-940771-12-0

Printed in the United States of America, 2014

For more information, please visit: http://www.upng.org
Or e-mail: upng@ung.edu

UNIVERSITY PRESS OF
NORTH GEORGIA

To the memory of Graham Greene, whose work is cherished by many and which has been for me inspirational.

FOREWORD

Readers familiar with *The Quiet American* (1955), Graham Greene's politically-charged novel that anticipates U. S. involvement in Vietnam, will recognize parallels with Creina Mansfield's title: *The Quiet Soldier: Phuong's Story*. Mansfield's novel rewrites the other; readers therefore will see overlap in the plots, with one powerful difference: unlike Greene's novel, Mansfield's provides the perspective of Phuong, the young Vietnamese woman at the center of both stories. It functions as a critique of not only *The Quiet American* but also other of Greene's works. Greene was not known for fully developing strong female characters—*The End of the Affair*'s Sarah Miles is the most notable exception, followed, perhaps, by Aunt Augusta in *Travels with My Aunt*. Greene's female characters generally appear in supporting roles, and some, one might argue, can be taken as caricatures: the superstitious and snoopy Ida Arnold in *Brighton Rock*, the self-indulgent and spoiled Milly in *Our Man in Havana*, the sanctimonious woman at the jail in *The Power and the Glory*.

But this is unlikely a reflection of Greene's views of women, as his interactions with them suggest something more complicated: he associated with intelligent women throughout his life—his wife Vivien, his cousin Barbara, Elizabeth Bowen, his lover Catherine Walston, and others. Perhaps Greene didn't see the problems of the world in terms of gender—though this is too easy an explanation—or that, in spite of his regard for women, he didn't believe that he could develop them as well as he could men. Perhaps he intended Phuong's disposition to remain out of the reader's reach, thereby maintaining the focus on the conflict between Fowler and Pyle. In any event, one observation is clear: Graham Greene created very few fully-developed female characters over the course of a prolific career.

The Quiet Soldier

Likewise, Greene certainly must have cared about the Vietnamese people, but *The Quiet American* isn't about them, and none of his Vietnamese characters play central roles, except Phuong, who is more a prize in the novel than a personality. One of Greene's most important novels, *The Quiet American* concerns the conflicts of western involvement in Southeast Asia in the 1950s. The original story is really about western civilization—western men—fighting out their battles in somebody else's backyard, and they—the Vietnamese people—don't really count for much in terms of being treated like three-dimensional characters. It might be harsh to compare the Vietnamese people in *The Quiet American* to the Africans in *Heart of Darkness*, but that's the parallel that has always come to mind for me: the Vietnamese characters are figures in the plot, not complicated individuals like Fowler or Pyle. Just as Joseph Conrad's text harshly indicts western culture— "all of Europe contributed to the making of Kurtz" (2.29)—so also does Greene's.

In *The Quiet American,* Phuong is a microcosm of the conflicts in Vietnam, as an Englishman and an American—neither of whom can ever fully understand the Vietnamese people—fight for her as a kind of prize, and so she becomes a pawn in the tense clash between Fowler and Pyle.

In *The Quiet Soldier: Phuong's Story*, however, Creina Mansfield develops a Phuong who is a complex character with intelligence, conviction, and courage. And grit. The reader instantly realizes that Phuong is not the meek girl slated to fulfill her older sister's plans to get her married off to any man who will prove a profit to her family. Unlike Greene's Phuong, Mansfield's Phuong has much more on her mind than fixing Fowler's opium pipes and otherwise waiting on him, for this is *her* story, as the title confirms.

It is the mark of the great works of literature—those that have stood the test of time—to resist closure and leave questions unanswered, to leave the reader wondering, to leave stories yet to be told. John Gardner retold *Beowulf* from the monster's point of view, thus adding to the classic myth with *Grendel*. Shakespeare's plays have been continued in retellings: Tom Stoppard's *Rosencrantz and Guildenstern Are Dead* has become its own classic version of *Hamlet*, while Lee Blessing's *Fortinbras* turns the same great tragedy to a comic sequel. More recently, *King Lear* was the inspiration for Jane Smiley's novel, *A Thousand Acres*, set in modern-day

Iowa. Francis Ford Coppola brought Joseph Conrad's *Heart of Darkness* to the screen in a retelling set, interestingly enough, in Vietnam.

And now, Graham Greene is placed in that revered group of writers whose work has been appropriated, revised, rewritten, and adapted as the basis of new literature. With Creina Mansfield's *The Quiet Soldier,* a new dimension is added to Greene's classic novel. But her novel stands on its own as an original work: the comparison to *The Quiet American* is clearly appropriate and necessary, as it comments on the ideas and ideologies of the past, but one can read *The Quiet Soldier: Phuong's Story* apart from Greene's original work. It is moving, a joy to read, and—like Greene's novel—it leaves prospect for the story to continue.

Joyce Stavick
The University of North Georgia
February, 2014

ACKNOWLEDGEMENTS

I would like to thank those who read all or parts of the novel in its early stages. Dr. Ian McGuire and Dr. Howard Booth, and all my compatriots at Manchester University, in particular Dr. Veronica Turiano, were encouraging and supportive. So too was Dr. Neil Sinyard of Hull University and my thanks to Dr. Patricia Dunker for suggesting I extend my use of epigraphs. Surgeon and fellow Greene enthusiast Ramón Rami-Porta very kindly read, commented upon, and corrected a number of details in the chapter where Dr. Tin operates underground.

Thank you to the leading lights of The Graham Greene Birthplace Trust who have encouraged me in my project and to Graham Greene's family for wishing me well in this enterprise.

Especial thanks go to Dr. Joyce Stavick of University of North Georgia for her immediate enthusiasm for *The Quiet Soldier*; without her there would be no book, nor too without the work of April Loebick and all those at the University Press of North Georgia.

To you all, my heartfelt gratitude.

CHAPTER 1

South Vietnam 1967

Phuong sees water spill across the red earth as she pulls herself out of the three-foot tunnel shaft. The fallen rain spreads across the bed of leaves on the forest floor. She feels the water too as it trickles onto her black pyjamas and blots the black and white scarf coiled about her neck. There was a time, her Saigon years, the time of liaisons with journalists and diplomats, when stains would have mattered. Now she fights like those she envied—with knife and gun. It is ten days since she last climbed up to the ground, and she welcomes the sweet dampness, her senses overwhelmed with light and air. She has reached the surface and has found the land under which she has hidden—her land, land of her ancestors and of her birth—to be fresh and crisp in the early morning sun. She blinks in the sunlight as she swiftly pushes the trap door closed and rearranges the foliage on top to conceal the entrance. An American soldier might stride right over it without detecting it. A Vietnamese puppet-soldier would know but walk on: he would not venture down into the dark to have his throat cut by his countrymen.

The scream that has lain within her since the road to Ba Ra rises to her throat. How she would love to let it free, to feel it sail on the wind across the trees, releasing her from her shame.

But she must be silent. She straightens and, with her cherished AK47 slung over her shoulder, runs across the open ground, swiftly putting distance between herself and the tunnel entrance. A soldier, she knows that she must be sacrificed (her great sacrifice already made) rather than endanger the tunnel. Yet the tunnels are not as important as the supplies and material concealed in them. The storerooms house weapons, food, and first aid equipment that were acquired at great cost. Even so, they would be

The Quiet Soldier

abandoned to save the fighting force still below. Her comrades are awake beneath her feet, mending garments or weapons, assembling booby traps and bombs, whispering together. Some, like her, are natives of Cu Chi district, descendants of those who first began to burrow into the strong red earth to evade their French overlords. Some have come from far away to a part of Vietnam that is strange to them, ordered here by their superiors in the north. Although the people of Cu Chi died in great numbers during the struggle against the French, they would have fought for another thousand years to regain their land. Only the land itself is indispensable; it is the essence, to be preserved whatever the cost, nurtured by the blood red water.

She reaches the cover of the trees and crouches, gun ready, listening intently. She hears a rustle amongst the leaves. Someone with greater stealth lays waiting: Kha, her ten-year-old messenger boy.

"Phuong," he whispers, only that he may say her name. Kha's devotion is the closest she will ever be to love now. He thinks her beautiful, though her body has been whittled down to muscle and sinew. Today, her complexion is more pallid than usual because she has lain in the underground hospital for over a week while the injury to her thigh healed. The wound, made with a switchblade, was long and deep. Surgeon Tin took the time to sew the jagged flesh neatly together again with precious cotton thread and the sharpest needle he could find. The neat bluish scar has begun to itch.

Kha looks at her adoringly. The only females he knows are peasants and fighters. All have roughened hands and grimy nails. None wear the *ao dai*. No colorful flowing slit tunics, just shapeless garments identical to the men's. Some have scars and burns, and there are worse wounds he knows, that adults speak of only in whispers. His own mother clawed her way out of the rubble when the B52s came, flying so high they hit without warning. She survived until the thickened petrol, the napalm bombs. Kha saw her burned to oneness with the bodies of his brothers and sister.

He gestures to Phuong to follow him. She smiles, draws close and touches him briefly on the shoulder before they move off together through the trees. The political cadres would disapprove of that touch: it speaks of affection beyond the cause, of a loyalty that might prove awkward or even disastrous were woman or boy to hesitate in abandoning the other in battle. Phuong touches because she is no longer commanded to touch. It is her gift, a sign of freedom that she carries with her as she speeds through the forest where once, when she was Kha's age, she played under the watchful eye of her older sister Lan.

However cautiously Phuong and Kha move, the forest responds to their steps with the hiss of snakes and the flash of wings. They make their way through thick undergrowth to the nearby village. The women have risen and are feeding the livestock. They see Phuong but do not acknowledge her. They do not need to look at her scarf to know she is VC. Phuong is as familiar as the morning sun. They knew her as a child; only her whereabouts in the years after her father's death and Lan's sudden leaving are unknown to them. They avoid eye contact because any hour the Americans might come demanding to know when they have seen *Charlie*. Better to tend the pigs and perfect the art of the blank stare.

Phuong finds the man who goes by the name of Chot and, with Kha waiting outside, receives her orders. Though Chot reveals nothing about himself, she knows from his accent that he is a northerner. He slurs his vowels as Heng used to do, and he reminds her of her Saigon controller in other ways too. He is abrupt and brutal, but his left sleeve hangs empty at his side and she guesses he nurses his grievances until they hurt in the same way that he rubs constantly at the stub of his arm. He cannot like leaving the action to her—today her orders are to lure the enemy into an engagement to delay their assault on the VC stronghold of My Tinh. The intelligence is, as always, detailed. Chot's contacts work within the American base. Last year, an important man visited the base to entertain the young American soldiers. He made one joke that so delighted the VC that many of the barbers, cleaners, and cooks carried it back to the tunnels. As he stood on the stage, the big American said, "We're so close to the fighting we had to give the Viet Cong half the tickets." How they laughed in the tunnels at the notion that they needed tickets.

Chot did not laugh at the joke then, nor does he smile at Phuong now. There is no small talk, no *good luck, comrade*. He refuses to recognize her as a woman or as a fellow human being. She is merely functional; his orders require that tomorrow she stand in the way of American tanks. These rasped instructions are more welcome than endearments. He demands only that she risk her life.

She leaves Kha in the village sharing the villagers' breakfast. She smells the manioc boiling and knows there will be salt and sugar, even sesame seeds to accompany it. They would share with her too, but she will not take from them. She has her daily ration of cooked rice wrapped in a cloth and, anyway, she wants cleanliness more than food. On the outskirts of the village is the lake where water buffalo stoop to drink and by their hooves chickens wander in the mud, seemingly oblivious to the mighty creatures above them. On the far side of the lake is shelter, with trees overhanging the water, their roots twisting and coiling above the shimmering surface. There Phuong discards her clothes and slips in. She dips and glides, then floats on her back. Finally she rises up and walks towards the lake's edge, coiling her hair to squeeze out the moisture. She retrieves her clothes and plunges them in the water, rubbing and squeezing out the worst of the grime and sweat. There's no time to dry them in the sun. She must dress immediately and return to the village for Kha, fresher than she has been for weeks, the thigh wound no longer irritating. She glances at the mottled scar on her arm. The wound was inflicted long ago when circumstances forced her to tend it herself. She covers it with her tunic then picks up the leather strap for her wrist. Replacing it affirms her as a soldier once more, for the crude bracelet is there to enable a comrade to drag her body if she is injured. Maybe it will be to haul her to safety and medical care, but if duty demands, her comrade will pull her out of the way and abandon her. This she knows and accepts. She picks up her rifle and returns for Kha.

He follows her out of the village. She will instruct him on the messages he must carry before the operation begins the following night. They travel through patches of dense vegetation, tall trees, and then through the sharp thick elephant grass taller than them both before they reach a patch of open ground. Phuong sees something glinting in the sunlight. She was about to step on that very spot. She carries the map of the mines in her head and knows there should be none here. It is a pristine Coca-Cola can. Kha prods it gingerly with the sharpened punji stick he carries. He's watched in the workshop as such objects are being booby trapped, but still he's drawn to touch it. His comrades might have laid it there to trick a foolish American, or the beautiful vessel might have been discarded carelessly by the enemy. Phuong has told him that Americans are so rich they can do this, but secretly he wonders why those who have such means need to plague his land. Why do they fight to take Vietnam when they refuse to drink its water? Kha scoops the Coca-Cola can up on the punji stick before

Phuong can stop him. It is empty and, for a moment, he is any boy idling his time in the sunshine, but his face clouds as Phuong grabs the can. The GI who threw it away could be close at hand, and he will not be alone. She pockets the can and gestures to Kha. Alert now, they track the Coca-Cola drinker and his comrades through the disturbed grass.

She senses rather than hears the patrol, and then they come into view. They are intent on their own task. She knows them to be tunnel rats—specialists in finding and destroying the tunnels, but not so expert that one of them has failed and left a trail as obvious as a billboard on a Saigon boulevard. These men are smaller than most Americans, shorter than Pyle and slighter than the blacks that her comrades fear cannot be killed with bullets. They have found a tunnel entrance and the first, a wiry man with red hair, disappears quickly in. Phuong raises her gun. Five men are left on the surface. If her first shot kills one of them (she already knows which will be first, not the one with the sergeant's stripes, but the most dangerous—the murderous looking one) then she has a chance of killing the other four. Kha with his punji stick will be little help unless they meet in close combat. Even then, if they "take the enemy by his belt," Kha will be easily overcome, for the men are small but more powerful than the ten-year-old boy. Killing these men is not her mission. They are a distraction. Chot will be displeased if she fails to carry out her orders tomorrow because she has been injured in this encounter. Yet six men invading the tunnel complex will wreak havoc. She thinks of Ngoc, who had pains yesterday that might be the start of labor. If she has at last taken to bed in the underground hospital, she will be unable to fight. Phuong thinks of her diminutive friend with her rounded belly lying in the chamber hung with American parachute nylon and decides. Kha tries to read her expression, surprised at her inaction. He expected her to fire by now.

Still she waits. Another man eases himself down into the tunnel shaft. Phuong gestures to Kha. Realizing what she means, he tightens his grip on the punji stick. Another GI descends. Phuong mimes to Kha, in case he has misunderstood, but now he shakes his head. She pulls his punji stick from him as the fifth GI, the bulkiest, struggles into the hole. There is only one man left on the surface now, and by chance it is the murderous one, the one with most trophy scalps slung on his belt.

The Quiet Soldier

Holding the punji stick like a spear, Phuong watches as he eases himself into the shaft. When he is shoulder-deep, she rushes forward, silent, implacable, and plunges the stick into the man's gullet. It skewers him, emerging through both sides of his neck. He gurgles first, like a child about to cry, then shrieks and goes on shrieking, clutching at the stick, a terrified cork in the bottle neck of the tunnel complex. His screams alert those he sought to surprise. The Americans' enemies move through the dark towards them, armed and ready.

The other rats hear his screams too. They are trapped, their retreat blocked by their skewered companion. They can escape if they pull him down, killing him in the process. Since he cannot survive, to spare him pain, they should stab him through the heart immediately. While he lives and screams, they are imprisoned in the tunnel. If they choose to kill him, they can come out fighting. One, two might live.

Lying on their stomachs in the long grass, Phuong and Kha wait. She has her AK47 trained on the tunnel entrance to see who might emerge fighting. He remains writhing, so they rise, turning and running until they hear him no more.

They run through the open scrubland and only when they reach the cover of the forest do they slow down. The midday sun shines through the trees, and they stop to rest against a tree trunk. "Why didn't they kill him?" asks Kha, delaying the moment when he must speak of his own failure.

"He's an American, like them. They care for their own." She wishes she could explain their curious caring natures and strange beliefs. The first American she knew wanted to spare even her blushes, believing her to be the delicately brought up daughter of a mandarin from the ancient capital of Hue. This isn't a bit suitable for her, he had objected, as if an entertainment could hurt. From the first, he presumed to know what was suitable. But how can she explain such enigmas to Kha, who found only remnants of his family to bury? She tries, "Each one is precious. They say—an individual. Each American," she amends.

"But he will die anyway," Kha objects. "Slower if they leave him, quicker if they pull on him and stab him. I would stab you," he boasts.

"They do not like to be close to suffering. They inflict pain... differently."

"From airplanes." His nightmares are full of the burning sky.

"Sometimes." She hands him her ivory-handled knife. "Better have this until you can sharpen another punji."

His eyes well with tears. He hates Americans completely and irrecoverably, so why could he not plunge the stick into the man? "Phuong," he asks humbly, "did you always know how to kill Americans?" Her duty is to tell Chot of his failure, and he will be disciplined. His age will not save him.

She gives him a smile. "Don't worry. You did well. I will tell Chot that you found the Coca-Cola can which led us to the rats. Many supplies and fighters have been saved. And no, I did not always know. I could not always do what I do now. I learnt slowly."

CHAPTER 2

We were all living on fantasies.
—Tobias Wolff

Having sent Kha on his way, Phuong enters a small clearing in the forest and crouches, eyes ahead scanning the distance as she feels amongst the fallen leaves. A margouilla lizard scuttles away as she raises a trap door and descends into a tunnel shaft. She is miles from where she emerged into the sunlight that morning. She knows the geography of all eight miles of the tunnel complex and has chosen the location closest to the position where she will launch her attack at dawn. Securing the trapdoor, she crawls along a communication tunnel until she reaches a small enclave big enough for her to stand in. In the darkness, she pulls a grenade from her waistband and waits to see if she was observed entering. The first sign will be a flashlight. Immediately, she will pull the pin and roll the grenade.

Nothing. She replaces the grenade in her belt, turns, and crawls on until she reaches a chamber the size of a small room. In it, she finds three of her comrades still working. By the light of small lamps, they are preparing claymore mines of the very sort she will need tomorrow. As she gently rests her AK47 against the wall, they greet her and exchange news. They have no telephones or other modern method of communication, but throughout their dark day, information has rippled by word of mouth around the complex.

Ngoc has not yet had the baby, though her pains have continued and her commander has allowed her to rest throughout the day. She asked to be allowed to go to the surface for some fresh air but was refused. With patrols known to be about, it was deemed too dangerous. Ngoc might have fooled an American patrol, but if they had a local collaborator with them, he would know just who she was—Ngoc the singer and dancer who entertains her comrades in a cramped cavern, on a bare-earth floor with songs such as *He Who Comes to Cu Chi, the Bronze Fortress in the Land of Iron, Will Count the Crimes Accumulated by the Enemy*. Phuong's informant chuckles, "She is a great one for fresh air, that Ngoc. It is all that singing she does! Let's hope the baby is not so finicky." Giang is an old woman of fifty. With her husband far away in the north in the regular army, she likes to grumble, but her heart is in the right place. She has taken risks to acquire salt to supplement Ngoc's rice diet. Her excitement spills over in her chatter about yet another baby to be born in the tunnels. One of her comrades interrupts to tell Phuong that all five Americans were killed in the first communication tunnel that they entered. Three were dispatched with grenades and two knifed. Good news. They destroyed nothing and yielded valuable resources—flashlights, knives, handguns and, most precious of all—"Two AK47s," she tells her, "returned to us." The rats never take their standard issue rifles into the tunnels, instead trying to confuse by using captured weapons. Phuong and Kha ensured they never got to use them.

"I shall ask if Kha can have one of the knives," says Phuong. "He did well today..." The third comrade, Day, proudly shows her part of the haul that has reached them. Day is a born organizer, a great placer of objects into straight lines and neat rows. Phuong picks up one knife with a bright red handle. To have this one carries a risk, for it is clearly an American product. Whoever has this knife will pay an extra price if they are captured, alive or dead. "I'll take this one," she says, resolving to tell Kha he can keep the ivory-handled knife she gave him. She took it from her first attacker; now, at last, it's time to let it go, and who better to give it to than a boy she wishes was her son? She takes out the Coca-Cola can and hands it to Day. "Here's something else for you to work on." Delighted, Day places it on an alcove shelf. It will be filled with pieces from exploded bombs, TNT and a detonator, and then left where some American soldier will pick it up in a careless, last moment.

She leaves her comrades still working. She must rest, in order to be ready at dawn. There is no hammock for her in this part of the complex. She would not oust one of the other women from her resting place, for she has bathed today and had the added luxury of fresh air. She opens a trap door in the floor of the chamber and descends a further level. There she crawls along another communication tunnel until she finds, as she knew she would, a space hollowed out to the side that is the size of a body. She clambers up and lies on her back, arms folded in front of her. Some movement above sends specks of soil onto her face. She listens for an alarm, her hand reaching for the new knife slung in her waistband, but none comes. She settles again, resisting the temptation to scratch her thigh; the wound has begun to itch again. There, in the red earth, she closes her eyes and waits for sleep.

She wonders where her brother is laying his head this night. It is better not to wish for anything, she knows, but she does wish to see him once more and to know that he is safe. To him she would dare to boast, "Look, I have found my courage." Most of all she would want him to know about Lan and to hear if he has a wife.

Once, she had asked him, "Where do you find your courage?" Nam was born fourteen years before her. Even Lan, ten years her senior, seemed raw and unworldly compared to their big brother, though Lan was a beautiful young lady in charge of their father's household.

Phuong asked him about courage after one of the huge tearing arguments with their father. Phuong and Lan heard him shouting and Nam daring to shout back. That alone had seemed to Phuong to be courageous beyond imagining. To contradict Trung Van Co, official in the French government in Cu Chi district, who had once met the governor-general himself. To yell as Phuong had heard Nam yell, "You don't know what you're talking about! The world is changing. Vietnam is changing and you're too blind to see it!"

Nam was, his father complained, giving up all the advantages of his birth and his intellect. Upon him had been bestowed the honor of a French education. He studied in Paris. No expense had been spared. He was as fluent in English as he was in French (his Vietnamese and Chinese not worth mentioning). He read Western philosophy. He could expect to rise through the ranks of the French civil service further than any Vietnamese before him.

"And I'm meant to be *grateful* for that?" Nam had yelled. "Why shouldn't a Vietnamese advance in his own country? If war comes in Europe—and it will—that will be our opportunity!"

It was one of many bitter quarrels that divided the Trung family and cast a sadness that seemed even greater than when their mother died. Then, their father spoke stoically of her resting peacefully with her ancestors, but his concerns about his son led him to talk of Shame and Disgrace. And, whereas sorrow for their mother receded as the years went by, the trouble with Nam only worsened. Every time he returned home it was clear that he had made a further step along the road to rebellion. He had acquired a further new idea, read another outrageous book, or discarded another vestige of conformity in his dress and manner. He had a perpetual glint in his eye, so that even to walk along the road with him was to meet trouble.

Once he confronted a French policeman beating a peasant and shouted, "What about liberty, egality, fraternity, hey brother?" He shoved the policeman as the peasant scurried away. "Forgotten those?" On that occasion his father's position saved him from jail, but Trung Van Co's French associates stopped calling the young Nam "a boy with promise." He became "a lad with some strange notions." The French governor of the province, himself a graduate of the Sorbonne, honored his subordinate with a visit to his home one day and for his pains was challenged about French rule by the son and heir. The governor had tried to laugh it off. "Voltaire should not be taken too seriously," he said, wagging his finger, but Nam refused to see the joke. As soon as the front door had closed behind him, their father bowing his visitor to his chauffeured car, Nam had called him "a silly pompous French ass."

"If you don't like the French, then why do you keep going back to Paris?" Phuong asked him. To her six-year-old thinking, there was no sense in spending so much time with those who were clearly nasty. Though there were many French in Vietnam, there must surely be even more in Paris, so Nam should stay away from them, as she stayed away from the rough boys in the village who pulled her pigtail if they had the chance.

Nam laughed and stroked her hair when she asked him this. When she thought back to that time, he was always tender, but bitterly so, as if he knew that the family would not stay together and that there were tough times ahead. Each year that he returned from his studies, he teased her less and advised her more. She had a terrible sense of time running out for them. Finally, he explained to her why he ventured to France. "Little sister," he said, "remember this—your enemy is your best teacher."

The year after the provincial governor's visit, things improved for a while, for Nam brought a fellow student home with him. Ngo Quang

Long was, her father said approvingly, "From a fine family. Just the sort of friend your brother should be making. His father is a mandarin in Hue." Quang Long had a fine, handsome face. His eyes were round and his hair luxuriant. He wore Western clothes—light colored linen suits that displayed crisp white collars and cuffs. He had impeccable manners and treated Phuong and Lan with solemn kindness, as if they were fragile and priceless. He and Nam went out most days and sometimes were not even back when their father returned from his duties, which caused him to complain, "I didn't know your brother kept so many acquaintances in this area. I thought he had outgrown us all." But he was cheerful during Quang Long's visit, at least until the final day.

The times Nam and his guest stayed home, they walked in the shade of the trees in the orchards, books in hand, talking and laughing, and when it became too hot at midday, they would discard their clothes and swim in the pond. And those days (there were probably no more than six, but forever memorable) would end in the evenings with the family and Quang Long sitting under a pagoda roof in the gardens and eating a meal that the daughters of the house had helped prepare. Dressed in their finest *ao dais*, the sisters would serve course after course and then, as the servants cleared away, would dance, re-enacting legends of the district. Long particularly was delighted and would guess at the meaning of their movements. "Was that about the neighborhood's guardian spirit? And you Phuong, were you the princess spirited away? I'm glad you were saved!" Later the men would sit and talk, whilst Lan listened intently and Phuong draped herself around her father to be kissed and petted.

After one meal, Quang Long, looking directly at Lan, said, "Lan, that was the best fermented fish sauce I have ever tasted. A man would be a fool to seek anything closer to perfection than that fish sauce." Lan blushed with pleasure while her father beamed indulgently and Nam grinned. Something was happening that Phuong did not understand and knew she should not ask about (being "a matter of great delicacy" as her great aunt would say), not as they sat at the dining table. It seemed rather extravagant praise, even for a good fish sauce. Clearly sauce was more important than she had realized.

So she spoke up and said what was true. "*I* helped make that sauce!" Everyone laughed, as if she had said something very witty, though she was sure she had said wittier things than that. Then Quang Long did the most wonderful, the most terrible thing that he could do. He grabbed her round the waist, scooped her up as if she weighed nothing and sat her on his lap, just as Nam or her father might do. With everyone watching, he kissed her on the cheek. "Little Phuong, how lovely you are." And he smiled across the table at her sister, who smiled back.

In the tunnel sleeping bay, Phuong stirs restlessly, her dreams of the past fighting her future. There should be only tomorrow.

CHAPTER 3

My father was a gentle man who understood life and its values. He taught us how to extract the goods and materials from Mother Earth, and how to preserve the land's fertility after yielding crops, year after year.
—Le Ly Hayslip

For many years, the village of My Tinh was known for its gardens. Two local mandarins vied with each other to produce the most amazing display of delicate flora. One was a specialist at bonsai, in the Chinese style, the other an authority on orchids. On opposite sides of the village, separated by the thatched-roofed dwellings of their poorer neighbors, their dark wood houses faced each other in unspoken, decorous rivalry. The outer perimeter of each establishment was lined with bamboo, palm trees, coconut trees, and bushes to prevent the villagers' pigs, ducks, and chickens feasting on the gardens' produce. Whilst the villagers worked in the paddy fields and tended their mango and pineapple crops, the garden owners refined their art. The bonsai expert pruned the roots and branches of his plants, wrapping their tender shoots until they lignified, smiling to himself as he produced intricate shapes and elaborate meanings. More and more was crafted into less and less.

But his rival answered with color and perfume. In his garden, festoons of purple *dendrobium litiflorum* spun around canes reaching above the height of the tallest man; the speckled yellow *paphiopedilium concolour* hung luxuriantly at shoulder height. Visitors brushed against the jewel-like *cheirostylis cochinchinens*, dizzying with its aroma even before they approached his *pièce de résistance*—an orchid never before glimpsed at such low altitude. Only by traveling to the Highlands could a lover of beauty hope to glimpse the *coelogyne nitida*. He would hazard large gulleys and gorges before he saw its exquisite drooping white flower, splashed with red and gold. It was said that the orchid grower avoided any activity that would warm his hands, so that he might be able to handle his prize without harming its delicate flower.

For many years, the village of My Tinh was known for its gardens. No more. The bonsai are trampled, the orchids crushed. The mandarins are mandarins no longer and their houses long ago became firewood. My Tinh has become a Viet Cong stronghold, its inhabitants notorious for withholding valuable information about enemy movements. Twice attempts have been made to eradicate My Tinh's existence. The whole village was relocated to an area some twenty miles away, but the villagers found their way out of the camps and trickled back to their land. All but the youngest and oldest of the men have been conscripted into the South Vietnamese army, but desertion rates are appalling. They show no great enthusiasm to fight for their Country, let alone die for Democracy. Some, having fought for the Viet Cong, have availed of the offer to rally to the other side. These have been the most disappointing of all. For, when the superior food and conditions provided by the South Vietnamese authorities has restored them to health and vigor, these Railliers return to the Viet Cong, their hearts and minds stubbornly unaltered.

Clouds of dust announce the approach of the American tanks, even before they can be heard, though soon the roar of their engines is like thunder in the rainy season. Crouched in a spider hole, watching them advance, Phuong again wonders at the noise with which they choose to announce an attack. They bring their colossal weapons, but at what cost? Even if she had not reached the village just after dawn and warned the villagers, the phalanx of M113 troop carriers would have announced the enemy's approach. In the village behind her, a few remaining inhabitants scurry about, snatching up their possessions and dragging those too young to walk, before they disappear into the forest or the tunnels. One will stay behind. An old man, who lost his legs in a raid last summer, instructs that he should be placed by the village pig pen. Obediently his daughter hauls him to the spot he has chosen before she turns away mournfully. She takes her child, the old man's only grandson, in her arms and leaves.

Squinting into the dust-filled sunlight, Phuong counts ten armored personnel carriers thundering towards the village. She knows that each one will be carrying an eleven man squad ready to disembark and fight on

The Quiet Soldier

foot. .50 calibre machine guns are mounted on the top deck. She breaks cover and runs towards a tunnel entrance. The leading M113 takes the bait, turning to follow her. Machine gun fire spatters the ground around her as she leaps into a tunnel entrance.

The first claymore mine detonates as the leading M113 rumbles over it. It flips over, spraying those inside with molten fragments. The explosion briefly deafens Phuong, but she is already slithering through the tunnel, in a direction away from the village. Having lured the first M113 to destruction, she sets about the others. She anticipated that, once the first tank was destroyed, those behind it would swing away from what they would assume was a mine field. They have not yet learned that their enemy does not squander resources as recklessly as they do. Had they driven on past the first smouldering M113, they would have found the ground clear. But by swerving away, they drive onto a second mine. The hit is less direct than the first. The explosion blows a hole in the side of the vehicle, sending pieces of metal plate flying high. There are cries from the men burning inside. Fearful of suffering the same fate, men clamber out of the vehicles. Some sit atop, some jump to the ground. Phuong watches until she has a clear view of three soldiers who rush towards their burning comrades. They manage to drag one out and, as they try to douse the flames, she raises her assault rifle and takes two down before retreating below ground again.

Now they are angry. Men who come to destroy are driven to rage by retaliation, and their anger is useful because it will make them careless. Already she hears the machine guns firing randomly. Even the buffalo are not safe from the deadly indignation of men who feel this is not how it should be.

Small earth-falls slow her progress as, subterraneously, she crosses the path of the M113s. As she pokes her head out of the tunnel, she sees that even the drivers are visible, maneuvering their vehicles by using improvised levers connected to the steering and throttle. She cautions herself against staying too long in one place to cut down these sitting targets. However many she kills, some of the soldiers and the tanks will still reach the village. Chot knew this too. Her orders were to delay the assault, giving sufficient time for the political cadres staying in the village to evade capture. Documents have been destroyed, key personnel escaped, and the women and children gone.

She fires at a driver. He is so close that she can read what he has painted on his helmet: *This sucks*. He topples from the M113. Then she feels the blast from a machine gun so near that it deafens her. She is more vulnerable now. As she crawls back through the tunnel complex, she knows that she will not hear if a grenade drops in. Many of the shafts have been exposed by the force of the tanks rolling over them and by the persistent fire from the .50s. She does not fear that these soldiers will descend into the tunnel system. They are all too big. And American tunnel rats, she knows, are exceptional for more than their slightness of build; they can tolerate the encompassing darkness. The men above her, who have arrived in juggernauts, will stay on the surface to wreak what havoc they can.

She risks emerging one more time. The remaining M113s are close to the village now, and the soldiers are using them as cover to approach. She pulls the pin from a grenade and hurls it at the stragglers, not waiting to see whether it hits a target. The earth shakes as she descends again. Now all she can do is wait underground. When her hearing returns, she will be able to detect the surviving tanks retreating. First, she knows, the village will be searched. The soldiers' farewell will be to use their Zippo lighters to burn the thatches.

She descends to a further level of the tunnels and lies down in a sleeping booth much like the one she used the night before. Then, she dreamed about Lan and Quang Long, but now she must go over the details of her ambush. Chot will expect precise details, particularly of weapons destroyed. Three M113s, at least a dozen men killed and as many men injured. Chot should be pleased—if such as he is capable of pleasure. Most importantly, he will expect confirmation that the village was successfully evacuated and that nothing and no one of value has fallen into American hands. To confirm that, she will have to check the village.

She wonders where her brother is at this moment. There is a bigger war up north and has been for years, armies fighting armies. Here, only in the last few years have troops arrived in great numbers. It is possible that Nam is alive and still fighting. The prisons, the journeys, the brutal battles in the Red River Valley—he might have survived them all. She pictures him in a smart uniform, with insignia on his sleeve. He's not like Chot, shabby, hiding like a fugitive, but doing great work openly. Father said Nam was special. Somewhere, in the cool of the northern region, Nam is addressing his subordinates. They listen entranced to his fine, well modulated voice. They love him, of course, for his dignity and dedication to duty. Though they know they should not be impressed by his French education, they are, of course they are! For their commander (General perhaps?) has given up so much to lead them. "He always believed," they tell each other. "When we were still under the French yoke—and then the Japanese—General Nam was already working for our independence." They might even ask themselves—in the gaps in fighting when it is no dereliction of duty to have gentle, familial thoughts, "Does General Nam have a sister perhaps? Of course he will not have seen her for a long time. But he must think of her often. She will be a credit to him."

Some of her hearing has returned, and she also feels the rumble of the M113s as they drive away. Slowly she ascends the tunnel and emerges into the daylight. Dust still lingers in the air, and the heat of the midday sun is supplemented by the burning thatches. Cautiously she approaches the village. The Americans have taken their dead and injured, but the husks of three tanks still smoulder. When they have cooled, the returned villagers will search them for usable items.

In the field she sees three dead buffalo, but the village is deserted. It looks as if there was little for the Americans to find. Finally, there is a body. An old man without legs lies face down, his back ripped open. There are no pigs in the nearby pen, but Phuong guesses why he was put there. Villagers often locate a tunnel entrance in a pig pen, having discovered that Americans are fastidious about searching there. Perhaps his family escaped that way and the old man protected their flight.

The straw in the pig pen looks as if it has been recently disturbed. Phuong wonders whether the Americans found the trapdoor and left a surprise of their own. She will check to see whether the tunnel entrance is now booby trapped. If it is, the body of the old man will be blown sky high when she detonates it, so, shouldering her rifle, she turns him over, ready to drag his body further away. When the villagers come back, they will be able to bury his remains. She looks at his face as it flops over. Is it the smile that is familiar? She knows the look on a dead warrior's face that says *my last duty is done*. But then she looks again. She does recognize him. Her father used to bring her to My Tinh to visit an esteemed friend. Before she can remember exactly, she knows they were happy days. She recalls a fragrance. At first she thinks it is a Guerlain perfume, but such things came later in Saigon; they were unknown to her in childhood.

Then she remembers. The man had a garden. He used to cultivate orchids.

CHAPTER 4

The superior man, when resting in safety, does not forget that danger may come. When in a state of security, he does not forget the possibility of ruin. When all is orderly, he does not forget that disorder may come. Thus his person is not endangered, and his States and all their clans are preserved.
—Confucius

Vietnam, Cu Chi district 1940

What a ceremony it was to be when Lan, eldest daughter of Trung Van Co, united in matrimony with Ngo Quang Long, son of a mandarin from Hue! Co was delighted when the young man formally asked for his daughter's hand in marriage. Mindful of the teachings of Confucius, he was aware that no great store should be set on worldly success and riches. Nonetheless, his heart swelled when he pictured the procession of the groom's family as they received the bride. As custom dictated, the procession would be led by a male representative of the groom's household, a man with a good manner of speaking and of high status in society. Since the father, second in order in the procession, was himself a mandarin, then who might lead the way as a worthy representative of so august a family was a matter of delightful speculation. The young man had been reared in Hue, the magnificent ancient Imperial city, so was it too fanciful to imagine that a member of the royal family might honour them all with his presence?

Co stood in his study, looking out on his formal gardens, and saw himself, in the years to come, welcoming the finest members of Vietnamese society to his *humble abode*. The phrase sent a tingle of alarm through him, for he saw from his window that there was much that was inelegant and untidy about his property. He would have to set his servants to work to ensure that the phrase would be understood as the gracious humility of a superior man rather than an accurate summation of what he had. He clapped his hands to send for Van, his senior servant.

When the old man stood before him, bowing, Co pointed out the window, asking peremptorily, "When were those borders last trimmed? And is that eucalyptus to be allowed to spread in every direction?" Van briefly looked at the offending plants before returning his gaze to the polished floorboards. His master let forth, "The place is a disgrace! Where is the order that denotes harmony? Things have been allowed to slide." At that moment, a cockerel strutted into view, picking his way in front of the house, as if in mocking support of his assertion. "I say again—a place for everything and everything in its place!" Co surprised himself with the force of his irritation; of course the engagement was wonderful news, yet unease niggled away at him. He sat down at his desk and considered its source. Ngo Quang Long was a remarkable young man, personable and charming—in fact, alarmingly charismatic and wont to spout an awful lot of nonsense about reform. His favorite phrase was *the need for change.* For all his fine family and education, he was rather given to fanciful statements on the nature of society, which at the very least might stir Nam up again. At worst he might jeopardize his own social standing and that of those associated with him.

He wished he could discuss such matters with Van, who had lived under his roof for fifty years, but how to explain the strain of the times to one who had never left the village? How could Van be aware of the tumult in Vietnam or in the wider world? He knew the seasons, good harvest and bad, nothing of the war in Europe, how France herself was threatened by her old enemy, Germany, and that her loyal colonies would be called upon to send resources to protect the Mother country. There were no words to explain to Van that men of good sense were frantically applying themselves to their duties and praying that the storm would pass.

Co looked up at the abject figure before him, his tone mellowing as he said, "You've all had a great deal to do lately, what with our guest, but see to it that the gardener cuts back those plants. And do something about the altar cloth at the shrine. It's threadbare."

Van raised his eyes and nodded obediently.

Co sighed, "Ah, how much my wife and yours are needed now!" Van's wife had tended Co's in her confinements and in her final appalling illness. She had been wet nurse to Phuong, dying when the girl was just a few years old.

Van spoke for the first time. "They would have enjoyed planning Miss Lan's wedding. Remember how much time they spent sewing? They wouldn't have been content until the bride was wearing the best *ao dai* ever seen in Cu Chi!"

"I have instructed that it is to be of the finest silk," Co boasted. "Red and beautifully embroidered with the imperial symbol of the phoenix. And the outer cloak will be even more extravagantly decorated. Of course she'll wear a *khan dong* as high and flamboyant as anything ever seen around here. I often wonder why brides don't get headaches from balancing those on their heads!"

"It will be a great occasion," said Van.

"Without doubt," agreed Co, full of doubt even as he said it. Why did he suspect that he was the chief dreamer, that the young people themselves were curiously detached from the wedding arrangements? Even at dinner the other night, they had preferred to talk politics rather than of processions and ceremonies. Nam and Long had discussed whether the French could withstand the Germans, almost as if they relished the chaos they anticipated. Long had said that France was weak because there were Frenchmen in positions of power who sympathised with fascism against communism. That France would *fall*. Co shuddered as he recalled Long's words. What sane man would stand in the path of the hurricane? Such pronouncements would be worrying if they were not uttered by a scion of so noble a Vietnamese family. His remarks were not just immature; one could, one *had* to forgive the idealism and impetuosity of Youth, but from another mouth they would be... unwise. More than unwise, revolutionary, the sort of rubbish that Nam spouted before he came to his senses.

"I rejoice that my daughter has found a husband of worth," said Co. "One who pleases her as she is duty-bound to please him." Van knew better than anyone that Co's wife had given him little joy. Why she had irritated him so continually was now obscure. Her slender body and delicate features had not been framed for blows. She had been obedient and meek enough, uncomplaining too, but he had often felt the need to shout, curse, and hit. She had absorbed pain like a sponge; she had drawn suffering to her.

"They seem well-suited," Van assured his master.

Co nodded in agreement. He dismissed Van and stayed in his study. Memories had only deepened his unease. He did not wish his daughter to marry as harsh a man as he had been in his impatient youth. Something had indubitably changed since the engagement. Though Long and Nam still spent most days out and about, and though they often returned when the household had retired for the night, to be in the presence of the betrothed couple was to be conscious of a power more heady than any fragrance, more irresistible than any decree. There was no *touching*, of course, nor even attempts to touch. Such attempts, Co conceded to himself, would have been almost forgivable, for though his daughter's virtue was beyond question, as had been her mother's, he remembered the frustrations of his own engagement and would have forgiven his illustrious son-in-law to be a few surreptitious kisses and even an embrace or two.

Unless, of course—here was a concrete worry to fix on—more was going on than he realized. Could it be that the young couple were more cunning than he had imagined? Any fool could see that they were smitten with each other. The most trifling observation from Long was received by Lan as if it were from the Master, Confucius himself.

Co found his unease taking the shape of reflections on the lustfulness of young men and the naivety of well brought up young girls. He remembered his own crafty maneuvers. A walk in an orchard. *Let me pick you some fruit from this tree*—an arm brushing up against a soft breast. A confused apology to cover his quickened breath—*I'm so sorry*. Seizing of the hands, then a small body pulled towards him. A battery of kisses, an artful pressing of fragile hips against his tautened form. In his younger days, he had plucked a great deal of fruit.

Clearly he was missing something. Perhaps these protracted days, when Nam and Long journeyed who knows where to see heaven knows who, were nothing more than a sham. Supposing that as soon as he had departed to pursue the many tasks associated with administering the district (tasks that were becoming increasingly difficult, because nowadays, it seemed, under every stone, there was a subversive), his son and his friend returned to his house? *We won't go gallivanting today. Far better to stay here with you*. Nam would not protect his sister's honor. A bride's virginity was, no doubt, one of the many traditional standards he thought out of date. Furthermore, lascivious young men enjoy the conquests of their fellows; knowing it was being done nearby carried some of the pleasure of doing it. Lan would not be able to resist Long, with his elegant manners, fine Western clothes, and bedroom eyes. *Let us walk in the orchard. Let me pick you some fruit from this tree...*

Co decided that he must act. An occasional kiss and a cuddle before the wedding was one thing, but now he saw that debauchery was taking place under his roof, or rather, amongst his trees. He resolved to stop it. He could not stay home, as his duties were becoming more onerous every day. As well as his habitual tasks, he was aware that his superiors planned some drastic security maneuvers in the district. A friend or two had hinted at matters that went as far as provincial governor level. Some of those wretched trouble makers were in for a shock.

Co pondered. He could not be in two places at once. Even if he did delay his departures or return unexpectedly, it would not be enough. He needed a second pair of eyes. He needed a spy.

He called Phuong to his study. Since the engagement, she had been subdued, which Co understood as the effect of contemplating the loss of the sister who mothered her. Lan would depart, as custom required, to become part of her husband's family.

"Phuong," her father said, "this is a happy time for us, is it not?"

Phuong nodded. "Yes, a happy time, a wedding... the happy couple."

Co was unsure how to proceed. How could he broach with a daughter the subject of sex when his very point was that daughters should know nothing of such matters? If only the veil of ignorance could be lifted just briefly and then dragged firmly down again. "Yes indeed," he tried. "Your sister is about to be married into a very fine family, the Ngos. We Trungs are, of course, a very fine family too, but the Ngos, well, they are *aristocrats*. This is all the more reason why the wedding must not be... anticipated. Phuong," he said gravely, "have you seen any signs that Long and Lan have anticipated their wedding?"

Phuong nodded. "Yes."

"In the orchards?"

She shook her head.

"Where?" cried Co, feeling the sweet indignation of confirmed fears. "Surely not in my house?"

Phuong nodded.

"When was this?" he demanded.

"Now," she answered quietly, alarmed by her father's tone.

Co leapt up. Outrage took him as far as his study door, before he paused. He had seen Lan sitting quietly by herself in the garden, reading a book, and Long and Nam were making one of their mysterious visits. He took Phuong by the shoulders, "Anticipated in what way my child?"

Phuong shook as she answered. "They have prepared the garments. His and hers."

"Ah, I see." He smiled at the confusion even as he felt a lingering unease. He looked at Phuong's solemn expression and drew her to him. She was a serious one, perhaps because she had her older brother and sister leading her out of childhood too quickly, or maybe because she had inherited her mother's sombre view of the world. He hugged her. "You are a good little girl." What a fragile little bird she was! He wanted to tell her not to worry, that life would be kind to her and that she would gain her heart's desire.

But she was too much like her mother for him to do that. He thought again of the woman he had courted, his dead wife, mother to his three children, and how he had always intended, one day when he had fewer cares, to love her.

He could only caution their young daughter in the hope of protecting her from the vicissitudes of fate and the exploitation of rapacious men. "Listen and watch, my little Phuong, listen and watch."

CHAPTER 5

In what way is a man's true character hidden from view?
—Confucius

    On what was to be Long's final day as his guest, Co knew that etiquette required he stay home. Nam had left on another unexplained trip, though he knew his friend was about to depart for Hue, in order to prepare his own household for the arrival of a wife. Co, therefore, would have to show how things should be done and so, despite pressing matters concerning the administration of the district, here he was roaming amongst the trees, quietly reflecting to himself in the morning glow and fanning away the wasps that busied themselves nastily around the fermenting fruits. Lately, in any spare moments he could squeeze from his busy days, he found that he was drawn to the orchards. He noted that the young people were still in the house, despite the increasing heat of the day. Phuong was never far from the engaged couple nowadays, and Co was pleased that she was following his instruction to watch them, although she was a poor informant, for she rarely said a word.
    The wedding ceremony itself was only three weeks away, the red silk *ao dai* and *khan dong* now complete. Now at last, to his satisfaction, he detected signs of alarm in the young bridegroom, which was just as it should be. However grand his family might be, however extensive the Ngo properties in that wonderful city, to take on the responsibility for the comfort, security and general wellbeing of another person was more than onerous; it was a trifle awesome. A certain agitation—sweaty palms, an anxious peering round corners and hesitation to enter or leave a room—was only to be expected. Co was quite delighted when he noticed that Long had also developed a nervous tic by his left eye. Lan's future happiness seemed guaranteed by such evident conscientiousness.

She would be happy, but far away from Cu Chi. She would bid farewell to all that she had known—the elegant, dark wood house, the surrounding garden and orchard and the shrine to her ancestors, which had formed her daily existence since her birth seventeen years before. All would be but memories. Most of all, she would be separated from those she had loved and tended. Despite her good looks—her pale skin and delicate oval face epitomized beauty—Lan was not vain or self-absorbed. She was a capable young woman who had helped maintain his home ever since she had had to step into her mother's shoes. He had no worries on that score. She would attend to her wifely duties diligently and would carry her exalted rank with modesty. Already her devotion to Long was apparent. She would follow him through thick and thin. There would be no *thin* of course, but for form's sake, it had to be said. No man wanted a fair-weather wife. The women of Vietnam were renowned for their loyalty and Lan, her father saw, would be ferociously so. When he visited the Ngos (royal circles, no less!) he would have to be careful about how he reacted when Long began talking about "the need for change," for the balance of... not power, for he would always be the elder... the obligation to respect would have shifted. He saw himself sitting as honored guest in the rich surroundings of a Hue mansion as Long indulged in his idealistic ramblings. He would remain graciously silent, to show his daughter that she should revere every word that came out of her husband's mouth, however foolish, just as his wife would have done had he ever been less than wise.

Co hoped that Nam's absence did not mean that he was being drawn into some attachment with a girl from a local family. With Long as his brother-in-law, he would have every opportunity to marry well. And how typically thoughtless to be away from home as his friend was about to depart! Manners were all the more important in these troubled times. They were the fabric that held society together. Friendship did not excuse such informality.

This family event had wider consequences that a man capable of strategy should consider. With Lan gone, the house would be without a mistress. The servants were well and good, but a wise man would not leave the ordering of his household to the paid help. He would soon find the best of his possessions scattered on the other side of the village. Phuong was clearly too young for such responsibility. She had some years of schooling to

The Quiet Soldier

complete, and he was no minor official who needed to curtail his daughter's education and matrimonial chances by prematurely imposing such duties upon her. Was it not time for him to take another wife?

Ideally, he should seek out a capable woman who would care for his household and be a mother to Phuong. His little bird needed a female confidant, someone less oppressive than his sister, whose sense of family duty was exemplary, but, he had to admit, she was not the most perceptive of women. He blanched at the thought of an increase in her extended visits. She would shower Phuong and himself with fatuous advice, take credit for all that went right while volubly blaming him for anything that went wrong. Co fanned the wasps away with irritation as he planned his future.

When they all traveled to Hue in a few weeks time, he could cast his eye amongst the unattached women of the Ngo family. He might find a young widow or some unfortunate woman with a squint and no flesh on her bones. But no, he need not settle for second best. With his fine house and status in the district, he could dare to hope for a fresh young bride to breathe new life into his existence. This time, he would be kind and patient.

Cries from the servants shook Co out of his reverie. He heard the sounds of breaking bamboo and thought with annoyance that once again his neighbor's buffalos had smashed through his fences. The gardens would be trampled, the laying hens alarmed, and the cook in tears. He did not run as he left the orchards. Already he saw himself calming his own servants and admonishing his neighbor's, and so restoring order through sensible application of his authority. But when he came into the courtyard, he saw with incredulity that a Sûreté agent stood in front of the house, barking orders at a dozen uniformed men, some of whom were training their guns on his house, while others were charging into it.

"What is happening here?" he demanded. He recognized the man for a notorious Métis, embittered by his French father's abandonment of him, who relished every opportunity to make it clear that he was no mere native. Ignoring Co, he shouted orders at his men as they searched the house. Co moved forward when he heard crockery breaking and shrieks from his cook, but the agent barred him with his stick.

"I will not be prevented from entering my own house!" protested Co, pushing aside the stick. A rifle butt jammed into his stomach, and he found his arms pinioned behind him.

"Shut up, old man," ordered the agent, as Co regained his breath and started to protest again. Undaunted, Co was about to threaten the agent with the wrath of his superiors, when he heard gunshots coming from his house. He broke away and moved as fast as he could towards his house. This time it was the agent's stick that felled him. He crumpled on his knees, bewildered as the Sûreté agent towered officiously over him, looking with triumph as Long was dragged out the doorway by two soldiers. Blood trickled from a wound to his left cheek.

"Stop!" rasped Co. "Do you know who you have there?"

The Sûreté agent swaggered closer. "I do. The question is, do you?"

"This man is Ngo Quang Long, son of a mandarin from Hue!" cried Co.

"He is a professional agitator, for all that," the agent sneered. "And he goes by many aliases. Where is your son, old man?"

Co scrambled to his feet. "My son has nothing to do with this."

The agent snapped, "He has everything to do with it. Either you are a fool or you're an agitator too."

"My son is a graduate of the Sorbonne. He is the future of our country," Co answered.

The agent bristled, "He is a Communist. He's suborning peasants all across the district. He's recruiting every malcontent he can find. And this is another of them." He used his stick again, this time raining blows on Long's shoulders. Long collapsed with scarcely a sound. It was his self-imposed silence that, for Co, confirmed the agent's accusations. Long's elegant Western clothes were crumpled and blood-soaked, his round eyes suffused with pain, but what had changed most about him was his manner. Prison or worse lay ahead of him, but he did not deny what for him were not accusations but achievements. A mask had slipped and what radiated from him was an awesome determination. He had prepared for this.

Co thought, he will die for his cause.

The agent shouted at Long as he was forced upright by two soldiers. "Where is Trung Huu Nam? Come now, surely you want some company in your prison cell?"

"He is not part of this. I scarcely know these people," Long answered dismissively.

Co looked about him. Four of his servants cowered as the soldiers' rifles were trained on them. The fifth, his cook, had a wound to his shoulder as he was dragged from the house. Van and his daughters were missing. He watched as the soldiers continued to search the house and its grounds. He stayed quiet, waiting for them to discover Lan and Phuong in some hiding place, but finally the soldiers returned without them, though not empty-handed, for they pillaged as they searched. One had already cut the throats of the cockerel and a chicken and was wearing them hanging from his belt, the blood dripping onto his uniform. Another carried out Lan's wedding *ao dai* and *khan dong* in grubby hands. But when Co saw the silver candle-sticks from the shrine to the family's ancestors being carried out, he protested, "This is sacrilege!"

"This is what you get for associating with revolutionaries," the agent said, indifferently. "You have two daughters. Where are they? Or do you allow them to wander wherever they choose?"

"Wherever they are, they are better off than watching this," said Co as Long and the cook were hauled away. A trail of dust lay behind them as their feet dragged pathways to a waiting vehicle.

The agent came close to Co and said, almost gently, "You know, even in the best families, there are black sheep. You'd do yourself some good by turning them in."

Co suppressed the trembling of his limbs as he replied, "Black sheep there may be in your family. There are none in mine. Those men are your prisoners. Treat them as you should. If I hear that they have sustained further injuries, then I shall speak to your superiors. Remember who I am."

The agent laughed insolently as he gestured to his troops to follow him. "Do you think that matters to me, you old fool? You've been harboring a professional agitator that we've been tracking for months. He's corrupted half the peasantry in this god-forsaken place. Where he's going, he'll pray for death, and you'll be lucky if you don't join him there."

Trung Van Co gasped. His world was crashing down when, moments before, he had feared only the collapse of fences he had watched Van and Sinh build.

CHAPTER 6

If one learns from others but does not think, one will be bewildered. If, on the other hand, one thinks but does not learn from others, one will be in peril.
—Confucius

Darkness came. Co was alone, save for the four servants who had witnessed the Sûreté raid. Lan and Phuong were still missing, as was Van. When the agent and his soldiers left, the master of the house stood in the courtyard, staring after them. He was as still and quiet as Ngo Quang Long when he was dragged from the house, transformed from the son of a mandarin from Hue into the agitator Long, the prisoner Long. The servants had already begun to set the place to rights as best they could. The bamboo fences were repaired, and the remaining poultry chased and caught. When it had become too dark to work in the grounds, they lit the lamps and went indoors, while Co remained gazing into the distance. He was a vain man and one too prone to value his possessions and his position in society, but in the miserable, shame-ridden years that lay ahead, he never doubted he had made the right decision in protecting his son. In his shattered world, it gave him faith that, in a crisis, he knew where his loyalties lay. He hoped to goodness that his children knew that too.

The tabernacle was restored and the altar tidied. Then the furniture was righted and smashed crockery swept away. Only when the blood-stained floorboards were scrubbed clean did they send for him. "Master, come inside. You'll catch your death out here," his servant chided. "They've gone now. They won't be back...Not yet at any rate."

Co caught the allusion to his son. "Nam," he said, "if he returns..."

"He won't." It was said with certainty.

Co lifted his arms despairingly. "How did this all happen?" he cried.

The Quiet Soldier

With solemn literalness, the old servant began telling Co what had occurred as he wandered outside that morning, dreaming of a new bride. "The young people were in the reception room—all three of them, little Phuong too. I was clearing away the breakfast things, when suddenly Miss Lan said, 'There's someone out there.' He was brave then. Her fiancé, I mean. He took out his revolver..."

"He had a gun!" Co exclaimed. He pictured Long in his elegant linen suits. How easy, he realized, to reach into a Western-style jacket and pull out a weapon. How much he had missed.

"He took out his revolver and said to me, 'I'll hold them off. You take Lan and Phuong to safety.' He knew, you see. He knew they had come for him."

The servant spoke with such sadness that his master looked at him as if for the first time. For years, there had been talk of ordinary working people being recruited by the communists, but he had always felt such rumors were exaggerated. Communists were wild-eyed fanatics, weren't they, hiding out in the jungles and the hills, occasionally swooping down to inflict atrocities on the population? Was it possible that domestic servants and peasants stooping in the fields had heard an attenuated echo of communist dreams? He recalled that, a few years before, this servant had learned to read. Co had briefly wondered why he had wasted his spare time on acquiring a skill so unnecessary for domestic duties, but now he considered who might have encouraged and taught him. When Nam used to return from his studies in Paris, full of wild ideas of national freedom, his father's greatest fear had been that he would spoil his chances of getting a job in the civil service. It had never occurred to him that theories and dreams—new *ideas*, would impinge on others around him. Only yesterday, he had thought of communists with dread. Could it be that he lived among them?

There would be time enough to adjust to this new reality. The future was not to be consumed in wedding processions and mixing with the aristocracy.

"Where are my girls?" Co cried.

"Van took them to safety. He will return soon. Master, why don't you rest?"

As if he were a child, Co let himself be led into the house and put to bed. In the darkness and the quiet, he thought back over the events of the day. That vile Sûreté agent had called him a fool. There had been no respect, not for his property or his person. He was just another native to be pushed around. His years of service to the state counted for nothing. When Nam had warned him of such things, he had not listened. Where was Nam now? He might already have been arrested. Long would be interrogated about his friend's whereabouts. Co prayed that he did not know, for torture could weaken the firmest resolve. He shuddered as he thought that the punishment for such crimes was the guillotine.

He slept fitfully, jolting awake as he was gently shaken. Co jumped up. "Where are my girls? Are they safe?"

They are safe," he was assured. "Though Miss Lan must get away from here."

Co considered this. So his daughter *knew*. She had knowingly become engaged to a communist. She knew what she was marrying into and the risks she was taking. His older children had brought violence to his home. The house was probably being watched now! He knew how they operated, those bastards. He had approved of strong-arm tactics in the past, but had not thought of himself—or those he loved—on the sharp end of the stick.

If his children were safe, he could bear all the rest. He saw that Disgrace had come to the Trungs. He would be flung from his office like a messy gizzard thrown from the kitchen to be devoured by swine. "How," he asked, "how did you manage it? How did they escape from the house?"

"There are the tunnels... We have an entrance..."

"On my property!" exclaimed Co. Like every inhabitant indigenous to Cu Chi, he knew that the earth of the region was remarkably suitable for tunneling, and, as an official in the colonial government, he had heard rumors of tunnels being extended by the insurgents. The authorities, himself included, considered them typical of the sneaky, underhand methods of those who sought to destroy French Indochina. Burrowing away like moles, instead of fighting like men. Now he was thankful that such tunnels existed, for they sheltered his own girls. He tried to picture them. He saw them cowering, hungry, cold, and frightened. They would have heard the gunshots as they were spirited away. They would not know whether Long had been shot dead as the soldiers burst in. Lan would have understood some of what was happening, but for little Phuong there would have been only terror and confusion.

The Quiet Soldier

Co yearned for the events of the day to disappear, to return to his dreams of a splendid wedding. What a ceremony it was to be when Lan, eldest daughter of Trung Van Co, united in matrimony with Ngo Quang Long, son of a mandarin from Hue. "Could it all be an error?" he asked. "Mistaken identity perhaps. That agent is known as a hot-head."

"No mistake. Master, we've found Sinh's body. They tortured him."

Co sunk down at the news about his cook. "Sinh! He has been with me since he was a boy! What did they want with him?"

"They wanted to know how to get into the tunnels. He would not tell."

His cook had known what he did not. Co realized that he himself had lived only on the surface. Secrets had been kept from him because his own loyalties had been in question. Perhaps, only when the Sûreté agent had demanded to know where Nam was, had they known for sure which side he was on, because only then had he known himself.

"I must see Lan," he said. "Will you take me to her?" He asked with some humility, aware he could not command in this matter.

"Van will come soon," he was assured.

But it was dawn before Van returned alone. "Where are they?" Co demanded, placing his hands on his diminutive servant's shoulders.

"Safe—but it's unwise for Miss Lan to return. Come." Van led his master through the formal gardens, enveloped in the morning mist. Dew lay on the grass and he smelt the sweet aroma of lilies as he trod them underfoot. How innocuous the unruly plants seemed to him now! Co and Van skirted the orchards and went round behind the piggery. Even the swine seemed disturbed by events of the day before as they squealed and grunted, butting their heads against the wattle fencing. Lan appeared quietly from behind a small outbuilding and Van moved away.

"Father!" She bowed to him formally, her arms folded, as in apology.

Co reached forward. He drew her near and looked down into her beautiful tear-streaked face. She smelt musty, like damp earth. He shook her forcefully. "What have you been up to? Do you know what you have done? They've ransacked the house, did you know that?"

"Times are changing, Father."

He let her go before he rattled her teeth from her jaws. "Oh, I've heard it all before! *The need for change!* Why couldn't you be content to marry and settle down?" What a ceremony it was to be when Lan, eldest daughter of Trung Van Co, united in matrimony with Ngo Quang Long, son of a mandarin from Hue! "Why couldn't you and Nam just be good Vietnamese?"

"We are, Father, we are. We see a different Vietnam." Though Lan spoke gently, her words shocked him, for he had based his life on the belief that truth and honor lay in the past and that the future could do no better than imitate it.

"Then you are rejecting me and all I have stood for! Are women to be like you in the future then—harsh and duplicitous?"

"Father, forgive me," she said. "I hoped to be all that you wished me to be, but believe me, this is my destiny. If Long lives, we will be married one day."

He tried to dissuade her. "We will say that you knew nothing, that he deceived you. They dragged him away as if he were a common criminal."

"I know. They will not believe that I knew nothing. For Phuong there is a chance here. She is still a child. We have tried to protect her, but I will be arrested, if only to pressure Long and to get to Nam. Your position in the district has given us a little time, but that is all. Father, I must go now. I put others in danger by delaying."

"Where will you go? How will you live?"

"There is an organization, Father. I will be part of it. If Long survives interrogation, then they will send him to the Ba Ra penal camp in Thu Dau Mot province, north of Saigon. I will stay close by, but it is better you do not know exactly where I am."

Co marveled at the way his finely reared young daughter could speak of interrogation. Only yesterday he had been planning a prestigious marriage for her. Now, she was going out into a dark, dangerous world, which she seemed to understand better than he. She would be hiding in tunnels, running in the dark from rough men who sought to do her harm.

She turned to go. Co reached for her and swung her roughly towards him, as if pulling her back to the safety of his world. Van stepped forward. "You have to let her go! Send her with a blessing!"

Co sighed. He kissed Lan on the forehead and said, "I haven't read those new works that you have put your faith in. I know only the ancient teachings, so I say to you, *Wheresoever you go, go with all your heart.*"

As she walked away, Co let his tears flow. Only when she was gone did he ask, "Where is Phuong? I cannot lose all three children in one day!"

Van answered, "Phuong will be home soon. Don't be concerned. She cried, mostly for Long, and she worries about Nam, of course, she always does. But we comforted her. She asked what would happen to Long. I told her that they will interrogate him, but that he is prepared for the struggle. Nam may be safe, though none of us shall see him, perhaps for a long time."

"So now I have only my silent little bird!"

"She is being looked after by those who are my comrades—your friends too at such times. I left her in a tunnel. Don't be alarmed. She is sleeping more soundly than she has done for ages. I think she likes it down there."

CHAPTER 7

In actual fact, Vietnamese peasants and workers were not sitting around waiting for landlords and businessmen to experience a moral awakening.
— David G. Marr

February 1945

"You are growing beautiful," her father said. The words were uttered sadly, for ever since that distant day five years before when Long had been arrested, when Lan and Nam fled, Trung Van Co viewed both assets and deficiencies with a jaundiced eye. What he had lost, he lamented, and what he still possessed, he worried that he might lose. That Phuong was becoming as fine-looking as her sister was to be regretted, because all hopes of a good marriage were gone, and Beauty would be preyed upon. The unguarded flower would be violated by a wayward bee. Already some of the young men of Cu Chi eyed his fourteen-year-old daughter with desire. Those that he had overheard call her comrade were scrupulous in avoiding lascivious looks. Perhaps they were men of iron, who had conquered such base cravings. All he knew was that his younger daughter, who had barely spoken for a year after Lan's flight and Nam's disappearance, was most content when she associated with those who knew the tunnels, and so he turned a blind eye to her mixing with such dangerous companions.

Through the tunnels news of Long filtered back some months after his arrest. He had survived interrogation and had indeed been taken to Ba Ra penal camp, as Lan had anticipated. She lived somewhere near the prison and was known to be part of a group that petitioned for the release of political prisoners. When the Japanese swept into the country, they had hoped that they would pardon those who had opposed the French, but the administration had been left in Vichy hands, and Long and his comrades still languished in their cells.

Phuong accepted her father's remark without comment, aware that it was a lament rather than a compliment. She had entered the study where he spent most of his weary days, though the room was now denuded of books. The shelves had been emptied, along with the best of the furniture in the house, to pay taxes that were demanded as soon as Co lost his position in the district bureaucracy. He had been stripped of his title, robbed of his possessions and denied an income. The provincial governor no longer stopped by. Stooped and shabby, Co had been gazing out at the tangle that had once been his garden as Phuong entered. "The times have not been kind to our master," the servants were wont to say, but they stayed on nonetheless, though there was precious little left for them to tend.

They remained until the famine came. The French tricolor still flew in Vietnam, but it was the Japanese who now called the shots and, to feed their great war-machine, they had decreed that crops other than rice should be grown. That had plunged the country into shortages, which were bad in the south, even though rumor had it that northerners were faring much worse. It was not just the peasants who felt perpetually hungry. Everyone, except those who wielded the big cudgels, spent their waking hours searching for food and their sleeping moments dreaming of it. The rounded stomach that Co had carried before him with pride was gone, his traditional robes hanging loose on his wasted body. Phuong's skin stretched taut across her cheekbones, threatening her insipient beauty. Even the laying hens had been slaughtered and eaten, for it was impossible to think of tomorrow when today's need was so great.

Eventually the servants had departed in distress, to fend for themselves, knowing that Co had no further largesse to bestow. Even Van had gone, though he was still close at hand. Within a week of the servants going, Co had found a small cache of grain left on his doorstep. Then it was his turn to weep, for he had no doubt that it was one of his former employees who had returned surreptitiously with the gift. When he later heard that a band of forty men and women with firearms, identifying themselves as the new revolutionary organization known as the Vietminh, had broken into the nearby grain store at Ben Suc and made off with its contents, he wished that there had been more for them to steal.

"Father, come and eat," Phuong coaxed. "We have some food." The grain had long gone, and they had not had rice for weeks, but she had found some manioc to boil. The last of the salt had been eaten, but if they could force it down, it would give them strength. Listlessly, Co followed her.

She led him out into what had been the garden. It was a warm night and the house was stifling. The pagoda had fallen into disrepair, but they sat at the table where once Ngo Quang Long, son of a mandarin from Hue, had sat as honored guest.

In the crumbling ruins of the garden, stripped of all that was edible, father and daughter inhaled the bitter-sweet aroma of remembrance. As soon as they had eaten their meagre fare, they would begin, as ever, wondering what their loved ones were doing at that moment. Nam especially was a concern, for though Lan would be suffering many privations as she worked for Long's release, they knew her to be among her comrades. The authorities harried them, but they remained resolute. Occasionally a message of reassurance reached Cu Chi.

It was a marvel how such news came. The messenger might be a man, woman, or child, sometimes a stranger, sometimes as familiar as the morning sun. A child tugging at Co's sleeve would repeat, as he bent down, "Your friends say they are well and that they love you as they love their country," running away before a startled Co could straighten his aching limbs. In adults, Co and Phuong came to recognize a certain air of cautious intensity and would make sure they could be alone with the messenger. "Those who have traveled far greet you, honored father and sister." Co relished such messages, which were more precious than rice, but so much did he yearn for news that he began to fancy everyone was a carrier. Strangers calling at the once grand house, hoping for some scraps, would be unnerved by the immoderation of the old man's greeting and baffled by the repeated question, "You have news for us?" Phuong knew that caution was required, for some of the strangers could be Sûreté spies and even those they knew might be informants. The French were growing edgier, determined, if the Japanese left, as surely they must, to maintain their hold. Their network of informants was vast. People were not always what they seemed, she was learning.

There had been no message since the monsoons. Co and Phuong feared that Long might have succumbed to the harsh conditions of Ba Ra. The prisoners were fed only with what their friends could provide for them, and with times so hard, that was precious little. Lan's messages had never contained allusion to her brother, which was evidence of sorts that he had not been arrested. He had escaped, maybe to the north, where the movement was strong, though the famine more acute. It was too far away for any news to reach Cu Chi, where those who loved him waited.

Co looked up at the clear evening sky. "It will be cold in the north," he said, though he himself had never traveled as far.

"What do you think Nam is doing tonight, father?" Phuong prompted. He liked to daydream, and she liked to listen. Weeks before, at Tet, when the new year should have been welcomed in with solemnity, gaiety, and hope, there had been little celebration in the depleted Trung household, but father and daughter had observed the tradition of remembrance with relish. And out of remembrance, hope renewed. Though each kept the thought to themselves, both nursed a dream that those who had left their lives so abruptly would return one propitious day with equal suddenness.

"Busy, of course he'll be busy," Co began, weaving his tale out of the finest spun silk, cherished memories of his only son. "He always wrote so well, his teachers never tired of saying so. I think he will be employing that gift. His words will be chosen to awaken those who sleep under the colonial yoke, as I once slept." How bitterly Co resented his former colleagues avoiding him after Long's arrest. "When, in August 1940, Huynh Phu So predicted the imminent humbling of the French by the Japanese, the Sûreté put him in a psychiatric ward! But who was mad? Not he! These Hoa Hao knew which way the wind was blowing."

"But what of Nam, father?" Phuong urged, to deflect his angry reflections.

"Tonight he will be completing a piece he has written for his underground newspaper. He will be working late at his desk, his eyes straining a little perhaps, for kerosene is difficult to come by, even for a man such as Trung Huu Nam. But those around him will ensure no harm is done to his eyesight. He will have many devoted companions, so much so that he often wishes for a little solitude. Like Ho Chi Minh himself, he places duty first. He will work well into the night, choosing his words. Fine words." Co faltered. In the gloom, he thought he saw a human shape. In alarm, he looked across at Phuong, but her place at the table was empty. "Phuong? Is that you?" There was no answer, and now Co could see neither his daughter nor the shadow. "You have news for us?" he asked the darkness.

Then a figure that could be Nam appeared before Trung Van Co. His face was obscured, but he had the same bearing, that unmistakable mark of the man born to lead. Co tried to smile, though his face was unresponsive to the joy brimming inside him. He tried to speak. How foolish I was to think that you would be a scribbler! You are a soldier, I see, my son. Lead the people... He wanted to say so much, for in the years since they had seen each other, he had come to see that Nam had done far more with his education than work in the civil service, a lackey of the French. A man should strive for harmony, but when it does not exist, then he must work for change. But now he was pleased that the words had not been spoken, for he saw that the figure ahead of him, silently urging him forward, was not Nam at all. Had his enemies returned to torment him further?

"Why have you come?" he demanded. There was no answer, but from within the house, he heard the sound of the tiny bell hanging by the altar to his ancestors, and then he knew that this was no enemy, but a welcome friend, come to lead him to a place of quiet and rest: it was his own great, great grandfather, Trung Quang Vinh, a renowned scholar and soldier who had first built a house on the spot where the family's home now stood. Behind him gathered a small army of Trungs, silently welcoming Co into their midst.

Co reached forward towards his beckoning ancestors, and then he slumped, his head falling with a thud onto the table.

CHAPTER 8

Move
if there is gain.
—Sun-Tzu

The old family servant and Phuong stood in the dip of the valley under a canopy of broadleaf trees, next to her father's freshly dug grave. As he would have wished, Trung Van Co was buried in a propitious site, following geomantic laws, away from the pernicious White Tiger wind. "He is safe now," Van told Phuong. She had run to him after her father slumped in front of her, neglecting the rites that should have been performed straight away.

"I should have called him back," said Phuong, softly. Her jaw-line tightened, but she was dry-eyed.

Van's Party training had been long and hard; he was well used to the process of self-criticism and so was inclined to agree with Phuong. "Yes, you lost your head," he agreed. "But now his feet are towards the sea. And this place will suit him well. It is close to the mouth of the Dragon. A good decision. Your family will flourish because of it. You'll see."

He held the old beliefs along with new ones, but was concerned about more pressing matters than neglected traditions. With her father gone, Phuong was alone. It was true that she was known by the whole village and well liked, indeed too well liked in some quarters. Were she plain, some family might take her in, but she was not. Even as she had emerged into the clearing in front of his thatched dwelling, panic-stricken and disheveled from running so far, he had seen the beauty that her father had, in recent years, so often lamented.

As she stayed by the graveside, head bowed, he considered what to do with her. Like the rest of the young people in the village, she was already part of the Youth League that traveled around Cu Chi entertaining the villagers with patriotic songs and blood-curdling propaganda. But she was too reserved to perform; even by the standards of finely brought up young ladies, this girl was exceptionally shy. She wasn't lacking aggression though. He risked a glance at the delicate arms beneath the silk of her *ao dai*. She was stronger than she looked. He had seen her train with a punji stick, and she was a natural—swift and decisive. The youths practiced only on straw dummies, but if she could thrust and strike at flesh and bone in the same way, she'd be formidable. Let her become a guerrilla fighter, like the offspring of peasants. Party discipline would ensure that she was morally safe, he told himself. His own sons were part of the Vietminh. The time for gentility was gone; let his master's daughter tread the same stony path. "For freedom we must spend blood," he shouted, and Phuong looked at him with wide eyes. He remembered her baby cries for a mother that never came and thought, she isn't made for hardship. I must protect her.

As they turned away from the gravesite and began to struggle through dense mangroves to regain the path, he asked, "How is your esteemed aunt?" On her visits to her brother, Co's sister had been the bane of their lives as she shrilly re-arranged the household, but now it seemed to Van that the old shrew, petty, suspicious, and tyrannical, would guard her niece well. Her house was a few days' travel away, in the next province. He'd take Phuong to the battleaxe and be back in no time.

"She died before Tet," Phuong reminded him. "Her sons..."

"You cannot go to them." He spoke more sharply than he intended, but the girl's innocence made him want to slap her. He found he was adopting her father's tone. "Who knows in these times how their households fare? And how would you get there? You've never been out of the province."

Phuong stopped in her tracks and turned to him. "If I can't go to them, I'll seek out my sister. She'll look after me. We've had messages that she's close to Ba Ra."

"And you'll do this on your own? You wouldn't last five minutes." He looked at her *ao dai*. Though past its best, it was still clearly of the highest quality. No one would mistake this girl for a peasant. "What a child you are! You think the roads are paved with good intentions? At your age, your sister was cannier."

The Quiet Soldier

"Then I'll stay home and tend my ancestors' shrine. I'll be here to honor my father on his anniversary. One day, Lan and Nam will come back and praise me for watching over the house."

He couldn't bear to listen to her a moment longer. His age was heavy upon him, and he wished for nothing more than to curl up and sleep forever. The pain in his belly was insistent; it was worse than hunger or worms. It would devour him, if the needs of his master's daughter didn't do it first. He turned and scrabbled through the undergrowth. "Foolish little bird," he muttered, and he went back to his own home to sleep with the memories of his years at Co's side.

Next morning, he went to the old, ruined house. The ornamental arch that had overhung the entrance had fallen to the ground. It was no more than firewood now, but he found he could not pass beyond it to view the degradation that had befallen Co's property, so he stood and waited. It was some time before Phuong emerged from the house and approached him.

"If you still want to go to Ba Ra," the old man said, "I'll go with you. We shall travel as grandfather and granddaughter." Even the smile that greeted his words irritated him. What had she to smile about? As we travel, he thought, I will teach her circumspection and craft, lest there is no safe haven at the end of our journey. "We will leave tomorrow. Tell no one we are going. No, do not look like that. It is for their protection, for they cannot divulge what they do not know." He would not let her be the bait to catch Lan.

So, without farewells, they left, abandoning the house and its meagre remnants. All they took were straw mattresses rolled up on their backs, for there was no food to carry. "What we cherish at home becomes worthless on the road. We must not carry anything to tempt bandits." He ensured that their bamboo walking sticks were freshly sharpened. "We will avoid trouble whenever we can, but sometimes it must be confronted. When Trouble stands resolute, blocking your path, meet it head on. Remember, if you strike, strike to kill, as I have seen you practice."

For days they walked vigorously along pathways familiar to them, but as soon as they moved out of Cu Chi district, Van felt his strength diminish, as if its red earth carried his life's blood. They traveled more slowly, avoiding villages when they could and living off the land. They caught frogs and rats, roasting them over a fire. Van showed Phuong which berries could be safely eaten and which could not; where to seek out the yellow slugs that grew fat in the sandy soil close to streams; and how to chew even the most bitter of grasses. Nevertheless there were many days when they went hungry, some days when they were lost and others when Van was too tired to walk for more than an hour or two. Then they would settle on their straw mattresses, easing the pangs of hunger by sucking on cloth and talking intermittently.

"Do not dwell on the past," Van advised. "Consider the future and your sweet reunion with Lan. You will help her in her great work." When he questioned the girl, he discovered that more than six months had passed since a message had come from Ba Ra. Lan might well be dead by now. He resisted the impulse to tell Phuong how many dangers lurked between her and the tranquil existence she seemed to believe was a short distance away with Lan. Let her travel in hope. He noted the resilience of her beauty, despite the privations of their existence. Though he was covered in sores and his teeth fell from his mouth as readily as leaves from a tree, her skin remained clear and her fine features untouched. Her loveliness infuriated him as much as it had worried her father. For Co, her allure had seemed a temptation few men would resist, but Van believed it separated her from reality, from the hardships of life that every peasant knew. Had he braved this journey to throw her defenseless into fresh dangers? He feared so. One name he repeated to Phuong again and again. "When we reach Ba Ra, there is a man—Hoang Anh. He can be trusted. Remember Hoang Anh, but never speak his name."

On occasions, they heard gunfire in the distance and would hurry in the opposite direction. When they saw other travelers approaching they would hide. "Better to be alone than to put ourselves in the hands of uncouth strangers," Van cautioned. He thought that he initiated her in wariness but that process had begun years before on the day of the Sureté raid. He confirmed the trait in her and sought to provide fresh sweetness in speaking of the glorious cause for which they were all fighting. He told her wonderful stories of the valiant fighters on the Liberation Road. He spoke too of those who served in different ways, by long years spent in isolation and exile, denied even the use of their own names. "Vietnam's freedom will come slowly, for she has powerful enemies; only the Party could defeat them and serve the masses. We must be bold, yet humble."

As they trudged along, dirty and hungry, he loved to quote the Party's favorites maxim. "Eyes opened wide in defiance, gazing contemptuously at a thousand giants. Heads bowed, serving as a horse for small children."

She was a good listener, always had been, but he doubted whether he had succeeded in creating a loyalty that went beyond her childish heroes, Nam and Long. He could speak of manifestoes until his last breath, but she was a female when all was said and done. Lan had grit, whereas this little one had only her gentle love to keep her going. Maybe it was enough that she would fight for them. Perhaps he should have left her in Cu Chi amongst the guerrillas and saved himself this journey, where every step bloodied his feet.

Though the pains were worsening, Van's mood lightened as they descended one morning into a lush valley. Far away, there was a noise like perpetual thunder. "What is that?" asked Phuong.

"It is a great waterfall," answered Van, relieved. His eldest son, Sang, had described it many times. "We are close to the village where Sang received help when he was injured last year. Today, Phuong, we will eat warm food, and tonight we shall have shelter." He raised his punji stick to point at a group of thatched dwellings further down the valley. "That must be Than Thi."

They descended along a well-worn path towards a group of straw-roofed dwellings fenced around with bamboo. It was a meagre sort of place, with no timbered houses worthy of mandarins and not a buffalo in sight. The inhabitants would be poor folk, scraping a living from the soil and the rivers. Van ensured they approached in clear view, so that half a dozen men were waiting as they reached the hamlet. All the inhabitants were awake, most watching from the entrances to their dwellings, assessing the old man hobbling on ruined feet and the young woman whose clothes were so tattered that, for modesty's sake, she had wrapped her mattress around her.

Van knew the passwords that would gain them help. He spoke the right words, and they were welcomed. The children were allowed to gather round and gaze. Rice, cooked and salted, was offered, as if it were abundant. With thanks, Van and Phuong each accepted a small bowl, but declined more. They had dreamed of eating their fill, yet now found that to be amongst people was exhilaration enough. They would not be so discourteous as to be greedy. The women clucked around Phuong. Bolder children stroked her hair. Fresh garments were found for her and she washed with soap for the first time since their journey began. Van's feet were gently bathed and rubber sandals set ready for him.

By the afternoon, as the heat lessened, the villagers and guests sat on the ground in the shadow of the thatches and talked. The men asked Van about conditions in Cu Chi district. He told them, but he did not name his destination, nor who they hoped to find in Ba Ra.

Being closer to Saigon, the villagers had far more news than reached Cui Chi. "There have been momentous events!" a village elder announced. "The Japanese have taken over the administration of the whole of Indochina."

"From the French?" asked Van. His whole life had been lived under French rule. The Trung household had built its prosperity on a French stipend. The sky, it seemed, had moved.

"Of course from the French. Who else?" chuckled the elder, delighted at the effect his news had produced, and other villagers smiled good naturedly, although they themselves had needed some convincing when they'd first heard. Only when the sound of artillery fire came from Ba Ra and they'd witnessed a skirmish between retreating French troops and the advancing Japanese had they believed it. The local French customs inspector and his wife had also been killed. Good news indeed.

One young man rose up to say excitedly, "So much for the supremacy of the white races! Let's see them bleed now."

"The Japanese are also fiends," the elder reminded him, alarmed at such a frank display in front of newcomers.

"Of course," agreed Van, "fiends..." But at least they were not fair-skinned fiends.

Another villager voiced the thought, "We are still eating shit, but it is no longer French shit!" They all laughed.

"In confusion comes opportunity," said the young man, repeating the words of secret lessons. "As in a game of *co tuong*, victory often goes to the participant who takes advantage of a temporary gap in an opponent's defenses." His eyes flickered back and forwards to Phuong's face, to see what effect his words were having. She kept her head down.

"I spoke to a school teacher myself," another young man chipped in, not to be outdone. "He can get hold of newspapers, and they say that

The Quiet Soldier

Vietnamese is to be the official language of the state. The French flag has been hauled down and stamped into the ground!"

"They've lorded it over us for eighty years," said Van. "Is it possible these new masters, the Japanese, will grant independence?"

"When have we been granted anything?" an old man asked bitterly. "No, we won't be given our freedom. We'll have to take."

"Yes, we have more battles ahead," the elder agreed. "The Vietminh has increased its power-base. With confusion there is also danger. Let's not forget those prisoners that were killed."

Phuong raised her head. "What prisoners?" she asked.

The men, young and old, looked surprised at her intervention. "During the coup, the Japanese released political prisoners from the jails," one explained. "A few escaped, but others were killed."

"Was Ba Ra one of the prisons?" asked Phuong. The informant shook his head; he was not sure.

"My granddaughter asks because we once had a man from our village taken there," Van quickly explained, fixing her with a look. "That is a long time ago, girl. We do not need to drag up old stories..." He rose. "And now we must be going, with many thanks for your hospitality."

The villagers expressed surprise. "At least stay the night," urged the elder, "then start refreshed in the morning. It will be dark in a few hours." Van declined and the old man and the girl were soon leaving the village. The children followed them for a mile or two, but turned back when their home lay in the distance.

"I should not have mentioned Ba Ra," lamented Phuong, "though they were so friendly."

"Friends all, I hope," said Van, "but you must choose your words for the one enemy that may be listening."

Phuong bowed her head in acceptance. One must save one's friends from knowledge, it seemed, and also evade one's enemies by keeping quiet. Silence was the answer to everything.

CHAPTER 9

The unguarded flower will be violated by a wayward bee.
—Vietnamese saying

    The roar and echo of the waterfall increased as they approached it. Dusk had come with a full moon. A pangolin already stirred, dragging its scaly body across the path in front of them, as if aware that they posed no threat. They had traveled for two days since Than Thi. Van eased himself by the side of the pathway. The pain in his belly was worse than ever. "Find a dry warm spot among the bushes where we can rest," he instructed. Regret sprung in him. They had been together on their long, grim journey, but still she was not ready to face the world. "I know, Phuong. We are too close to people, but tomorrow..." Too tired to point, he leaned his head to one side, towards the glow of kerosene lamps not far away. "That is Ba Ra. We will wait here until the morning to enter."
    Obediently, Phuong stepped off the path into the forest as Van closed his eyes and tried to plan their entry into Ba Ra. He feared that Long had been killed in the prison breakout and that Lan had gone. Even if she were still in Ba Ra, she would undoubtedly be using an alias, so how was he to find her? If Long was no more, she might be traveling back to Cu Chi, a journey he knew he would never make. His bloodied footsteps would be in this direction only. He listened to the sounds from the forest: the distress-call of macaque monkeys and the chirping of geckos. Had Phuong caused such disturbance?
    There was the sound of flapping wings as a flock of birds took flight. He looked about in the gloom. Shadows and faint scraping noises surrounded him. Small animals scurried for cover and beyond was the rush and roar of the waterfall. Phuong was taking a long time to find a place for the night. By now she should have returned and be helping him to his feet. With

the aid of his punji, he pulled himself up. Cautiously, he did not enter the thicket directly, but skirted to the side. He saw the shape of the stranger before he saw Phuong. Moonlight fell on him as he stood on the rocky precipice in front of the waterfall.

The stranger was dressed in soiled peasant pyjamas, but the knife he carried on a belt around his waist had a finely carved ivory handle. He was urging Phuong towards him, with sounds rather than words, as if she were a recalcitrant mule to be coaxed. With his left hand, he gestured that she should come closer, while his right hand lay on the hilt of the knife. Phuong stood as if transfixed, her punji stick held slackly across her body. She shook her head but did not utter a sound. Foam from the waterfall sprayed them both.

If only Sang were at his side! The sight of a young, seasoned warrior would make this bastard think again. With the aid of his stick, Van pulled himself into view as quickly as he could. What a curse it was to be old! Seeing him, the man showed his teeth, laughing gutturally, "What, Uncle?" He pulled his knife from his belt and ran at Van.

"Strike!" called Van as Phuong raised her punji, but she drew back and held the stick in her right hand to beat the man about the shoulders. It was too late: his knife sliced Van's chest. Blood pumped from him. Dimly he saw the man turn back towards Phuong and grab her by her hair. She was shaken until her feet left the ground, then punched on the side of the head and pushed down. Van fell to his knees, then dragged himself towards the twisting bodies, guided as much by the first sounds from Phuong— screams as the assailant fell on her.

Van tried to pull the man away, but a blow from an elbow jerking backwards struck him in the eye, sending him reeling. He fell back and, for a while, there was blackness. When he tried to stand, he felt Phuong's discarded punji beneath him. He grasped it as firmly as he could and tried to plunge it into the man's back, but his blow sliced ineffectually at the neck. A punch sent him toppling over, as he saw that Phuong's clothing had been ripped away as easily as cobwebs.

Summoning all his strength, Van felt in the long, wet grass for the punji again. Instead, his hand found the ivory handle of the knife. He grabbed it in both hands and struck at the body raising itself from Phuong. As the first blow struck, the man turned. Weakly, Van dug the knife into the upturned face, again and again. He sunk down exhausted. He could not see Phuong, only hear her sobs. Then he recognized her small, delicate hand taking the knife from him. His sight was dim, but he heard the man's final rasped breath as Phuong used the knife on his neck the way she had been trained to do.

"Why did you not call out?" Van asked. He knew the answer. She had chosen to protect him. She had taken her chances rather than risk his safety. It will always be so, he thought.

Even the thundering from the waterfall diminished; all became remote, and he felt a terrible coldness. His jacket was soaked in blood, yet the pain was receding into numbness.

He heard Phuong crying, "I should not have hesitated."

As he died he thought of the blood-red soil of Cu Chi and of his sons who fought for it.

* * *

Phuong knelt beside Van's body and rocked with grief. Even in her sorrow she was fearful of uttering another sound, in case her attacker had companions close by. A violation committed once could be committed many times. Though Van's wound gaped in front of her, she could hardly believe that he would not wake. He would admonish her, even express disgust, but anything was better than being alone.

His spirit might return if she did the right thing. It could re-enter his body if she opened his mouth by placing chopsticks between his teeth.

She should have carried chopsticks. The scars of her father's death reopened. *You lost your head.* Crying, she struggled to raise Van to a sitting position. Her hands became sticky with his blood as she pulled his tunic over his shoulders and head. Wrenching, she pulled it free. Van's body fell back. Phuong stood up, with the tunic in both hands. She waved it in the air. Come back, she begged silently. Come back.

Van's spirit did not reply and, finally, Phuong curled up by his body and slept fitfully.

Shortly after dawn, a gust of wind blew a spray from the waterfall and woke her abruptly. She saw the two bodies and leapt up, drenched, looking around her. She had to leave in case companions of the attacker searched for him. But she would not abandon Van alongside his killer, as if they

The Quiet Soldier

were equal in death. And yet he would not want to be buried in this alien land. The river flowed towards Cu Chi, nowhere near as far, but at least in that direction. She dragged the half-naked body towards the ravine and pushed him over the side with her foot. His body bounced off a rock, hit the water, buffeting in the foam, and then disappeared.

She searched the long grass and found the ivory-handled knife that had been by her side as she slept. She wiped the blade clean. She had no way of securing the weapon at her waist unless she took the dead man's belt. She forced herself to look at him. The slashes to his face had torn his lips and his nose, so that he seemed to be sneering, *you are no fighter*.

He was right. When she had gone in search of shelter, she had become distracted. First, she had wandered to a *bi bai* tree and picked some sweet berries. As she ate, she glimpsed some orchids that she had seen in a garden in My Tinh, near home when her father had taken her visiting. She was picking one, with its exquisite drooping white flower, splashed with red and gold, when the stranger stepped into view, smiling and predatory. Though he had coaxed her with promises of safety, she had known Trouble instantly. Why then had she not called out as if there were a dozen able-bodied helpers close by? And when Van had appeared and ordered her to strike, why had she still been reluctant?

She forced herself to look at the face of her attacker. Even in death, he was mocking. He possessed her body as his last pleasure. He had triumphed over her, torn away her pride and made her unmarriageable. Phuong undid the belt and then tugged on his tunic, pulling it over his head. She kept it bunched in her hand; his spirit she would not invite to return. The garment was intact, though stained and foul-smelling. She stripped off what was left of hers and put on his. He had been large for a Vietnamese, and the tunic reached her knees. She buckled the belt on her bare waist and slipped the knife under the leather. She could hear wild boar foraging in the undergrowth. Soon, they would enter the clearing. Let them eat away that sneer.

CHAPTER 10

History is not all epic events: 'small' people doing seemingly inconsequential things can sometimes influence the course of affairs.
—David G. Marr

Ba Ra was an old provincial capital. The central street was wide and lined with plane trees, which had been planted by French civil servants to remind them of home. Traces of the turquoise and salmon-pink paints, sent all the way from France to adorn the stucco work, could still be glimpsed in the rubble of the mansions that had been destroyed by cannon when the Japanese commander had opened fire on the day of the coup. At the north end of the boulevard stood the square in which stupefied colonial troops watched their surviving officer beheaded on the orders of that same Japanese commander who had been infuriated by the level of his own casualties. Months later, fragments of the *Proclamation of Martial Law* signed by General Tsuchihashi still clung to the trees. Citizens, both French and native, were ordered to remain calm, to go about their normal duties, and to avoid doing anything prejudicial to the interests of the Imperial Army.

As Phuong entered the town, she tried to copy the walk of the other women out in the streets—small, unassuming steps rather than the bold strides of the traveler she had become. She must not so obviously declare herself a stranger. She would listen, too, before she spoke, in case her accent marked her out. In all things, she would have to work out what Van would have advised. She had discarded her punji stick before entering the town, but she still had the man's knife. She could have bartered for food with it—she had eaten only grasses since the rice at Than Thi—but it was more comforting than a full stomach. She would put it to use one day, she hoped.

The Quiet Soldier

The sun was still low in the sky, and there was a breeze that chased scores of russet leaves around the streets, but perspiration dripped from her. She had skirted the town noting its layout, as Van had taught her, and then entered. She kept her conical hat on, though she had a headache and its weight was heavy on her. She feared the locals would know her to be a stranger. Even if she saw Lan in the streets, she would have to be cautious about approaching. Yet the thought that her sister might be moving amongst this sea of strangers made her want to scream her name. Phuong shivered, wishing it was certain that Lan was here in Ba Ra.

She saw that many women of the town were heading to the market across the wooden bridge that spanned the canal. She joined them, involuntarily lifting her head as the sweet smells from the market reached her. The longing for food returned. The produce was less meager than that of Cu Chi in recent times, a delight to the eyes as well as the belly. Vegetables were displayed in rows, like fallen soldiers; pumpkins were piled high and shrimps and cockles floated in barrels. Headless frogs still jumped as the boy selling them picked each one up to strip it of its skin. A goat stood tethered to a post next to its owner, who bartered the sale of some fertilized duck eggs—a great delicacy that Phuong had not seen, let alone tasted, since Ngo Quang Long, son of a mandarin from Hue, had first visited the Trungs. Most enticing was the cooked food, ready for any customers with the piastres to pay. Pickled pig's ears were piled up to be chewed and crunched. *Pho Bo* bubbled in a tureen, stirred by an old woman who turned away every few minutes so that she could, with an air of great delicacy, spit green phlegm from the side of her mouth. Phuong would have eaten that soup, spittle and all. She gazed at it yearningly.

"Hungry, little sister?" Amid the rapid chatter of the traders and customers, she did not realize at first that the words were addressed to her. "Come over here and try some *canh*." He was young man. He smiled, revealing long yellow canine teeth, as sharp as claws. He lifted a ladle of the clear soup in the pot before him. Phuong shook her head, but lingered. What would she do for some of that soup!

What would she have to do for some of that soup? Her thighs were bruised from yesterday's assault. A smile could prelude an attack. Was this the inevitable bargaining now that she was alone and unprotected? "Look, dumplings. Very tasty."

The careless gossiping and haggling of the market stopped abruptly, and the man's fangs disappeared. Phuong turned and saw that a Japanese officer was approaching, flanked by two soldiers with rifles over their shoulders. The officer had a harsh expression on a face that was flat and round like a skillet. His boots tapped violently on the baked ground as he strode through the market. Instinctively, Phuong moved out of his way by going towards the soup seller; she stood a chance with a Vietnamese, but a foreigner with such a face was beyond comprehension.

Those in the market watched the Japanese soldiers covertly. None looked directly at them, so that, when the officer halted by the goat and shouted, it took some minutes for the trader closest to him to realize that he had asked for some fertilised duck eggs. Bowing, the man handed them over, declining the money that the officer held out. He bowed lower as the officer barked words of demotic Vietnamese and lower still when the money was flung at him.

As soon as the soldiers were out of view, the buzz of voices began again. "Bloody Japs," muttered the soup seller. "At least you know where you are with the French. They take anything worth having. This lot think they're doing us a favor."

As the duck egg seller picked up the piastres flung at his feet, the soup seller ladled out some *canh* and handed it to Phuong. She tipped the bowl and drank without stopping. She tasted shrimp, watercress, and a wonderful hint of chicken. It was almost the same as the *canh* of Cu Chi. It would have been made with fish sauce. *A man would be a fool to seek anything closer to perfection than that fish sauce.* She had no chopsticks to scoop out the dumplings. She hesitated as the grinning soup seller watched. Using her fingers—what would her father have said? But Van would have approved. He'd wanted the edges knocked off her, he'd said. Well, she'd had more than edges... She plunged her hand into the bowl and scooped the dumplings out one by one, finally licking the grease from her fingers. The yellow canines came into view again as the man laughed. "You are fine lady! And you were hungry, little sister!"

He was hazy before her. In Cu Chi, *little sister* was an adult's homage to childhood. Did it guarantee familial respect here too? Yesterday's assailant had goaded Van with *Uncle!* Was she being mocked now? Would he lead her away, to shake her off her feet, and then commit that violation too

The Quiet Soldier

terrible to name, as the man yesterday had done? Van could not save her then and now his body was drifting towards Cu Chi or had come aground in this black, alien soil. She wished she could read the signs here aright, for she longed to confide in the shape standing over her, blocking, it seemed, the whole world from view.

She wanted to say, I am alone. I am only fourteen. Will you help me? She wished she wasn't fourteen. She wanted to be less than ten so that it was alright to cry helplessly. She wanted to be back in Cu Chi with an older brother spoiling her with presents from Paris and a sister telling her stories to lull her to sleep. Had she only imagined that life with servants and a busy, important father, who occasionally spared a day to take her to visit their neighbors? Trung Van Co is on the best of terms with the provincial governor, yet nothing is more precious to him than his little Phuong, which means *perfection*. *Perfection*, which she possessed back then. Her hands shook as she struggled to untie the straps of her hat under her chin. She was oppressed by her headache and the strange coldness of her itchy skin. Dare she say, I am seeking an old man called Hoang Anh? Can you tell me where to find him?

But this might be more Trouble standing before her. When she thought that the stranger who could be trusted, Hoang Anh, could die because of her words, she wanted to be silent forever. She gave up trying to untie her hat. Her legs were heavy; her thighs ached. She fumbled for the ivory hilt of the knife at her waist. As she touched her tunic, the fungal smell of its previous owner assailed her. Giddy with nausea, she heard Nam calling her *little sister* as he walked in the orchard with Long, books in hand, talking and laughing. *Little sister* they called her in the evenings, as they sat under a pagoda roof in the gardens. *Little sister*, when she draped herself around her father to be kissed and petted.

She fell at the soup seller's feet.

* * *

Cups of green tea rattled as a bent, elderly woman hobbled on rounded feet across the room with a tray. None of the men acknowledged her as she settled its contents on an upturned box next to the mah yongg board. The vast room contained no furniture—just assorted junk and innumerable people, from babes in arms to aged squatting figures. There was the muffled sound of voices, yet no one seemed to be talking. Even those children old enough to walk tottered quietly from object to person. Hammocks were slung in one corner and a haze lingered in the rafters.

Phuong awoke to the clink of the cups and the sharp ricochet of the mah yongg pieces. It was suffocatingly hot in the miasma of opium smoke. A lined female face, more ancient even than the bearer of tea, looked down at her. "So you're awake at last. When you're ready, there's tea." Her accent was different, but from her words she might have been any great grandmother in Cu Chi. She asked no questions, showed no curiosity, simply poured some hot green tea into another cup and gestured Phuong towards it.

Phuong felt at her waist for the knife. It was gone. The belt hung across the side of the hammock. She rose up and swung herself to the floor. The men continued their game of mah yongg.

She knew she could not ask questions without answering some and found it difficult to think what might be dangerous. She took the cup and bowed her thanks. Had they heard her speak? But they seemed already to have accepted her. Perhaps, she thought, someone has ordered them to keep me here, but for what purpose? She stayed quiet. Some of the women brought food—plain rice with some tepid, sour vegetables. The men stopped their game to take their share, and Phuong was handed a bowl and chopsticks too. The children scavenged from the adults, scooping rice from the bowls, gulping it down.

She felt better for the food and walked to a high window to look out. No one tried to stop her or showed interest in her movements. Perhaps I am not a prisoner, she thought as she gazed out on the busy street below. The sun was sinking in the sky and inhabitants of the town were returning to their households. She dared a question to the men who had returned to their game of mah yongg. "Is this Ba Ra?"

They nodded. "Are we close to the prison?" There were some slight movements, like a communal shrug. When she repeated the question, one of them adeptly made his move in the game before answering, "You must wait for Mr Heng."

"Mr Heng?"

"He brought you here. You are safe because of Mr Heng."

The old woman who had peered into the hammock added, "Mr Heng is on the Committee."

CHAPTER 11

[Mr Heng] was obviously a man who took a tiresome pleasure in giving instruction.
—Graham Greene, spoken by Thomas Fowler in The Quiet American

"Remember that day in the market, your first day here? That Japanese officer who tried to buy the duck eggs and was insulted because the seller tried to give them as a gift..." Mr Heng smiled grimly at the memory. He was talking softly to Phuong in the corner of the attic room that had been her home for the three months since she had arrived in Ba Ra. Small children idled close by, waiting for the first meal of the day. The hiss of steam came from the stove, as the old women prepared rice and tea. Old men waited like the children but kept their distance from Heng and Phuong, knowing that he was instructing her.

Phuong nodded. She remembered it all. She had her own hammock now and a place on the rota of domestic duties, but only light tasks so that there would be plenty of time for this—this preparation.

"That's Captain Kaneko. He runs the prison. In civilian life, before the war *forced* on Japan by its incessant need to gobble up the rest of the world, he was an antiquarian bookseller. He's very lonely. He misses his wife, his mother and his books. We natives are not as friendly as his studies of foreign cultures and languages led him to believe!"

The sharp teeth flashed as Mr Heng smiled again as he gazed down at her. It was a long time since Phuong had thought of him as the soup seller, but today he would take that role again. When she had waited for Mr Heng from the Committee, as the old people had told her to do, she had been taken aback when the humble market-trader appeared. But, she reflected afterwards, she should have been ready. People are rarely what they seem. If the son of a mandarin from Hue can be a revolutionary, then so too can a young man selling *cahn* from a market stall in a garrison town. So too can a young woman with freshly braided hair wearing a vermillion *ao dai*, if her will is strong enough.

"Yes, Phuong, I'm afraid to say that Captain Kaneko is grievously disappointed with us Vietnamese. We are completely ungrateful, and untrustworthy into the bargain! Poor man, it's almost as if he and his army have done something to upset us!"

Phuong smiled. She had learnt to smile again. She knew that Mr Heng had a dry sense of humor and that he masked his hatred for the enemy behind these little jokes. And he liked her to smile. Men liked her to smile, evidently.

He would not try to touch her, she knew that too. Perhaps it was because he was totally committed to the cause and she was one of his soldiers. Or perhaps the old women who had tended her had told him of the bruises on her inner thighs, of the blood and the tearing, and he would not touch such tainted goods. The filthy tunic had been burnt, the wounds had healed, but what had happened could never be erased.

"He speaks *dreadful* Vietnamese. Obviously you should try to look as if he is making sense. You may have to cry a little but don't overdo it. You have to be charmingly and helplessly in need, not a nervous wreck."

Phuong nodded; her vulnerability must be charming. Despite the reason for her being so attractively dressed, it was still pleasant to be out of rough clothes. The vermillion silk caressed her skin. She was perfumed with sandalwood. Even her hands had regained some of the softness that had been lost since the days of plenty. Mr Heng had ordered her not to practice with a punji stick, so that she would have no tell-tale calluses. "You are a lady, Phuong," he had told her. "I knew that as soon as I saw the way you ate the soup. We can make that work for us." Only *us* and *them* for Mr Heng; he made you choose.

"I'm going now. Follow in a little while. Don't eat breakfast. You might have to eat *canh* all day before he comes. And if you need any help and I'm not around, signal to the man trading herbal medicines. He's one of us. Ready?"

"I'm unarmed," she said boldly.

"You're not meant to *hurt* him. Get the information, that's all. And if he helps you, he's compromised and we have a hold over him. This is the best chance to find your relatives."

"I agree." How foolish she had been to think she would walk in to a town like Ba Ra and find them waiting for her. Fainting in the market had been a blessing in disguise, for how else would she have been given a place to stay and comrades? As for finding the man Van told her to trust, Hoang Anh, how had he supposed she would do that? "I understand my mission. But shouldn't a soldier always be armed?"

He laughed so loudly that some of the children chortled in chorus. "You're more pleasing to the eye than most soldiers! Here..." He held out her knife. He'd had it ready, so maybe he'd expected her to ask for it back. "But make sure you strap it to your waist securely. You don't want it clunking to the floor as you're recounting your tale of woe."

She gazed at the ivory-handled knife in the palm of her hand, then grasped the handle and ran a finger down the blade. He'd kept it razor-sharp. No blunt knife would kill the Japanese officer, for she would be lucky to manage one blow. Whatever Heng's orders, if the price of finding Long and Lan was another violation, she would kill Kaneko.

She looked about her as Heng left the attic. In the months since her arrival in Ba Ra, as she recovered her strength, she had quietly observed the group that had taken her in. The clutter of battered furniture never diminished, nor was the vast room ever empty of people. Babies cried, were fed, then slept in rush baskets hanging from the rafters. Old women squabbled about the chores and prepared vegetables, while old men played mah yongg until the opium quietened them. The able-bodied and able-minded came and went without comment and without, apparently, exciting any curiosity about what they were up to. Some never came back. Even now, she wasn't quite sure who was related to whom. Finally, she realized that it wasn't a home; it was a base camp. They were all soldiers under Mr Heng's command. Even the youngest child, born since her arrival in a corner of the attic, had a place in Heng's small army.

If a raid threatened, they would de-camp in minutes. The ties that bound them were invisible and indissoluble, though they might separate for lifetimes. She had been taught the rules. Trust each other and no one else. Die rather than betray one of your comrades. Go down fighting.

With the knife strapped to her waist, she left the building. Her heart beat faster as she reached the street. She struggled to control her breathing. This is dangerous, but I must do it. If I die, my soul will be free. No shame, no fear. I am closer to Lan, and not only her. Let him be alive! He must be alive, for if he had been killed, then I would surely know it. She forced herself to consider how she was behaving and reminded herself that a lady in an *ao dai* should take small, delicate steps. She should deport herself elegantly and modestly. She slowed her walk, aware that her fine attire drew looks as she crossed the canal bridge and made her way towards the market with the early morning customers.

Heng had taught her how to observe without seeming to show the slightest attention. He had moved more quickly than her and was already in place behind his soup tureen. Her eyes did not rest on him. She noted the dangers—the blocked exits, the strangers, the known informants. Demurely, she walked by the traders, gaze down, listening. When she had mapped everything, she walked slowly across the market towards the stall selling herbal remedies. A young lady could idle quite some time at such a stall. What decorous ailments could she have? She considered her cover story for Kaneko, her "tale of woe" as Heng called it. She was a young lady who had been returning to her home in Hue when her only companion, her maid, had been arrested and thrown into Ba Ra jail, all due to some horrible mistake, which a kindly Japanese captain could sort out.

Palpitations of the heart and fatigue seemed appropriate. She would ask the medicine seller holder for advice. His stall was busy. Half a dozen customers leaned over his merchandise, grabbing handfuls of what they wanted. *Choc gai* was selling briskly and so too was clustered fishtail palm. The malarial season was close.

Deferentially, the peasants moved aside as she approached, waiting to hear her words. She told herself she need not worry. He was, after all, *one of us.*

It happened in an instant. One moment she was framing a sentence about *something to help me sleep* and the next she was gazing into a pair of round, light-brown eyes. She had not seen such intensity since Long's arrest. In fact, he looked very much like Long. Words drained from her. To gain time, she looked down at the small mounds of herbs. His hands were reaching out to pick up some *thien ly* leaves. Why were those simple movements so compelling? Fine hands, yes, not small but well-shaped and the fingers fluttered a little as he moved the leaves. He was left-handed, and this made his actions curiously pronounced and appealing. She looked

The Quiet Soldier

up at him and found him already regarding her. "I'm having difficulty," she started, "difficulty..."

His smile! Even the way his lips drew over his teeth made her falter. His expression was full of kindness and understanding. She feared for him; surely anyone could see that he was more than a market trader? Then he spoke. "How can I help you?" She knew at once that he was a northerner, and she detected too the intonations of someone used to speaking French—another sign of his breeding. She thought, if the invaders ever got to know us, they could subjugate us forever.

He repeated his question. "How can I help you?" Over the years, she recalled that simple sentence, and it never failed to send her heart pounding. When she had to pretend that some other man's endearment had pleased her, she'd repeat those words in his accent to herself. *How can I help you?*

She was about to ask for some *cai ma*, since he didn't seem to have some, when she heard the clatter and hiss of a large soup tureen crashing over. Hot *canh* had sprayed half a dozen customers, and Heng was making a show of mopping them down and apologizing. She saw why he'd done it. Kaneko, flanked by two guards, had entered the market on the soup seller's side and, as he strode by, Heng tipped the tureen over. Kaneko, legs planted stoutly apart, stood waving his cane as he sorted out the incompetent natives.

A complicit look passed between her and the herb seller as, heart pounding again, she made her way across the market. Slowly, slowly, she told herself.

Kaneko was raging at Heng. "You idiot! Lucky for you the soup not soil my uniform." He pushed his cane into a complaining customer. "Quiet!" His eyes lighted on Phuong as she approached. His tone changed. "All quiet now. Go on your way."

Instinctively, she knew what would captivate him—sympathy. The bigger the brute, the more he feels sorry for himself. She gazed up. "*Tu es troublé,*" she said gently.

Did his eyes water as he thanked her for her concern? His large, flat face disgusted her and his Vietnamese was truly appalling. He barked when he should sing. In his execrable accent, he asked her if she was alright. Had the idiot soup seller splattered her—may he be permitted to say—beautiful outfit? A foolish question, since she had clearly been nowhere near the soup when it fell. *How can I help you?* She coyly thanked him. No, she had far bigger worries.

She wondered whether the herb seller watched as Kaneko led her away to "a quiet place where I can hear what is troubles you."

It took all her resolve to walk beside him. Though he wasn't much taller than a Vietnamese, his thick-set frame intimidated and revolted her. His head was shaven, but she could see hairs sprouting on his hands and on his neck. He was little more than a gorilla and smelled as fetid. She raised her hand, as if to brush some insect away from her face, so that she could inhale the sandalwood lingering on her sleeve. Resentment hardened.

He slowed down to match her sedate steps, and she longed to run. Kaneko growled at his soldiers and they drew back. Phuong remained keenly aware of their armed presence behind her. She knew they wouldn't shoot; given the order, they'd fell her with rifle butts. Her countrymen averted their gaze as the group approached. They saw her, of course, and thought her a bourgeoisie collaborator walking alongside a Japanese officer. They allowed themselves small expressions of disgust that foreigners would miss. A man on a bicycle gave her a hard-nosed stare as he pedalled close by. An old woman sweeping vegetables slapped her own head. Crude words fell like sighs as she left the market. Whore, daughter, and granddaughter of vermin...

This was the price of finding her sister. Let it be the whole price.

CHAPTER 12

There are Five Sorts of Spies: Local, Internal, Double, Dead, and Live.
—Sun-Tzu

Approaching the bleak, foul-smelling camp on the outskirts of the town, she could see the freshly repaired gash in the wire fence through which prisoners had crawled on the day of the Japanese coup. She was sadly moved to think that those she loved may have escaped that way. If they had trod where she now walked, she was closer to them than she had been since the Sûreté raid. She forced her thoughts to the task in hand—Heng had warned her about daydreaming when she should be most alert. "Concentrate on what's happening around you if you want to keep that pretty little head of yours on your shoulders," he'd advised. She stared at the prison ahead. What a legacy the French had left the Japanese! There were about twenty brick-built huts with small apertures through which innumerable faces stared. Holes had been dug in the ground and covered in bamboo to form cages—they would be the isolation cells for those singled out for special punishment. A few prisoners, the lucky ones, allowed some respite from the suffocating heat of the huts shuffled about outside, yoked to night-soil buckets, too listless to raise their eyes to see the girl in the vermilion *ao dai* entering the camp with the prison commander.

The guards at the gate straightened to attention as they saw Kaneko with Phuong at his side. Heng had said she would not get this far so quickly. He'd said she might have to meet the captain a number of times, working on him until he invited her into the prison, but Kaneko had needed little persuasion. He had paused briefly under the shade of a plane tree and begun to ask her about her troubles, then abruptly invited her to his own quarters. A man could be made to do almost anything, she was learning, if he thought you acquiescent and simple-minded. She gave him a vacant half-smile and saw his face contort with pleasure. He started lecturing her, in his abominable Vietnamese, on something or other. His arduous duties, the burdens of responsibility. This disgusting, over-fed porker was whining.

He led her into a wooden hut, and she quickly surveyed the room as he scrambled to remove some books from the easy chair. By one wall, sheets lay crumpled on the narrowest of beds, so she knew he was quartered alone. He had a desk with papers and ledgers like the ones her father used to have, relics of French rule that sent a pang to her heart. How precious Father had once believed those records of his collaboration were! Kaneko's ceremonial sword hung on the wall beside his bed. There was another exit door that would be closer to the perimeter fence, and through the small window, she counted three guards patrolling.

With her hands demurely folded in her lap, she sat on the chair and said, "My father, who is a mandarin in Hue, has many books." That was enough to set him talking about his books, his business, and something he said was the study of his life and sounded like *poultice* or maybe *poultry*. After her *tu es troublé*, he'd replied in French, but she had not been able to understand a word, so she'd asked, was it possible, because he looked such a learned man, that he spoke Vietnamese? He'd puffed with pride at that and told her he spoke Vietnamese immaculately. What a fool, but at least a fool who'd kept his distance so far. He stood surveying her from the other side of the room.

"How am I to find my maid?" she asked slowly.

He took a large ledger off his desk, without taking his eyes away from her. "What is her name? We keep full records." Heng had told her that if she got this far she was to go close and look at the ledger herself. He'd made her memorize names she should look for. He'd had wider interests than her relatives.

But who was taking the risks? Not Heng. Let him find his own names. She asked, "Have you lists of those who died or escaped on the day you liberated us from the French?"

He shut the ledger. "What interest in that?"

"That was what concerned my maid. She was arrested for asking about her former employer. He was from Hue too."

He re-opened the ledger. "Fifteen dead and forty two escapes. Come here and look."

The Quiet Soldier

She forced herself to move towards him. His gaze was amatory. She could see the names only by standing close, so close that she heard his quickened breath. She knew that to find *Ngo Quang Long* even in the list of escapees would not be good news, for if he had been listed under his own name, it was because he'd been informed upon or broken under torture. He would have used an alias, so she was looking for clues to his identity—a coded reference to his family, or her own, for she hoped for some sign of Nam. Father had never allowed the possibility that his son had been arrested on the same day as Long, but she had come to realize that it was likely. He too would have had to withstand brutal interrogation. Her finger shook as she ran it down the list of dead. Kaneko was mumbling in her ear about her beauty, his being far from home...

She turned to the list of escapees. There was no *Trung Huu Nam*, nor *Ngo Quang Long*. Neither had broken and given up their names. Kaneko mistook her look for encouragement and placed his gorilla hand on her shoulder. She turned away as if to see the list in a better light and Kaneko moved with her, begging now. The only word she could understand was *comfort* and she knew full well what comfort he wanted.

The names were in front of her but this revolting foreigner was demanding her body. Far from home? Then go home! He pressed against her at the moment she saw the name that she realized was Long's alias.

Kaneko flung an arm round her back, as his face convulsed with self-pity. "You want this. It is why you spoke to me." She heard the rush of the waterfall, the sarcastic *What, Uncle?* and smelled the acrid body odor of her first assailant. Kaneko was stroking her, scratching the silk as his thick fingers thrummed her shoulders, her back, and her bottom. His hands roamed close to the knife at her waist.

She pulled away. "Not here," she said, "...among the books."

"Yes!" He pushed her backwards onto the bed. He wouldn't wait any longer. She threw up her arm trying to grab at the sword on the wall, but missed. Kaneko raised himself to undo his trousers and with the weight on her lessened, she managed to scramble from under him, falling heavily off the bed. He yelled furiously in Japanese. Looking behind her, she saw that two guards had burst into the room. He swore and, as they jabbered back, she realized he was angry about more than being interrupted. He rushed out. She went to the back door, opened it, and looked about. Whatever had caused the commotion had drawn the guards away from the rear-perimeter fence, at least for a while. She had one task to perform before she ran towards the fence and plunged down. The sharp wire ripped through her clothes as she slithered underneath it. Then she ran for the trees.

She did not dare look back until she was deep in the undergrowth. Still breathing heavily, she turned and saw black smoke curling up from the prison. "Over here!" It was Heng. She followed him through the forest without a word. Finally, he stopped and kicked away some leaves to reveal a hole just large enough to crawl into. She went in and he followed.

How this drew her back to memories of the damp soil of Cu Chi. This was no more than a hole in the ground, the soil black and crumbly; it wouldn't make a network like the blood-red clay of her homeland, but it was safer than anywhere on the surface. If the Japanese searched the forest, she and Heng would hear reverberations well before the enemy was upon them.

She sank back against the wall and winced as the soil stung the wounds on her back. Heng edged round towards her. "Let me look." It was an order, not a request. She bent forward. "The skin is hardly broken," he said dismissively. Was he laughing? "You should have seen their kerosene supplies go up! What did you find out?"

As relief and fear subsided, irritation grew. She deserved some expression of concern. The herb seller with the kind eyes would have asked, are you alright? Heng may be a true believer in the cause, but he also enjoyed the danger for its own sake, like a boy playing a game.

She'd exact a price for her services. "The comrade in the market, at the herb stall, who is he?" she asked.

Even in the dark, she knew he was grinning. "You don't need to know."

She thought of Van telling her that she could not be made to divulge information she did not have. But to know his name, even his *nom de guerre*, would be something to cherish. She stayed silent, letting Heng realize the name was her price.

He cursed. "I got you out quickly, didn't I? I could have left you there until morning. You'd have come away with more than a few scratches on your back."

Had the women told him of those other injuries? She was meant to be grateful he'd helped her get away from Kaneko, but he'd sent her there in the first place. She wouldn't concede anything.

The Quiet Soldier

He cursed again. "In love, are we? Take it from me, Phuong, love is a waste of effort. You've been listening to too much *dàn bau* music." He started humming quietly about love. "Alright! He's called Bui Hien."

Bui Hien. It suited him; Hien meant *nice, kind, gentle*.

"Stop daydreaming, Phuong. We don't have time for soppiness. What did you learn? And if you say nothing, I'm going to wring your neck."

"Fifteen died and forty two escaped on the day of the coup. My brother-in-law escaped." She fell silent, thinking of Nam. She was no further forward in finding him. As Heng chivvied her, she reached to her waist. "And I got these." Before she'd run from Kaneko's quarters, she ripped some pages from the ledger. She handed them over.

Heng took them, but there was no light for him to read. "So what are these?"

"Lists of detainees, perhaps the prisoners you're interested in."

"Good. And we've compromised the captain. He'll have some explaining to do. You say your brother-in-law was on the list of escapees?"

"Not his real name." She remembered Van lecturing her about true revolutionary leaders. What sorted them from the rest was the will to withstand torture without breaking. Long had managed it. Born into wealth and privilege, he'd shown character, fulfilling the promise of his youth. Lan would be proud, yet she felt sick at heart.

"So you recognized his alias?"

"Yes, I knew it." Remember Hoang Anh, but do not speak his name, Van had told her. When she had seen *Hoang Anh* on the list of those who had escaped when the French fled, she knew her brother-in-law was free. In the dark, dank shelter, she covered her eyes and wept. Long had survived.

CHAPTER 13

A bastard combination of bookish internationalism and chauvinistic patriotism, a melange of intellectual Marxism and primitive social demands, corresponding exactly to the aspirations of a section of the backward masses of these
Asiatic deltas.
—French intelligence-analyst's assessment of Vietnamese Independence Day speeches on September 2, 1945

The infiltration of Ba Ra prison was the first of many similar missions. Dressed in an ao dai, she became bait for some predator easily taken in by her faux-trusting manner. It was amazing just how much a man would say to a woman he believed to be wonderfully ignorant. Little changed when the Japanese retreated and the French returned. If anything, Frenchmen were easier to dupe, since they had long treated Vietnamese women as playthings.

She kept the ivory-handled knife sharp and practiced with it. As a rule, it was not in Heng's interests to order men like Kaneko killed—better to compromise them. He did not want more attention than was necessary, but she knew if it suited him, he would order her to use her knife. She began to wait for the order.

Heng's attic army became her family. She learned to prepare pipes for the old men, heating the brown gum into amber as she listened respectfully to their tales. They had all lost someone and now, she understood, needed to lose themselves. She chatted with the young mothers and helped with the children. But she was closest to two unmarried young women, Tha'm and Mai. Both were away on missions when she had arrived. When they returned and found her there, the peasant girls resented the newcomer and her refined manners, but thawed when the old women whispered about her injuries. And they saw for themselves that she was resourceful and brave. With her fine features and elegant deportment, she drew attention wherever she went. When Heng sent Tha'm to entice a French captain, he'd ignored her. "You wear the ao dai better than me," Tha'm admitted to Phuong on her return. "You walk like a mandarin's daughter. I've worked in the fields too long. My mother got it wrong when she called me discreet grace."

Her talents lay elsewhere. She carried a double-bladed knife and could kill so efficiently that the wound had to be searched for. She could conceal herself in small spaces. Once, she'd hidden under the floorboards in the regional court house for more than a day before assassinating a member of the French High Criminal Commission and then returned to her hiding place until the building was empty. She could walk in a crouch position for miles and swim underwater with ease. She'd pace an area and map it accurately from memory. She was fascinated by the weapons the French possessed. Her ambition was to seize a French rifle and be allowed to keep it. Heng was forever telling her to slow down and be patient. Yet he valued her skills and her loyalty. "However sharp it is, the knife will never cut its own handle," he'd say about her.

Mai had a gentler soul. She had briefly been married. She was frail, with a small distended stomach—a legacy from the famine that had killed her husband and child. She liked it best when she could stay and help with the cooking and child care, but one day she was sent on the type of mission they all dreaded. While at the market, she had caught the eye of a Sûreté officer. She became his mistress and lived in his apartment on the other side of town. After that, Phuong would see her in the street or the market sometimes. Not a word or a look could pass between them, but occasionally Phuong would go close and let her garments brush against her friend's to say, you are not alone. Mai had no visible bruises and put on weight, so maybe the policeman was kind to her, or at least not unkind, but if Heng ever wanted him dead, Tha'm and Phuong would have fought over the chance to do it. More likely, the Frenchman would tire of Mai one day; the stream of information would dry up, and with luck she'd come back to them.

The old people did not comment on the young women's comings and goings, but they talked of greater matters openly and eagerly. Tha'm wasn't interested; she knew all she needed to know. It was simple: she hated landlords, puppets, aristocrats, and foreigners. However, Phuong listened as avidly as she had once listened to her father discussing politics with her brother and Long. She heard their bitter laments at the return of the French. That the Nationalist Chinese had swooped southwards to aid the French had been no surprise. They'd pillaged even when they found the population starving, but who were these British and why had they helped the enemy in the south? No one could understand it. If British troops had not "restored order" until the French arrived back in force, then Vietnam would have broken the imperialists' shackles.

But there was some good news. The puppet emperor Bao Dai had abdicated and, best of all, their leader Ho Chi Minh had declared Vietnamese independence. Accounts traveled from the north via the political cadres who risked their lives to share his inspiring speech. "The entire Vietnamese people are determined to mobilize all their physical and mental strength, to sacrifice their lives and property, in order to safeguard their freedom and independence." Young and old rejoiced when they heard how, dressed like a worker, he'd stood proudly in Ba Dinh Square in the Ascending Dragon Citadel and begun by quoting the Declaration of Independence. "All men are created equal; they are endowed by their Creator with certain inalienable Rights; among these are life, liberty and the pursuit of Happiness."

"The Americans are our friends because they believe in freedom, as we do," old Mr Kim told her. Even Heng had been impressed when he heard about the American planes flying over the crowd. Though he never tired of saying that Vietnam must be self-reliant, he could not conceal his pride that such a great nation had saluted the fledgling government.

She'd never seen a plane and could not follow his boyish descriptions of these Lightnings that appeared, which was the event that most impressed Tha'm, but Phuong understood the Declaration. She repeated it to herself. It was like a promise addressed to her personally. Life, liberty, and the pursuit of happiness. She was pursuing happiness, for she was searching for Lan, Long, and Nam. She tried not to hope to meet Bui Hien again, but still she daydreamed about doing so and finding that he carried her memory in his heart as she carried his.

She knew better than to ask Heng anything more about the herb seller, so what she did not know, she made up. With Tha'm snoring in

The Quiet Soldier

the hammock next to her, she'd lie awake devising a life for him. He was from a bourgeois family, as she was. Like her brother, he was clever and sent off to France to be educated. She recalled the problems that had caused in her own family and so imagined a different sort of father from her own, one who would not speak of Shame and Disgrace when his son said the world was changing. Nam had been right and her father wrong. She gave her beloved a scholar-father like her renowned ancestor Trung Quang Vinh, one of the intelligentsia, not a bureaucrat. Perhaps son had followed father and become a scholar too, before the call to arms. She did not want him in danger, though what refuge there was in Vietnam she did not know. She would like to make him a poet, but saw the agony of composition in such times. If only he could write of love and nothing else! Perhaps, as those kind eyes suggested, he had chosen a profession dedicated to helping others. Yes, his herb selling was more than a cover; he knew about traditional remedies because he was a doctor, a doctor who never lost a patient nor saw gruesome war injuries. So young a man would be unattached, but not like Heng, not married to the cause. The brief moments at the market became whole conversations. She saw him in Western clothes—light colored linen suits with crisp white shirts. He had impeccable manners and treated her with solemn kindness, as if she were fragile and priceless. Even before the French were finally driven out, he'd have the courage to marry. But here her dreams dissolved. She could not be that wife. Such a man deserved a chaste bride.

What would Lan think if she found her? When she had fled Cu Chi after Long's arrest, she had left behind a little sister who had been naive, trusting, a child. She would be reunited with a duplicitous and cunning woman, one to whom lies came more readily than the truth. She never said a word to an outsider that was not contrived and, even with those she trusted, she weighed her words. She had corrupted all the feminine virtues. When she was self-demeaning, it was a ploy. Worst of all, she knew how to be enticing. The veil once lifted could not be replaced. Phuong held to the hope of finding Lan again but began to dread her sister discovering what she had become.

Years went by and Heng's army decamped from Ba Ra. They knew the Sûreté was closing in when Mai's body was found floating in the canal. They moved to Long Binh, leaving only the infirm behind. As feared, these remnants were arrested and interrogated. Phuong added those who died—Mr Kim, his wife and Hiep, a boy with an abdominal wound, who had been younger than her—to the list of spirits to be honored on their anniversaries. She hoped that one day she would say prayers for them, her father, and Van at the family altar in Cu Chi.

In Long Binh, she came closest to finding her family. The Committee there whispered of Hoang Anh, a man much respected for the years he had spent in prison. He was accompanied by his wife. So they have married, Phuong thought when she heard the news. But they stayed only a few months in Long Binh before an informer forced another move. The closer they got to Saigon, the more virulent the Sûreté's network of spies. And yet their orders were to make the city itself their next destination. Heng could barely suppress his excitement when he told them. "Our work will be vital there. It's where the big decisions are made. We won't be dealing with provincial types. We'll be hitting those who make the policy."

"Can't I stay?" asked Phuong. Alone, she would be able to achieve little, but she could not bear to think of moving further from Lan and Long.

"There's no question of that," said Heng, angry at the request. "You'll be arrested if you stay. Don't worry little sister, your relatives have probably moved too." She saw his sharp canines as he smiled. "The whole world is converging on Saigon. You might find them there."

Some days later, as they were on the road to Saigon, he walked beside her for a while. Tha'm drew back before Heng spoke. "I expect your mother taught you to dance?"

"Not my mother, no, but my sister." She thought of those evenings when they'd both performed for Long. He'd guessed that she was dancing the role of a princess spirited away.

"And you know English as well as French don't you?"

"I understand a little."

"I'll see if I can get you some books. You must practice."

When Phuong told Tha'm what he had said, Tha'm asked, "What sort of fighting needs dancing and English?"

CHAPTER 14

They became as dangerous as they wanted to be, they never knew how dangerous they really were.
—Michael Herr

The people of Saigon were surely another species. They rushed around their vast, teeming city hollering and gesticulating in ways that would have been condemned in any village. Towards strangers, they managed to be both insolently curious and insultingly indifferent. The streets were dangerous. They were not only full of bicycles and trishaws, but also cars such as only the military and police had elsewhere. Even Tha'm was frightened. "There's so many of them," she complained. "I'm a village girl. I thought Ba Ra was big."

Phuong remembered Nam packing up and going to Paris when he was her age. He must have been intimidated, but he'd never shown it. He would just come home exhilarated with new ideas. "Where do you find your courage?" she had asked him once. Wherever he was, he needed it still, and so did she.

When Heng's contact led them to Cholon, the Chinese district, they were all appalled. Of course there were many Vietnamese who were ethnically Chinese, but could they really be trusted? Hadn't the Chinese been the first and most tenacious of Vietnam's oppressors? But Heng treated Mr Chou with such deference that Phuong realized the old man with the three-strand beard was his superior in the organization. "Don't worry," she told Tha'm, "Heng protects the tree that gives him fruit."

The army settled down in a room on the Quai Mytho. It was smaller than the one in Ba Ra, but they managed, as only the very young and old were confined there. Often, Tha'm and Phuong would sleep on a flat section of the roof. They could see the bustling streets below and the shape of the Mekong River as it snaked through the city. They got used to the curious habits of their Chinese neighbors and started to learn the ways of their new quarters. "It's a different sort of hiding we're doing here," said Tha'm. "I could attack someone in the street and get away with it."

But only Phuong had been given a task so far, and it was to improve her English. Heng returned one day with some colorful magazines, some in French, some in English. "Here," he said, "study these. They'll help with your languages." He read aloud from one called *Vogue*—a French word but the language was English. "Her Majesty the Queen and her daughter H.R.H. Princess Margaret are photographed in color by Cecil Beaton, both wearing magnificent gowns by Norman Hartnell. Vivien Leigh, meanwhile, appears with a blonde hair-do for her role as Blanche in Laurence Olivier's London production of *A Streetcar Named Desire*." She was surprised that he could speak English so well and wondered whether it meant he'd had a privileged upbringing like her own, and if so, why he lost no opportunity to tease her about being a lady.

"Why should I speak English?" she asked. To converse with some man, of course, what else could it be? Some English Kaneko.

"Not speak it, understand it. In fact, you should conceal how much you understand." Should she tell him that she already understood the language well, because Nam had spoken to her in English as much as French? But she was in no hurry to embark on snaring another man. "We're interested in Thomas Fowlair, a British journalist. He's more independent-minded than the Americans, and we may be able to do something with him."

"He's sympathetic to us?"

The fangs showed. "I wouldn't go that far, but he's not biased against us. His reports are fair. A strange man—with some influence, but disappointed with life," said Heng, adding bitterly, "Do you think, Phuong, that every man escaping boredom comes to Vietnam?"

"I do not know what men are like beyond Vietnam. I've never been anywhere else," she said, refusing to bond in contempt for foreigners when it would be she who had to let them touch her.

As soon as Heng left, she stared at the photographs. Who were these people and what lives did they lead that their colored pictures traveled the world? The women had curious shapes. The younger ones had tiny waists and garments that billowed out to abrupt, premature hems. Their bare legs were clearly visible, the exposure emphasised by strange, tilted footwear on their large feet. Their shoes had never tramped through jungle or waded through paddy fields. The royal women had blue eyes, the type that the Chinese believed could see through the surface of the earth. Perhaps it was a true mark of their breeding, those round, azure eyes. Their curiously colored hair was cut and curled to frame their faces. The one called Leigh had hair as white as a *so dua* flower. Her breasts were almost as bare as a montagnard tribeswoman's, yet a luxurious gossamer-thin shawl coiled around her arms. She looked forlorn, like a pampered, unloved courtesan.

When Phuong and Tha'm finally ventured out into the streets, they saw such women. "Wearing magnificent gowns" and propelled forward by their tilted shoes, they spilled out of cars talking stridently, usually in French, but occasionally in English, in accents she had never heard before. They sat at the tables outside the hotels in the main square drinking alongside their menfolk. These Westerners had shops exclusively for them. No Vietnamese would have any business in them, unless to sweep the floor.

"We can be invisible, if we want to be," Heng would say. Tha'm and Phuong tried this out. Dressed in rough pyjamas and conical hats, they found that they could wait at the side of a bar or restaurant and be close enough to hear conversations, the speakers simply assuming they were messengers or servants. They were never accosted; Saigon prostitutes paraded in *ao dais*, not peasant clothes.

Tha'm became eager to start operating in this new jungle. "I could roll a grenade into the place and be back in the crowd before it blew," she offered, after she and Phuong had spent the evening outside Givral's, a noisy cafe across the rue Catinat from the Continental Palace Hotel.

But Heng cautioned her. "Saigon is full of foreigners, and we can't kill them all. As we found in the provinces some are more useful for the information we can glean from them."

Tha'm was scarcely satisfied by the small tasks he gave them. Mostly, he used her and Phuong as messengers. Any written material posed a danger, so usually oral messages were passed as quickly as possible through the network. Phuong's memory proved better than her friend's. Her task was to remember word for word what was said; Tha'm's skill lay in knowing when it was safe to approach a contact and when it was not.

Her boldness became rashness when she was enraged by foreigners. She despised their clothes, their manners, their presence in her country, their eyes, their money, what they brought with them, and what they took away.

They often saw Vietnamese women with foreigners. Some would even sit in the cafes, sipping drinks, even publicly holding hands. Once, a man with hair the color of sand and white, blotchy skin leaned down and kissed a young woman on the lips, as if sucking the juice from a mango. "Look at her," Tha'm hissed. "How can she stand that hairy giant?" Perhaps she's one of us, Phuong wanted to say, saddened by her loneliness. Even to give a single look of complicity might betray her, so she was alone in her world of deception, letting the foreigner think she was with him for his money while bearing scowls from Vietnamese like Tha'm.

They had been in Saigon four months. Heavy rain had been falling for days when Phuong and Tha'm were sent across the river to receive a message. Their pyjamas were soaked by the time they found their contact, an old man begging outside the walls of a Buddhist monastery. The river was swelling under the bridge as they joined the crowds crossing it. Both were thinking about finding the man to whom Phuong had to relay the message. They had no name but knew that they should look for him at a fish stall off the rue Catinat. Only if they judged it safe to do so, with passwords correctly given, would Phuong repeat the message. She was quiet, silently repeating it to herself. It made no more sense than the other messages she had carried, but she knew better than to change a word.

Tha'm grabbed hold of her arm in such a way that Phuong knew they were being followed. She quelled her impulse to run. The enemy would be on both sides of the bridge, so flight would suggest guilt and be futile. The rain was so heavy that she could hardly see to the river. The women in the sampans seemed harmless enough, but any one of them could be in the pay of the Sûreté. She reminded herself of who she was meant to be. The lies must come easily. She let the message slip from her memory so they wouldn't be able to prize that from her.

Suddenly, she heard her name spoken tenderly, "Phuong, little sister!" She turned. Maybe it was a trick. She certainly didn't recognize the man who had called. Through the gray mist, a peasant was limping towards her, one withered arm outstretched. Tha'm stepped to the side, ready to strike. But Phuong, with a gasp, held her back. She recognized the voice. *A man would be a fool to seek anything closer to perfection than that fish sauce.* It was feeble now, but still that of Ngo Quang Long, son of a mandarin from Hue.

CHAPTER 15

As the enemy has made waste of us, we will make waste of them.
    —Ngo Vinh Long and Nguyen Hoi Chan

"Not here," hissed Tha'm as Phuong flung herself towards the outstretched hand. She was right, Tha'm of all people was teaching her caution. Phuong looked down and forced herself to turn away. She held on to the bridge rail, shaking. For eight years, since the night of that Sûreté raid when Long was arrested, she had stayed alive for this moment. Seeing him again was to restore all that had been wrenched from her. Little Phuong, with no worries greater than a stern word from her father or a dread visit from her aunt, would regain perfection when she saw Ngo Quang Long. The cawing of cranes fighting for the fish that the fisherwomen were bringing ashore cut through the air. The mist hovered around her, and she remained afraid. "Wait," Tha'm urged her, as Long made his way across the bridge towards the city and they followed.

He was so slow that they had to keep stopping to maintain a safe distance behind him. The limp was no disguise, she could see. His left leg swung out from his hip as if permanently dislocated. His left shoulder hung low. Had they crushed that side of his body? She grieved at every step he took; he had been a young man imprisoned at Ba Ra but only this broken shell had escaped.

Long led them through narrow streets until pausing outside a shop where the air reeked of oil. An old man was on his haunches repairing a bicycle, spinning the front wheel. Long gave them a warning glance that stopped them following as he hobbled in through the narrow doorway. Tha'm shoved Phuong towards a shop opposite selling coral beads. "Look," she said, picking up a necklace of deep red, "would this suit me?" Phuong could scarcely play her part, for thinking who was in that

The Quiet Soldier

workshop. Long could be saying to Lan now, *I've found your little sister!* Her eyes were drawn back to the door, even as Tha'm shook the beads in front of her. Would Lan rush out, despite the risks, to take her in her arms?

Tha'm had made a show of considering every piece of jewelery on display before Long reappeared at the door and waved Phuong in. Tha'm crouched by the bicycle repair man, setting up guard beside him. It was cool inside, but the smell of engine oil lingered in the dimly lit room, which was full of dismantled bicycles, some parts hanging from the ceiling. "Little Phuong," said Long again. Once, when she was an innocent child, he had grabbed her round the waist, scooped her up and sat her on his lap, then kissed her on the cheek. She remembered his endearment—*Little Phuong, how lovely you are.* Now he took one hand in his, and she felt the roughened, broken skin. He was clearly part of the bicycle repair business. "Even when they told us that you were here in Saigon, we did not dare to hope, but it is you!"

"Yes, it is her," confirmed a voice from the shadows. Lan stepped forward. Much thinner, in peasant clothes, with her hair pulled back severely, but unmistakably Lan, still with the deportment of a lady. Phuong ran forwards. Her sister flinched at her first touch, and then put her arms around her. When Phuong began to cry, Lan held her back at arm's length.

"We must be strong," she admonished. "We have survived when many have not. What of father?"

While her friend waited outside, Phuong told of their father's death and of how Van had brought her as far as Ba Ra. Nothing seemed to surprise them. They did not applaud her courage or commiserate over hardship. The privations and dangers were, it seemed, much as they expected. They did not ask for details; they had details of their own, worse no doubt, for no one had ever tortured her or made her choose between her own life and a friend's. As they talked, she saw that Long's left hip bone jutted out as angular and sharp as the bicycle frames littering the room. He could not bend his left leg at the knee, so that it stuck out in front of them while the sisters, daughters of Trung Van Co, sat cross legged on the oil-drenched floorboards. Long could not seem to get comfortable and winced with pain as he moved. And those eyes, those round, expressive eyes were now rheumy and opaque. Had old age been visited on him prematurely like a sickness, or was he too close to tears?

He seemed more affected by the reunion than Lan, who, beneath an air of steely self-control, seemed exasperated. Perhaps she had been speaking to him as well when she said we have survived when many have not. Phuong wanted to ask if they were married, but such a question seemed too personal, too trivial somehow. Lan had scarcely been interested in weddings when their father had been planning all those years ago. Even then it was as if she had been schooling herself to accept suffering. Phuong longed to ask about their brother. Had Nam also been arrested on that day or had he escaped north as her father had believed? There had been no evidence of his being at Ba Ra, which was either the best of news or the worst. She had woven him into her dreams, so that, when she imagined Ho Chi Minh's Declaration of Independence, she saw Nam at his side, a loyal lieutenant.

But Lan's manner cast a cold, hard light on all dreams. When Phuong began to reminisce with *do you remember?* Lan stopped her and snapped, "The past is a shadow, sister. You must jump away from your shadow." A shaft of light from the open door lit Phuong's features, and Lan said, "You are beautiful, we always thought you'd grow up that way," as if to rebuke her. Finally, Phuong found that she had run out of things to say. She wanted to share her dreams of Bui Hien, but knew this Lan would admonish her for girlish hopes.

"I'd better go now," she said, rising from the floor. "Mr Heng, my commander, will expect us back."

"We know of Heng, but you should not speak his name unnecessarily," said Lan as she helped Long to his feet.

"You know him?"

"It is he who informed us of your arrival in Saigon."

Phuong was silent. The familiar anger with Heng flared as she realized he had known for months where her family was yet had not told her. And Lan, who had been in the city longer than her, had borne the waiting. Phuong shook her head and said softly, "Honored sister, every day since you fled, I have stayed alive so that I might see you again."

Lan retreated to the shadows. "The personal cannot take precedence over the political," she answered. Her tone did not soften as she added, "We shall see each other frequently from now on, little sister."

The Quiet Soldier

Phuong turned into the light and saw the crouching Tha'm look up at her expectantly. Never had she seemed so warm, so friendly, and so wonderfully easy-going. I am closer to her than my own sister, thought Phuong as Long followed her through the door. He drew her aside and said gently, "Your sister suffered a great deal when I was imprisoned. And she has given up so much for the struggle. Even now..."

Phuong nodded. All these years she had worried what her sister would think of her, the duplicitous young woman ensnaring men. She had never given a thought to Lan being less than Lan. *Listen and watch, my little Phuong, listen and watch*, their father had advised. When all the questions had dried in her mouth, she looked about her. She saw poverty and fear and a sister who was a middle-aged, hard-faced woman. It was Lan and not Long who repeated the well-worn phrases of revolution. She had the fervor of a true believer. She would die for the cause and expect others to do so too. Phuong wondered what role her sister played in Saigon. She was clearly not a fighter like Tha'm, for she hadn't the muscle that a warrior with punji develops. Her hands, as she had sat with them resting decorously in her lap, were white and soft as ever. Though she was dressed in peasant clothes, she still had the bearing of a lady. Phuong recalled that her sister's English was as impeccable as her French. Those skills would be useful in a city full of foreigners.

"That's your family!" said Tha'm, dancing beside her as they made their way back to the center of the city. The mist had thinned. They still had a message to deliver to the fish stall off the rue Catinat. "Did they have a grand ceremony when they married?" she asked eagerly. Despite her contempt for Phuong's privileged upbringing, she waited avidly for details of luxury and extravagance. Puppet landlords were disgusting, but their decadent habits were like salt on rice.

"I don't know if they are married."

"Do you think Heng will let you live with them? A family should be under one roof." There was no one left of Tha'm's family. Her younger brothers and sisters had been destroyed in a napalm attack with the women of the family. The twelve-year-old Tha'm had been out that night on a raid with her father. Weeks later, he was blown up by a mine as they sabotaged a road. Tha'm had finished cutting the ditch across the road before retreating.

"I don't know." Her friend's excitement exceeded her own. She need not dream of Lan and Long anymore; they were here in her present. She could find them at the bicycle repair shop whenever she wished. She put her hand on Tha'm's arm. "Don't ask Heng about me going with them."

"I won't. I want you to stay. Anyway, Heng doesn't listen to us, does he? He's got a plan. He's always got a plan."

CHAPTER 16

The danger season for self-expressive dresses is on us again.
—*Vogue,* June 1950

"You look extraordinary," he said. The sharp teeth flashed as he smiled. She was wearing a white dress of the sort she'd become accustomed to from the photographs in *Vogue* and *Paris Match*. But the others looked at her askance. The old, in particular, she saw, were shamed. "Like a whore," breathed Mrs Chou when Phuong had emerged from behind a screen in the dress that nipped her tight at the waist and reached only past her knees. Her legs were bare, her feet tilted. "You will have to dance in those," Heng had told her, pointing at her weird shoes. She pirouetted to show that she could balance and ended up facing Tha'm who was staring disgustedly at her. It was as if the western dress declared what she did beyond these walls: warfare through sex, sex that dishonored them all.

Heng caught her round the waist, took her right hand in his and held it out. "They will touch you like this," he said savagely, "and move you like this." He pushed her backwards. Dressed in a cream safari-suit, manouvering her round the room, he could be one of those puppets that hung around the Grande Monde, ingratiating themselves with foreigners. He spun her close to the hammock from which Tha'm glared at them. Heng stopped abruptly and pushed her away. "You need not go with anyone else," he said. "It's Thomas Fowler we're after. As a journalist with the London *Times*, he has accreditation. He often flies to the north to see the battles there."

"The north?" Bui Hien's north, the north where Nam may be, and a disappointed man was flown there! What made him so bored with his own life that he visited other people's wars for distraction?

"You can't walk through the streets looking like that. Go into the next street and hail the trishaw under the lamp." He thrust some piastres into her hand and raised his voice, as if he wanted all in the room to hear. "You're going to a gambling den, not a whorehouse. Someone will be there to chaperone you." The chores and past-times continued; no one seemed to be listening. Tha'm had curled away from them in her hammock, apparently asleep.

Slowly, Phuong put on the cotton gloves that matched her dress and tucked the piastres inside the left glove. Heng would have noticed that the tiny bag hanging over her arm was bulging, but he said nothing about her taking her knife. She had wrapped it in silk and forced it into the exquisitely embroidered bag because there was no place to hide it at her waist and she could not go without it. She turned to leave and suddenly Tha'm was at her side. "I'll be close," she whispered. She pulled at the dress. "I *hate* this."

Phuong shook her head. "Don't make me mind," she begged. "I've got to wear it."

Tha'm picked up a toddler waddling by and hugged it fiercely as if clinging to an innocence they both knew had been forfeited. Phuong went down the wooden stairs carefully in her heeled shoes, and then hailed a trishaw. As the driver pushed her through the traffic, she forced herself to consider the place she was going and the man she was to attract. Curiously, the Grand Monde was one of the safest places in Saigon because the drug traffickers, the Binh Xuyen, guaranteed it protection. Gambling losses might kill you, but not a grenade.

She had a description of the man she had been ordered to meet there. Fowler was tall, even for a European, with blue eyes. She thought of the icy cold of the royal eyes—an unnatural color for unnatural people. He was not young. When sober, he was distant in his manner but courteous. This, Heng told her, was the British way.

The streets were full outside the imposing splendor of the Grand Monde. The trishaw driver couldn't get near the curb because of the stream of cars delivering their passengers to the casino. They were nearly all foreigners, shouting loudly as foreigners do, hurrying through the wide oak doors. Ignoring the trishaw driver's scowl as he looked insolently at her dress, she paid him and sidled through the crowds to wait by the doors for her escort. Lan, now in a canary yellow *ao dai*, approached her. "I am Miss Hei," she whispered, "and you are my sister."

The Quiet Soldier

"Yes, I *am* your sister."

So Lan was to witness her degradation—more than that, she was to assist it. Even as they walked into the casino, a group of men shouting in English surrounded them. "Got a date?" one asked, leaning over Phuong. Lan drew her away.

"Come on Joe. Plenty more tail inside," yelled one of his companions. They burst through the doors, and Phuong and her sister followed into a high-ceilinged room full of enveloping noises and smells. She'd never been inside a gaming house before and hadn't been sure what the gambling tables would look like. All she could imagine was old men playing mah yongg, only with money changing hands. But the vast, high tables were surrounded by men and women shaking and throwing dice, then screaming and cursing in a babble of English and French. They seemed so stimulated that she was horribly reminded of sexual excitement. So this was what winning money, or the hope of winning, did to them. Many had lighted cigarettes in their hands, so that the air was thick with a bluish smoke that had none of the calming effect of opium.

Lan led her to a booth by the side of a dance floor. An orchestra played a tune that was slow and mournful. She watched the dancers. At least she was no longer the only Vietnamese girl in western dress. How many of them truly wanted to marry foreigners? Why would any girl who could find a husband at home wish to be taken to a foreign land? She wanted peace and prosperity too, but she wanted it in Cu Chi. Clearly the foreigners thought they had something to offer because, before Lan had ordered them drinks, bulky men were approaching the booth and asking for a dance. As soon as they had checked that it was not Fowler who was asking, Lan vehemently refused on her sister's behalf.

They had sipped their lime sodas for over an hour when a man, much like the one who had accosted Phuong at the door, reeled towards them. "Are you gonna dance?" he asked.

Lan shook her head but he persisted, bending close to Phuong, so that his sour breath became spittle on her cheeks. "Not asking you. I'm asking the pretty one. How about it?"

He toppled forwards and Lan leapt up to push him back. "Go!" she said and he backed away.

"Jeeze, only asked for a dance." He zigzagged back across the dance floor towards his watching, jeering friends. They began to throw cocktail glasses and shout mockingly at him. One glass jumped across the floor like a Bouncing Betty before shattering in front of a Vietnamese couple as they danced sedately round. The man manouvered through the debris, his expression unchanged.

"You might have to dance with some of them," Lan said quietly. "We'll invite attention if we sit alone much longer."

Phuong shuddered. "They smell," she complained, "and I don't want them to touch me." Maybe, if she spoke like a twelve-year-old, she could again be treated like one.

"Touch," said Lan scathingly, "you're worried about *touch*?" Abruptly her voice rose so that the drinkers at the next booth turned. "Where are my children Phuong? Have you asked? Do you care?" She stopped. A tall man was walking towards them, a glass in his hand.

When he asked her to dance, his accent was different from the others. "Would you care to *darnce*?" His blood-shot eyes were almost translucently blue. His manner was apologetic, respectful. Lan nodded, and Phuong rose.

He put his glass down to take hold of her hand and led her onto the dance-floor. Then he put his arm round her waist as Heng had illustrated, and they faced each other. As soon as he moved she knew that he did not care for dancing; he was indifferent to the rhythm of the music, but his hold grew so close that she knew she had aroused his desire, which was a victory, of sorts. She kept her eyes averted so that he would think her shy and so she need not look at his pallid, papery skin. He did not speak until the music ceased. "You dance very well," he said.

She guessed he meant she could follow his steps, however random. His breath smelt as sharp as the other westerner's. Close up, he looked older than she had first thought, older than Heng had described. Her dancing partner seemed weary but determined, like some soldiers she had known, and she wondered whether he fought for any cause apart from his own. "May I buy you and your, your mother a drink?" he asked as she moved back towards Lan.

"That is Miss Hei, my sister." She wanted to be alone with Lan, to ask what she meant about her children, but he followed her back to the booth and stood towering over them.

The Quiet Soldier

"Miss Hei, my name is Thomas Fowler." He turned immediately to look at Phuong, who had slipped into the seat on the other side of the booth.

Lan nodded graciously and said with icy correctness, "Mr Fowlair, this is my sister, Phuong."

Let me not have to go home with him tonight, Phuong prayed, attempting a smile. Her hands were shaking, so she took hold of her embroidered bag that she had left on the table and fidgeted with it. He watched. Was it his age or Lan's presence that made this so much more difficult than the previous times?

"Would you care to join us for a while, Mr Fowlair?" asked Lan, adding as he immediately seated himself next to Phuong, "No, not there please. Next to me."

He complied and sat talking for a while. He told them that he was from London and was a reporter. He spoke to *Miss Hei* whilst gazing at Phuong. She saw that she was reprieved. Lan or Heng, whoever decided these things, did not want her to return to his dwelling that night. He spoke of details that never reached the newspapers—and he was clever—too fine a source of information to be bled dry in one night. She felt him watching her intently with eyes that turned steely gray in the shadowy light of the dance hall. After a further round of drinks was finished, Lan rose abruptly and said, "We are leaving Mr Fowlair." A fight had broken out on the dance floor between some of the men who had earlier thrown glasses and a group of French officers. The orchestra stopped playing as two of the tussling men rolled into the wind section.

"I'm sorry you had to see that," said Fowler as he followed them out of the casino. He hailed a trishaw and asked what address he should give the driver. Lan gave him an address on the other side of the city from Cholon, and they set off.

After a while, Lan spoke. She could have been Heng, from her tone. This was Instruction. "We will not go tomorrow but the next day. He must believe that he takes the initiative. He enjoys the *pursuit* of women. He will be jealous of other men, but make sure that is the extent of his mistrust of you." She leaned forward and told the driver to change direction.

"Lan," said Phuong humbly, "what did you mean about your children?"

Lan halted the trishaw and descended before she answered. "I was in error to speak of the personal. I won't again. I'll walk from here." She moved away without looking back.

CHAPTER 17

A long and frustrating courtship.
—Graham Greene, spoken by Thomas Fowler in *The Quiet American*

She was reprieved for some months, permitted to return to the room in the Quai Mytho, to sleep untouched after evenings pressed against Fowler's insistent body as they danced at the Grand Monde. Other men approached her, and she learnt to distinguish between the accents of Americans and British. Even the singer in the orchestra became intelligible when she sang. *Baby face, you've got the cutest little baby face.*

Fowler was rarely absent. He hung about her like a smell and resolutely fended off all rivals. "Push off old man," he'd say, "the lady has a date." She came to understand what *a date* was—fruit of a different kind—an assignation between man and woman, the woman appropriated and devoured, like Cochin.

When the rainy season ended, she and Tha'm returned to the roof for the nights, looking over the river as far as the coconut fields and banana plantations where the Binh Xuyen held sway, yet from a distance it looked unsullied and safe. They would talk until they fell asleep, curled in a single blanket. When she could, Tha'm would follow her to the Grand Monde, blending with the servants and vendors outside the casino, her presence an unspoken doubting of Lan, who continued to accompany Phuong.

It could not last. The night would come, Phuong knew, when she would have to go with Fowler to his apartment. He told them he lived in the rue Catinat, and this they verified. He was not cautious. He mocked the journalists who thought they were safe from hand grenades by retreating to drink on the terrace of the Continental and was careless of his own safety.

He *was* safe, at least from her side, because he was a fount of useful information. As well as contacts in the military, he knew the Cao Dai and the Hoa-Hao. He was impartial in that he seemed to despise them all, though he had some sort of respect for the French. "They're the ones fighting this war. Do you know how many officers from St. Cyr are dying?" he asked.

Not enough, Lan's aloof expression answered (still his words were to Miss Hei and his looks to her), but he went on, "They're losing the best of a generation."

And yet how easily their army had capitulated to the Germans, she thought, recalling Nam and Long's prediction and her father's refusal to believe it possible. It had happened as Long and Nam had said, and this man was old enough to have fought in that war. What had he done when his own country had been in peril? Bored, Heng had called him. He had come eight thousand miles to follow carnage. Perhaps he saw it all as an adventure. Like Heng, he might enjoy the risks. "You are very brave," she said.

"It's easy to face danger when you've got a return ticket," he said. "It's a diversion, not enforced, as it is for the poor devils here." He shook her when he said such things, as none of her other targets had done, because he came close to recognizing who and what she might be. Such insights might make him more dangerous than brute soldiers like Kaneko.

While she could pass on fresh, detailed intelligence from such conversations, she hoped to ward off being alone with him. Twice he traveled north and came back with up-to-date news of the war. They fought battles up there, not just small skirmishes and clandestine operations. He spoke of their commander, General Giap's battalions, and she struggled to conceal her interest and pride.

Her curiosity about the north threatened to surge up and reveal itself so obviously that she feared he would notice. She wanted to ask about the climate, the landscape, the food, every aspect of the region. After his first visit, he referred to the calcaires that made the roads so hazardous for the French troops.

"Describe them please," she found herself saying.

"Well, they're tall limestone peaks that rise up abruptly by the sides of the road. They give the enemy great cover for observation and ambush."

"Why do the French not leave the roads to fight?" she asked.

"Because they have tanks—bigger than the armored cars you see patrolling on the streets here. They can't travel except on the roads," he explained, and she thought, how foolish to trap yourself inside such vehicles.

"A rich man's way of fighting," Lan said bitterly, when they talked of it later. "We must fight a different way. As Sun-Tzu taught: *The skilful warrior stirs and is not stirred. He lures the enemy into coming.*"

A week later, Fowler told them he was flying north again. He was gone for three days. On his return, he spoke openly of the fierce fighting. "The enemy's 174th and 209th regiments—about ten battalions—wiped out the French garrison at Dong Khe."

The enemy—Nam perhaps. "And this Don Khe, is it an importance place?" she asked indolently, smoothing the wide skirt of her pale blue dress and turning to watch the dancers. It was a noisy evening at the Grand Monde. The press were out on the town, celebrating their return from the north. One of them, a bullet-headed man with hair cut close, grabbed the microphone and sang tunelessly, *I wonder who's kissing her now*, leaving the orchestra in disarray.

"It's a key post," he explained, "placing the enemy astride the road they call RC 4 southeast of Cao Bang."

"You saw this?" Lan asked.

"We were flown over the battlefield, Miss Hei. Phuong, would you care to dance?" The orchestra's singer had regained his microphone when the bullet-headed man slumped to the floor. His friends were pulling him away by his feet, like an injured soldier.

"No, she would not. Mr Fowlair, what do you think will happen next?"

"A Legion parachute battalion is dropping at That Khe to fight its way up to Don Khe. That's a beautiful dress you're wearing, Phuong. Have I seen it before?" He took her hand across the table, turning to see her if her sister complained. She did not.

Phuong knew it was her turn to elicit information. "Flying above a battlefield is dangerous, I think. We are happy that you are returned safely."

He began to stroke her hand. Memories of past unwelcome fondling and pawing returned to her. She wanted to use the knife, which lay close to her fingertips. She willed herself not to pull away from him. "Do not worry," he said, "they fly us at 3,000 feet, out of the range of heavy machine guns."

"They have artillery?" She should not have used the word and to cover her error, she let his hand move up her arm.

"Yes, but I'm not going to bore you with such things! What have you been doing? Did you come here yesterday? Or the evening before?"

"We did not come, because we knew you would not be here," she said truthfully.

He looked relieved. "Princess Margaret," she said, "is a very beautiful woman, yes?"

"Not as beautiful as you, Phuong," he said desperately.

Lan leapt up beside him. "I am unwell. Mr Fowlair, may I ask you to escort my sister home?"

"No!" she tried to stay calm. "No. Sister, let me stay with you. I should care for you if you are ill."

"That is unnecessary," said Lan firmly. "You will stay with Mr Fowlair."

The order had been given. Phuong bowed her head, and when she looked up, Lan had gone.

Fowlair moved to her side of the booth. She saw raised blue veins on his hand as he caressed her thigh. "I will look after you," he said imploringly. He meant, she feared, that she would have to pretend to care assiduously for him. Further delay would only prolong the revulsion, the horror of his skin, his breath, and watery, rapacious gaze. Afterwards, she might be allowed to fall away from him, quiet. That was the moment she must seek.

"Will you come back to my apartment?" he was asking, and then the rushed words of confession. "I haven't been able to stop thinking about you. And I've been in agonies in case you were here dancing with someone else..." On and on, as if it mattered, as if his desire meant anything.

"Yes," she said. The orchestra began another song she recognized, something briskly romantic.

He led her out, putting his arm round her waist as he passed the table where his fellow journalists were arguing noisily. "Bill, you're a bastard..."

"So I'm a bastard! Why should I worry about the darned French? This is only a damned colonial war anyway."

Outside, it was still warm. A girl brushed past as Fowler summoned a trishaw. It was Tha'm, who must have seen Lan leave earlier and waited for her friend. In the trishaw, Fowler's knees stuck up absurdly in front of him. He was very tall, much taller than any Vietnamese. Too big, he would hurt when he entered her. She wondered whether he would recognize her pain if she cried out, or whether he would think he had given pleasure. She wondered whether she was to be the mistress of a man who would care about the difference.

CHAPTER 18

The wound has healed, but the scar is somewhat irregular.
—Dr. Vo Hoang Le, a tunnel surgeon who, with a punctured lung, sewed up his own chest wound without anaesthetic.

South Vietnam 1967

    The village of My Tinh burns for two days, and the villagers wait for the smoke to clear before returning to rebuild their hooches. Despite the doors, the smell seeps into the tunnel where Phuong lies on her ledge. She rests on her back, her arms crossed until she wakes suddenly. She coughs and bumps her head on the earthen roof as she rises up. Red soil covers her as her nightmare is broken. She was not dreaming of the men in the M113s that she so recently killed, but of her past violators, most now vague and nameless; only Fowler, Pyle, and the man on the road to Ba Ra clearly recalled.
    She crawls along the tunnel from her ledge to the workroom where some air remains. Ngoc is lying on the ground, her knees raised, her screams muffled by a dampened cloth in her mouth. Surgeon Tin kneels beside her, gently soothing his patient. "Midwife Giang is dead," whispers Day, her words reverberating in Phuong's bruised eardrums. "Fortunately, the doctor could get here."
    "How long has she been so?" Phuong asks.
    "Since the bombing. Don't worry. There's no infection in this room," says Day proudly through Ngoc's screams. "She's lying on a clean mat, and I've got a hammock ready for the baby. Look, sugared water in case she hasn't got enough mothers' milk."
    Phuong kneels on the other side of Ngoc. Tin looks across at her briefly. He is worried, she can see. He takes the cloth from Ngoc's mouth and her

The Quiet Soldier

screams ring out. He kneads her abdomen as if it were dough. Her screams become grunts as her breath quickens. She pants and then emits noises that seem to come from deep within her. The baby slips out onto the mat, thin, yellowish, and bloody. Tin grabs it by the feet, and it lets out a single cry. Gently he lifts the baby and offers it to Phuong. She takes it and wipes the secretions that block the baby's nostrils with a clean cloth. Then she holds it so that Tin can cut the umbilical cord. As he knots the cord, he explains, "The baby wanted to come out feet first." He takes the baby from Phuong, and Day raises Ngoc up so that he can lay the child on its mother's breast. "A boy." He smiles, "a boy."

Ngoc holds the child and gazes at it, amazed, as if it is the first she has ever seen. It is—of her own. Puffy and bog-eyed with exhaustion, her hair dripping with perspiration, she embraces him triumphantly.

As Tin returns to his patient to deal with the afterbirth and Day fusses over her small collection of cloths she has amassed to cover the baby, Phuong retreats and turns her face to a corner of the workroom. Her AK 47 lies propped against the wall and she picks it up, pretending to clean it. She's tasting again the bittersweet of a friend's achievement. Ngoc has given birth to a son. Her husband will love her for that—the family name will be preserved. One son is worth a thousand daughters. If Ngoc were her brother's wife, then the tiny baby suckling at his mother's breast would be her nephew. Nam's wife! Why does she concoct such fantasies?

Where are my children? Do you care? Lan scolded her when she did not want to dance with foreigners. In Saigon, her sister's bitterness was palpable; she wore it like a *khan dong*. It made her less effective as an agent because she could not fully blend in or effectively encourage men to confide in her. There were times when Phuong expected her to be unmasked, especially when she worked alongside CIA officers at the American Legation. Fowler for one had detected the bitterness and treated Lan warily. Yet had she more to complain of than her brother and sister? Who knew, as far as Nam was concerned. No word had ever reached them of his fate. Perhaps he died on the night of the Sûreté raid, all those years ago. Perhaps he was alive at this moment and crying *where are my children?*

She can always feel Tin's presence when he is near. His voice thrills her because of his northern accent, like the voice in Ba Ra market that seduced her. "Ngoc will be fine," he says reassuringly. "Day will mother her and fuss over the baby. But how are you?"

"Rested," she says.

"And the thigh?" So many men have touched her, but this one tends her wounds.

"Itching."

"A good sign. It is healing. But come to the hospital," he urges. "Let us check it, and you can stay for a while. You'll be a help. We lost two nurses in the bombing, so we could do with an extra pair of hands."

She wishes he would say *I* need you, not *we*.

"I should report to my commander." Three M113s destroyed and many enemy casualties will not be reason enough for Chot to allow her further respite from fighting.

"Don't worry," says Tin dryly. "You won't be difficult to find."

Ngoc has fallen asleep with the baby at her breast. Phuong says goodbye to Day and, slinging her AK47 across her shoulder, leads Tin through the tunnel complex.

When they arrive at the hospital, she sees why he invited her. Not for her company, but truly as another pair of hands. The long corridor is packed with patients. Mattresses are so close that they touch, and in the flickering light she sees the usual array of bombing casualties. Amputated limbs, burns, and eye injuries are most common. The most severely wounded would have died before they could be carried to the field-hospital, so Dr Tin's survival rate is actually very good. That pleases her; she knows how he suffers when he loses a patient. He is a child in that way, resistant to death.

His staff surrounds him, and instantly he must decide who to operate on. She wants to say to the nurses, let him rest, but that is the prerogative of a wife. Still, he needs her. "Can you take a turn on the bicycle?" he asks.

Not another pair of hands, but another pair of feet. She agrees with a nod. The only source of power is a bicycle-powered generator. Someone will have to pedal all night if Tin is to operate. She'll be close to him, watching him deftly use his improvised surgical implements, made from shell casings or aluminium from shot-down planes. She likes the way his healing hands transform scraps of weapons.

By morning, he has saved three more comrades, and she lies beside his most recent patients, trying to stay awake so that she can alert the

The Quiet Soldier

nursing staff if they deteriorate. Two have their wounds open and bloody. Tin discovered some time ago that there was greater chance of infection if certain wounds were sewn up. Arteries are litigated to stop the bleeding but the wound is left open, for the hardiest warriors develop new ones, *collaterals* as he calls them. She wonders if she has them and whether she will ever be injured badly enough to find out. As it is, she has learnt to see any part of the human body, inside or out, without flinching. She's almost touching Tin's first patient, a man lucky enough to get this far with an abdominal injury. She saw Tin return his intestines to his body as neatly as she used to fold her collection of scarves. I'll give blood before I leave here, she thinks, closes her eyes and sleeps without nightmares.

A day passes before she wakes. The abdominal patient has gone and in his place is a curled form groaning rhythmically. It's a curiously reassuring sound, as if the patient is not so much in pain as venting the strain of recent combat. She sits up. She hardly noticed when she arrived how the air has more than the usual fustiness of the tunnels. There must be decaying flesh nearby, severed limbs not yet taken above ground to be discarded. She must get out of the tunnels and breathe freely. She wonders whether Tin has slept or worked on despite his exhaustion. She rises and weaves her way across patients and mattresses, heading towards the ward entrance. Desperate to urinate, she'll not use the jars now she's minutes away from outside. She steps over a patient sitting upright, his one arm holding some grubby sheets of paper. It is her commander and he has seen her. She stops. No wonder Tin told her Chot would find her easily at the hospital; he must have already been a patient.

She waits, knowing he will expect to speak first. He wouldn't welcome sympathy, or even curiosity. She's close to smiling, she's so grateful for his dour professionalism, but her bladder is dangerously full.

"Ah, the doctor said you were here, helping out."

She nods, hoping he'll get on with it. He's not reading *Vogue* there. *Her Majesty the Queen and her daughter H.R.H Princess Margaret are photographed in colour by Cecil Beaton, both wearing magnificent gowns*—strange words from another world.

She strains in the dim light to see the lines and markings of a diagram he has in his hand; it looks like an enemy base, as if Chot is recuperating by planning an attack.

"You are to infiltrate the training center at Trung Hoa. Choose your own time, but do it before they regroup after this present wave." *Regroup*? The puppet soldiers have monstrous B52s on their side. As Chot reaches up to hand her the diagram, she glimpses the dressing beneath his torn shirt. He's got cuts and scratches everywhere she can see, so she guesses he's got shrapnel wounds to his stomach. He'll be in agony and, even if he's been offered pain relief, it's been in such short supply lately, he'll have refused it.

"And when I'm in?" she asks, looking at the sketch.

"*Reconnoitre*. You'll need to go in more than once. When you know it well, you'll lead a troop in to overcome the enemy. Clear?"

She hands him back the paper. "Clear. I'm going outside now, for a while."

"Just one more thing. Your comrades have requested a funeral service for you. When you're ready to go, we'll have it."

A drop of urine trickles down her leg. Her comrades rate her chances of surviving the reconnaissance mission as so slim that they want her "buried with honors" before she goes. She nods, doesn't wait for dismissal but gets herself to the surface quickly. She empties her bladder only yards from the tunnel entrance. They'll read the entire funeral oration with her listening. Even Tin, busy though he always is, might come to hear the recitation of her achievements—her medals and citations—but no mention of what cost her most dear. They'll talk about how sad it is she was killed in action.

As she pulls up her trousers and looks around her, she realizes that it's the first time she's come above ground without her AK47.

CHAPTER 19

She [was] lying beside me, a little out of breath, laughing as though with surprise because nothing had been quite what she had expected.
—Graham Greene, spoken by Thomas Fowler in *The Quiet American*

Saigon, 1950

He was not as big as she had feared. Repulsive, yes—his white, clammy body sagged on top of her—but one *dương vật* is much like another when there is no honor, and he did not hurt when inside, so she gave a little laugh of relief after he rolled off. She talked then, chattering away about trivialities so that she could forget what had happened—dresses and scarves, the film she had seen at the Majestic. Finally, he sat up and, amused, said, "You Annamites twitter and sing like birds." He encircled her wrist with his hand. "And you're so slight. I could snap you in two." He went to a shelf and poured himself a drink the color of morning piss, which he called Scotch.

Now his *dương vật* was flaccid, his conscience came to life. He began talking about how he'd taken advantage of her sister's illness—it was mostly apology, but a note of congratulation crept in. He clearly thought he'd been deft in his seductive manouvering. After cunning came the remorse. He sat in the only armchair and gazed at her limpidly. "I shouldn't have brought you here, but you're all I've thought about for months, since the first time I saw you in fact." Two trips north and the opium pipe she noted as soon as they'd entered the apartment told a different story, but she saw the way it was going to be. He convinced himself that he was devoted to—whomever—and believed in his devotion until someone else took his fancy. Then he began another obsession laced with guilt.

As she dressed, she wondered who he'd abandoned this time. There was no sign of female belongings in the apartment, nor photographs of family. Maybe, as he aged, he was finding it more difficult to pick up women. His apartment was shabby and neglected for a European's, so he was either mean with his money or he had financial burdens. She guessed a discarded wife somewhere, children too perhaps. He would not be good with children.

"Will you stay?" he asked, observing her closely as she buttoned her dress.

He was a watcher, and intelligent. She reminded herself to be careful. "I must return to see how my sister is."

"Won't you stay just tonight?"

No one would expect her back. She went to the window and gazed out into the night. In the rue Catinat, a couple of Legionnaires were aiding a third too drunk to walk. He was shouting profanities about the country and its inhabitants—another man sadly far from home. Then she saw the shape in the doorway on the opposite side of the street. It was Tha'm, waiting. If she signaled to her friend to come up, they could dispose of Fowler easily, and take the consequences with Heng. They'd continue looking over the river at night, chatting and falling asleep, heads touching. But for eliminating such a useful source of intelligence as a foreign journalist, they'd both have to answer to Heng and the rest of the committee. Worse, the Sûreté would investigate the death of a foreigner like Fowler, so everyone would have to move on from the Quai Mytho. They always lost the weakest when they fled. She shut the louvered blinds, sick with a sense of captivity. "I'll stay."

He did not want to repeat the act but nevertheless in appropriation slept with one hand between her thighs. It took all her strength not to push him away. Her embroidered bag lay on a small table where she'd placed it on first entering. Inside was her knife. She'd have to find a hiding place tomorrow, one that was accessible but where he would not chance upon it. She closed her eyes and pretended to sleep. It was the first time she'd had to remain with a man and share a bed. She feared what she might reveal if she dreamed and called out, but his Vietnamese was apparently as poor as he thought her English, so he probably wouldn't understand her cries.

Next day, to leave his touch, she rose and dressed before he woke. In the corridor, she heard Vietnamese voices. He'd left the key in the door, so

The Quiet Soldier

she unlocked it and went onto the landing. Three women crouching on the stairs stopped talking as soon as she appeared, but one, unsmiling, pointed to a curtain. Phuong nodded in thanks but the gesture seemed wrong from a girl like her in a western dress, *some tail*. She knew she could not immediately claim kinship with these women; she must assume they were puppets. She went back into the apartment and looked around. He lived in about the same space as the Quai Mytho room where, some nights, as many as twenty slept, but it was as she thought the night before—not an impressive abode for Thomas Fowler of *The Times*. The bookshelves were full, mostly of English poetry. Nothing in other languages, so Heng's information that her target spoke French badly and Vietnamese scarcely at all was probably correct. No political works, so if he was committed, he concealed it. Maybe it was true that he'd traveled all this way but did not care about the war or who won it.

He woke and scrambled out of bed, rubbing those penetrating, blue eyes and looking about for her. "So I didn't dream it," he said as he came towards her, arms outstretched, like a father to a daughter, but one who had done what no father should do. In the morning light, his white skin was lined and papery. Shamed, her eyes filled with tears. He slid his arms around her. "I know, I know, you've lost your virginity, but I love you, I love you."

She wriggled free and turned away, hating his use of sacred words. He looked pitiful in his crumpled underwear. He moved heavily into the corridor, and she heard splashes as he used the water closet behind the curtain. When he came back, he started pulling on the trousers that he'd discarded by the bed the night before. "I've got to go to work now. I'm already late, but..."

He was reluctant to go in case she left. She waited for him to solve his problem, and finally, as he threw on a jacket, he suggested that they meet later in the morning to have coffee.

"I do not drink coffee."

"Drink whatever you like, but let's meet at the milk bar on the Place Garnier. Do you know it?"

"I have never visited a 'milk bar'." She saw with delight that she was irritating him. Loathing would drive her on.

"But do you know where it is? The Place Garnier. Phuong, will you meet me there?"

She would be late, she decided, not much of a punishment for his fumbling and thrusting, but a start.

"Place Garnier? *Je ne suis pas sûr où c'est-à-dire.*"

"Don't know where it is?" He had an old man's irritability, or perhaps he spent every morning recovering his temper after vermouth cassis and Scotch. "Look, come to the window. It's almost in sight. Go down there, and it's on the left. Will you be there? Eleven thirty, Phuong?"

She agreed. "Now I must go to my sister's. She will be worried."

He embraced her, and she turned away from hot breath on her face. "Of course you have things to collect, but you'll come back won't you? Tell your sister I can provide for you. I'm not a rich man, but I can look after you. You'd like that?"

She would never ask him for anything. She'd starve rather than say thank you for what he gave. They went down the stairs, past the old women and into the street. At least he understood enough not to try to kiss her lips publicly as they parted. She saw him watching as she turned off the rue Catinat into a side street. Soon, as she expected, Tha'm was beside her. They did not acknowledge each other, for one was in peasant dress, the other with shameful bare legs, but went indirectly to the Quai Mytho.

Heng was not there, and the rest knew better than to ask where she'd been, though Mrs Chou gave her a mournful look. She changed into an *ao dai*, and packed her magnificent gown and tilted shoes. Even so, her possessions fitted easily into one large cloth bag. "I'll carry it back for you," said Tha'm.

"No," said Phuong, close to tears; Tha'm's unvoiced disgust shamed her. "Better that we are not known to each other there. Get to know the women in the building. Find out if they can be trusted." There was no clock or watch, but she guessed that, if she left straight away, she would reach the milk bar by eleven thirty. "Let's go on the roof one last time," she suggested.

The air was clear, and they sat and looked out at the river easing through the city. Eventually, the Nine Dragons washed everything away into the sea of oblivion. "What's it like?" asked Tha'm suddenly.

She didn't answer for a while. "I try not to be there, in my mind, when it happens," she said, "then it's not me they're touching."

The Quiet Soldier

Tha'm drew her dagger and stabbed at the roof tiles. Tiny chips flew about, like shrapnel. "One night," she said, "when you've drained him of all we want to know, I'm going to kill him."

Fowler was pacing outside the milk bar when she arrived. "It's past twelve," he said. "I thought you weren't coming."

"I do not have a watch." Sighing, he took her by the elbow and led her into the milk bar. When they were seated and he had purchased drinks with enough piastres to feed a family for a day, he asked, "What did your sister say? Is she angry with me?"

His face creased with concern, but again she detected pride, as if he had won at a game that he frequently played. She wished he knew that he was the fool, not Lan. "My sister is concerned about my well-being," she said, wondering whether, in truth, Lan had spared a thought for her during the night. When she had returned to Long, what had she told him? This is the night when little Phuong is to be debauched by another foreigner, a man old enough to be her grandfather? No, such things must be kept from delicate feelings. Crippled and broken he may be, but he was still Ngo Quang Long, son of a mandarin from Hue. He might pose as a mender of bicycles but, she thought, as she sipped sweetened pink milk through a straw, the depths of my degradation are beyond him.

CHAPTER 20

Neither envious nor covetous, how can he be anything but good?
— Confucius

"The Americans are noisy bastards. They throw money at a problem and shout from the sidelines." This was the third time Fowler had used exactly those words in as many weeks as he lay on the bed in his stuffy apartment. She wondered whether she should report it again to Heng since her controller retained a lingering hope that America's love of freedom drew them to Vietnam's cause. She was learning to know this man and his ways; drunk or sober he repeated himself, sometimes with modifications as if he was refining, but refining for what purpose? Surely *The Times* would not print such sentiments. Their correspondent lay in his underpants, slipping into contentment thanks to two pipes of opium, using precisely the same phrases he used the week before. "*So pleasant it is to have money, heigh ho!*" That again. The first time he said it, he'd drawn a book off the shelves and looked it up, but now he had it pat. He had money too, hadn't he? What did he think he was in this city of beggars—poor? A handwritten letter had slipped from the book as he'd declaimed. Now it was in her box under the bed ready to read when she could be sure he was out.

"Another pipe?" she offered. Three, and he would be impotent. Sometimes, he apologized.

"You care for me," he said, watching as she lit the lamp again and kneaded the opium. "I was so lonely before you came, so lonely. To be alone...*La solitude*," he added, as if his emptiness was worth translation.

So far from home, anyone would be lonely, but he had a return plane ticket if he wanted. "In London, is there a Waterloo Bridge still?" she asked, handing him the pipe.

The Quiet Soldier

"How do you know about Waterloo Bridge?" Even as he mellowed, he'd catch at some word or phrase that might have come from a rival.

"There is a film with that name. I saw it with my sister." In the Majestic, it was, in fact, Heng's shoulder brushing against her side, as, weak with longing and regret, she'd watched as her own story unfolded. She'd recognized the actress whose photograph was in the magazines she studied. Phuong reached under the bed and drew out the box. "I have seen her... here." Beneath the copies of *Vogue* and *Paris Match* was her knife. She touched it briefly, then selected the right magazine, flicked through the pages and showed him the photograph.

He was beyond focusing. His mouth attempted a smile. "Ah, Vivien ..." He drew in, exhaled slowly, and closed his eyes. "Waterloo. The British defeated the French at Waterloo, a great victory. Did you know that?"

"On the bridge?"

Another half smile. "You're so astonishingly, wonderfully ignorant. *Not* on the bridge. The bridge is named after the battle, when we defeated the French forces in an historic..." He began to doze.

When we defeat the French, we'll name more than a bridge after our victory, she thought. Victors do the naming, she knew that. There'd be no more streets named after French warships when their owners are driven away. As Fowler began to snore, she took her knife and the letter, then slipped out of the apartment, past the women on the stairs. Tha'm had spoken to them and reported that, although they should not yet be trusted, they were not hostile, and very curious about her and her old foreigner.

Sometimes Tha'm would be outside, or in a near-by side street, but this evening there was no one. She walked to the Quai Mytho. In *ao dai*, she drew attention, and a group of sailors followed her for a while, but she stepped quickly into a shop and left by the back way, the shop owner waving her through.

In the Quai Mytho, Mrs Chou sat in the courtyard and, using a palm leaf as a fan, gently rocked a hammock strung between two trees. She smiled forgivingly at Phuong. "Look, these two were born on the same day. Uoc had her daughter early, but Ly gave birth as we thought."

Phuong looked into the hammock. Two babies lay next to each other. Despite the heat, they were cocooned like two chrysalises. "A good omen," she said, but her heart constricted with envy. "They will be bound in friendship."

"Ly has a son," boasted Mrs Chou. She hesitated, and then added, "To have one son is to have; to have ten daughters is not to have." Phuong sensed her unease and waited for her to reach beyond aphorisms. Finally, after much fanning, Mrs Chou said softly, "I have something for you. Of value. You must put it inside you before, before..."

"You mean to stop...?" Phuong could not say it either. Reared without a mother and losing Lan too soon, there were words she'd never heard spoken. She looked into the hammock. Mrs Chou also peered into the hammock. "Thank you," said Phuong. Her face flushed. "Thank you." She followed Mrs Chou into the small room that she occupied with her husband.

The old woman took a small packet from the store cupboard. "I have it ready for you. It is made with crocodile dung," she said. "It works." Phuong took it and bowed in thanks. As she left, she thought she heard Mrs Chou whispering. The old woman had turned away and said something about dust.

She found Heng upstairs carelessly watching the mah yongg. When he saw her, he took her aside and she gave him the letter Fowler had kept. He read it aloud in his enviable accent. "Dear Thomas, I am sending this to the last address I have for you. When I asked your editor for your whereabouts he was not forthcoming. I know from your by-line that you are still stationed in Saigon. However, the cheques come via your solicitor and I thank you for those. Perhaps you feel that money fulfils your obligation to a wife you no longer love. That may be so. We cannot continue to argue, although my views on the indissolubility of marriage remain the same. There was a time when you too claimed to believe that we would be together for a lifetime." He stopped. "So you were right. He's left a wife in London. He's escaped to us!" He went on grimly with the letter as Phuong listened. "I am writing to you about another matter. Hugh was very ill this winter, Thomas. He had measles and nearly died. Some think of measles as a mild childhood ailment, but sadly that was not the way it was for poor Hugh. You will not need convincing of that, because I remember when you came back from one of your great adventures, you quoted the African saying 'Count your children after the measles'. Well, were you here to count, you would find that you still have two children. Regrettably Hugh's sight has been irreparably damaged. He now wears

The Quiet Soldier

spectacles and, to his distress, is unable to participate in sports. You have not been here sufficiently to know that he has no love of such activities, but unfortunately the headmaster's ruling only makes the boy feel more isolated at school. He has, I'm afraid, very few friends. It would therefore raise his spirits considerably to receive a letter from his father. God bless you. Affectionately, Helen." Heng handed the letter back, folding it back in the creases as it had been when she had given him. "Well, what do you think? Are we dealing with a man with a heart? He kept the letter after all."

"Or used it as a bookmark, forgetting its contents." She tried to keep her voice unforgiving. It was difficult to think of an abandoned wife and child as enemies. Useful or not, she wished Thomas Fowler would return to his responsibilities, or at least write to poor Hugh with the bad eyes. She considered. "He has a conscience, I think, but he likes it to sleep." She decided she should tell Heng how Fowler was still dwelling on the role of the Americans. His face clouded as she told him. "Can it be true?" she asked. "Why would the Americans get involved in our war? And if they did, wouldn't they be on our side?"

"Remember that film we saw at the Majestic? The one where the American and the French policeman walk away together, the start of a beautiful friendship?" He laughed bitterly. "It seems that the Americans are more afraid of Communism than anything. They've forgotten they used to disapprove of the French milking us!"

She absorbed this. "Fowlair says they are throwing money at the problem and shouting from the sidelines. What are the Americans giving our enemies?"

"It's your job to find out. Where is he now? How long have you been gone?"

"He's asleep. I fed him opium."

"One day he'll wake up and find you absent."

"Then I'll say I've been at the cinema with my sister."

"Then go to the cinema now. Find your sister and go with her. Keep your tickets and discard them where he will find them." As she went down the stairs, he came after her and called teasingly over the balcony, "You see, little sister, how we make lies into truth?"

She took a trishaw to a street close to the bicycle shop. As on the first time she approached, a look-out alerted the occupants and Long appeared.

Smiling, he supported himself by leaning his withered arm against the doorpost. He held a blackened cloth. Raising his good hand, which was covered in oil, he said apologetically, "Forgive me, I am hard at work." He did not comment on her new attire, but drew back to let her into the shop. Again, Lan was in the shadows and came forward as Phuong entered.

They had not spoken since the evening Lan had ordered her to stay with Fowler. "Honored sister, I hope you are recovered from your sudden illness," said Phuong, but Lan ignored the sarcasm. "We must attend the cinema, so that the old foreigner believes we do that habitually." She could not bring herself to use Fowler's name in Long's presence. Without dispute, Lan followed her, and they took a trishaw to the Majestic.

The film had started, and she had forgotten to note its name as they entered. She would have to look at the board before she returned to Fowler's apartment as well as committing the story to memory. On the screen, she recognized the dancing man once beloved of the woman that sang of bamboo trees. Now another woman was angry with him, for she thought he was married, but he was not married. She must love the dancing man to care so much, just as the one who sang of bamboo did. The dancing man was not handsome, at least no Vietnamese woman would find him so. He had a thin, narrow face and sticking out ears as it was joked was the misfortune of the men of Quang Tri Province. Yet many women loved him. Her thoughts drifted from the film to her own situation, where there was no love. She did not mind whether Fowler was married or not, but when she considered that Hien might have a wife, she envied that wife as she envied Uoc and Ly their babies. She felt despair too, for if Bui Hien were to appear now, if he were to declare that he loved her as she loved him, she would have to turn him down.

On the screen, the dancing man sang in praise of his hat, and then the woman who cared that he was married appeared in a magnificent dress made of ostrich feathers. Finally the woman learnt that he was not married, so they were both happy and danced together closely with abandon.

Top Hat, she read as they left the cinema. It was called *Top Hat*. She asked her sister Heng's question, maliciously, "Did the film please you?"

"There was no truth in it," said Lan contemptuously.

"Have you seen a film called *Waterloo Bridge*?"

"Another decadent film? Of course not."

She took a pleasure that was something like revenge in Lan's fury. "Careful sister," said Phuong. "We must do whatever we can to know our enemy." In the silence that followed, Phuong suddenly realized what Mrs Chou had whispered. Your child would be less than dust.

CHAPTER 21

Without wisdom,
it is impossible
to employ spies.
—Sun-Tzu

More American advisors arrived in Saigon yesterday, at the request of the Vietnamese government. They will join the thirty five who came last year following U.S. President Truman's Memorandum in March, stating that French Indochina is a key area that cannot be allowed to fall to the communists. French commanders have stressed that The Military Assistance Advisory Group, MAAG for short, will remain entirely non-combatant. The Americans will not engage in operations, but limit their role to advising on strategy against communist aggression and to the training of troops.

Furthermore, the French command is confident that they will soon regain the northern territory that was lost in the autumn of last year. The so-called 'disaster of RC4' in September and October 1950 was unprecedented. At Lang Son, the major depot for the border region, enough weapons and ammunition were abandoned to equip a whole Vietminh division. This led ...

That was all. He'd given up at *this led*, screwed the paper into a ball and aimed it at the fan. Some days, he stayed in the apartment writing at the rickety desk until the intense noon-day heat prevented him from leaving for his office to type what he'd written until late in the afternoon.

She hated those days, knowing that at any moment he might encircle her waist to lead her to the bed. She could only breathe freely in his absence. If, by mid-morning, she could persuade him to the milk bar that was half-way to his office, he'd walk on afterwards. Heng would be angry if he knew how assiduously she tried to get Fowler out of the

The Quiet Soldier

apartment, but she told herself that it wasn't the articles he wrote that reaped fresh intelligence; they would be published soon enough, and she was not the only soldier that spoke and read English better than the enemy knew. Anyway, they were now fully aware of the noisy bastards who shouted from the sidelines and threw money at the French. They knew too that there were to be even more of them. No, the Briton's value lay in the wealth of detail he gleaned from sources who spoke candidly to a fellow westerner.

She screwed the paper up and placed it on the floor where she'd found it. Then she went to her box under the bed and took out the cinema tickets and discarded them nearby.

There was enough of the day left for her to escape for a while, even if he came home early without stopping for a drink, so she went to the Quai Mytho. She found Tha'm, and they went onto the roof. "I have to meet a contact later," Tha'm told her. "Do you want to come?" They both knew that Heng forbade her such tasks now she was entrenched with Fowler.

"Yes," said Phuong. She changed out of her dress into pyjamas and laughed, "Fowlair wouldn't recognize me if I walked by him like this!" She hated him for assuming what was actually true—that she preferred the touch of fine silk against her skin to the coarseness of peasant clothes. Tha'm and Mai used to criticize her for her bourgeois origins, and she'd resolved to fight her trivial impulses, but they still lingered.

Tha'm sat on the roof and looked over the city. Phuong sat beside her. One day she would have to pay the price for having had more than her fair share. "I like luxuries, because of the way I was brought up," she said.

"Rice is better seasoned with salt," said Tha'm consolingly.

"And sauce as well." Fermented fish sauce, with the aroma of devotion and protection. "You know, as a child, I thought everyone had as much as we did."

"It wasn't your fault." Tha'm was in a forgiving mood. More than that, she was excited. Phuong looked at her enquiringly.

"This contact I have to meet, I think he might have orders for me. I don't know why, just the way Heng told me. This might be my chance to do something more than ferry messages."

"Not?" She could not bear to think of Tha'm as a foreigner's mistress. But a friend can hurt in ways that an enemy cannot.

Tha'm's eyes sparkled, and she hugged her knees tightly as she congratulated herself. "Not that! I wouldn't be any good at *that*. Maybe..." She chopped her hand across her throat. "Some important puppet."

"Is there anyone you wouldn't kill, if ordered?"

"No."

"Mrs Chou? Uoc's baby?"

Tha'm jumped up, angrily. "Don't be silly. How could Uoc's baby be the enemy?"

"He might grow up to be a puppet soldier." She wanted to shake Tha'm's complacency.

But Tha'm wouldn't stir. "Then Uoc will kill him."

Phuong rose too and brushed at her clothes—another bourgeois giveaway. She stopped. "Yes, you're right," she conceded. "Then Uoc would do it."

They left the roof and went into the street. Another truth—the past was your shadow. As they hurried along, she tried to make it better with her friend. "One evening we could go to the cinema if you like," she offered.

"A capitalist film? I wouldn't understand it."

"I'll explain it."

"I've seen *Cheo* theater loads of times. The actors came to our village. I like the one about Thi Hen best, the one where she tricks all those men. And she gets out of being dirty with any of them! Films can't be better than *Cheo*."

"Different. Even if you didn't like what you saw, you'd find out how to get into a cinema. You might be ordered to do that, and you wouldn't have a clue." She knew she was being spiteful.

Tha'm didn't answer. They'd entered the rue Catinat, which was busy with people emerging after the noonday heat. If Fowler had decided to return to his apartment at this time, they could bump into him on the pavement. Her boast about his not being able to recognize her would be put to the test. She pulled her hat further over her face, relieved when they turned into a side street. At a sign from Tha'm, she stopped. They wouldn't approach the contact point until observing it for a while. She withdrew into a doorway on the opposite side of the street and squatted like a servant, taking in every detail around the fish stall where Tha'm had been ordered to meet her contact. He or she was not known to either of them—only by an alias and password.

The Quiet Soldier

She signaled to Tha'm that all seemed clear, and her friend approached the fish stall where an old woman was bent over the white cat fish, carp, and live eels on display. Phuong watched as the old woman shuffled towards an alleyway. After a while, another figure emerged, and Phuong's heart leapt in recognition. She recalled their last meeting. *How can I help you?* She could not hear what he and Tha'm said to each other, but the movements of his hands were unmistakable as he handed her a parcel. It was Bui Hien. She wanted to rush across the road and say, "Look, it's me!" but she'd put everyone at risk if she did. And after *it's me*, what then?

Tha'm crossed the road, scowling, the parcel in her hands. It stank, so that passersby looked away. Hien left by the alley, but Phuong stared after him. "Come on," said Tha'm, and Phuong slowly followed. The stories she'd made up about Hien were so elaborate that she was shocked to see him much as he'd been before, now under cover as a fish seller instead of herbalist. Maybe he'd traveled no further than Ba Ra to Saigon as she had done. His reappearance suggested he was no passing contact but part of Heng's network. "That man, what was his name?" she asked, fearing her voice betrayed her warmth.

"He calls himself So~n," answered Tha'm disgustedly, stretching out her arms to keep the parcel further away from her nose. "He could have given me fresh fish. Mrs Chou would have cooked it for us afterwards."

Phuong laughed. How extraordinary that Tha'm should see Hien and not love him instantly as she had done. "Here, give that to me." She took the parcel that Hien had held and wondered how to raise Tha'm's spirits. They were less than a mile from the Quai Mytho and, as trained, they stopped to check to see if they were followed, squatting on a bridge over the Saigon river. "I'm going to tell you about a film I saw."

"Go on."

"It begins with a man leaning over a bridge, a bigger bridge than this. He is an old man with gray hair."

"A mandarin? A landowner?"

"A soldier, who has been fighting for a long time, since he was young. Looking over the water, he remembers his youth..."

"They have found a truth there. I think of being young when I look at the sampans. My father fished every day. Always we had fish, *fresh* fish."

"The soldier remembers meeting a young girl, a dancer. He loves the dancer, but he must go away to fight."

"Then she should go and fight too."

"The rulers forbid the women to fight. It's a foreign land, but a good land at this time, I think, because they hated the French."

"I've heard of it. Germany."

"No, it's where Fowlair comes from—Britain, but let me tell you about the girl and the soldier's love for her."

"Tell me the rest another time. We must get back. You've got to change, and I must report to Heng." Tha'm waved the parcel of rotten fish in the air. "This is a message I'll happily pass on to him."

They went to the Quai Mytho, and Phuong waited outside until Tha'm had ensured Heng would not see her enter in peasant clothes. As she slipped by the stairs on her way to the roof, she saw them in the small ante room bending over the stinking fish, poking at its entrails. She changed back into *ao dai* and waited on the roof for Tha'm, but she did not come, so Phuong went back to the apartment in the rue Catinat. Fowler returned a little later to find her looking at the pictures in *Paris Match*. He'd already had a beer. She smelt it on his breath. "Let's go to the Continental," he said, "and have a drink." Obediently, without a word, she rose and went with him.

CHAPTER 22

It is rare, indeed, for a man with cunning words and an ingratiating face to be benevolent.
—Confucious

    The Continental Hotel's marble floors were precarious, especially when wearing western shoes like those she had on tonight, the satin high heels matching her blue dress. Yellow light from the chandeliers flooded down, illuminating, she feared, what she was doing in such a place. She saw the Vietnamese staff in starched white jackets carrying suitcases, serving drinks, and delivering messages and thought, we have become servants in our own land. The Continental was intimidatingly colonial; in its foyer and bars the languages were English and French. American accents were still in a minority, but what they lacked in numbers they made up for in volume. Fowler steered her by her elbow as they entered, and she gazed about her. Yes, she recognized those at the bar as the Americans who regularly tried their luck at the Grand Monde. There was the one called Will, so small and wiry he could be Vietnamese, then the towering Abe and Mike and two more whose names she did not yet know, clearly all "advisors," with their crew cuts and military talk. Will was jabbing his finger at Abe and yelling, "Rag-tag farmers, godamit. They work in the paddy fields all day and arm themselves with rusty flintlocks when night falls. How long do you think..."

    She never heard the end of Will's question as Fowler leaned close to whisper, "Let's get a table over there," and led her away. He ordered their drinks, and they sat in silence. She strained to hear the conversation at the bar. It sounded as if Will was goading his fellow countrymen, as she'd heard him before. He would not rest until someone tried to punch him. She wasn't sure whether he believed deeply in some cause or wanted to provoke.

A man was striding towards them. He was unmistakably American, though he hadn't been at the bar with the others, having stepped from the terrace. No other nation produced men so flushed faced with hope and good food. He was taller than Fowler and decades younger, Hien's age, but how different from her gentle Hien. The foreigner stared at her as he approached but spoke deferentially, addressing his words to Fowler. "I was wondering whether you and your lady would step across and join my table..."

Any foreign arrival should be cultivated; the Committee would expect to be informed about him, yet she found herself willing Fowler to refuse the invitation. The sturdy American's politeness could not conceal a calculated resolve. She was glad to see Fowler hesitate, but then he accepted, and she had to accompany them both onto the terrace to join the other Americans. Joe, who she'd already marked as working in the embassy, was saying, "They have artillery that can only have come from the Chinese. Take it from me, it's Korea all over again." Fowler introduced her to the man who'd invited them over—"Alden Pyle." The name seemed stranger than other western names. She wondered if Heng, whom she suspected of mixing with more foreigners before the war than he liked to admit, would be able to place such a name. The unnerving newcomer took her hand and held it longer than etiquette required. What was it about him that worried her? He was quieter than the rest—but then, wasn't that what was said of her? Fowler was watching them closely. His mood had become brittle; something about Alden Pyle bothered him too.

As the conversation resumed, she gathered that the Americans were expecting their press corps to return from the north. At the mention of the war zone, Fowler became defensive about not going with them. Was he losing his nerve, she wondered, or did he refuse because of her? Had she known of the trip, she would have urged him to go. A commotion out on the street turned all heads towards the door. The journalist called Granger was lugging a shambling figure in with him.

Fowler had spoken one truth—Americans were noisy bastards. Granger was complaining loudly about the cost of his trishaw fare as he dumped his companion in the chair next to her. Trying to look as serene as they liked their tail to be, she tried to catch every word spoken. These men, except Alden Pyle, had what her father would have called *facile tongues*

The Quiet Soldier

and seemed to think she lacked ears to hear. They yelled at each other as they tried to work out the drunk's identity. She could tell from his haircut and clothes that he was French, but neither Granger nor the rest seemed to be able to ascertain as much, and the Frenchman was too drunk for speech. When Granger noticed her, he asked, "Who's the dame?" and Alden Pyle looked askance, as if a member of his own family had been insulted. She was surprised; what she had seen of Americans so far had not prepared her for such delicacy.

The conversation reverted to the battles in the north, and Joe said, "There's a rumor that the Vietminh have broken into Phat Diem." To conceal her interest, she picked up her drink and sipped it, looking into the orange pool as if it claimed all her attention. Phat Diem was news. The town was a Catholic stronghold, full of dissidents with their own army— natural allies of the French. If Joe's rumor was right, then the gains in the Red River Delta were continuing. She wished she could turn to Fowler and say, *so much for French confidence in reversing their fortunes*, but he thought her ignorant of the war and incapable of reading what he wrote. Now, she should try to verify the information she had heard before passing it on. She listened to Granger's vociferous account—he claimed he hadn't got close to the action. In fact, he boasted about his lack of first-hand experience of the war. The French only let him near their victories, he said, and that was fine with him. After all, it was only a colonial war. Maybe he's concealing what he knows from the rest so he can write the best article for his paper, she thought, but if he was as ignorant of troop movements as he claimed, how could she find out what was really going on in Phat Diem? Was it too late for Fowler to travel to the battle area? And how could she prompt him to go? She watched him and noted a fresh briskness in his manner as he asked Pyle what he thought of the rumor. Was it the mention of Phat Diem that had heightened his mood, or was he trying to evaluate Alden Pyle?

The American answered with shocking directness. "I'd like to go and have a look if it's important." She saw that she would have no need to urge Fowler to go: he wouldn't let this younger man outstrip him. But why was Pyle heading to the war zone? He wasn't a journalist. Was he yet one more newly arrived "advisor?" His build was military, but he was more subdued than the rabble at the bar, and Joe from the embassy treated him with respect, as if he held higher rank. She heard Fowler say he worked for the Economic Mission. She would have to find out what that meant. Alden Pyle had made Fowler competitive; it reminded her of her father's reactions to Nam. He'll go to Phat Diem to prove he's got as much courage, she thought.

As Granger announced brashly that he was off to a brothel, Alden Pyle turned away and invited Fowler and her to dine with him. Fowler accepted, and Pyle leant down to say to her apologetically, "I guess you get tired of all this shop—about your country, I mean."

She wanted to say clearly in his language, *this country is my shop, not yours. Get out of my shop*, but she hid behind puzzlement—"*Comment?*" He'll think me sweet and a little dense, she thought, but is he trying to appear the same? Is he playing the same game as I am?

Abruptly, pushing back the chairs, the men were on their feet, on the move. In the scramble outside, she tried to get into a trishaw with Granger, who was drunk enough to be valuably indiscreet, but Pyle put his hands on Granger's shoulders and steered him away. He is observant, she noted, but still she was not sure whether she was dealing with a chivalrous young man who wanted to save her from Granger's drunken hands or a trained operative who was protecting a fellow American.

As she rode with Fowler towards Cholon, she saw that the French army was out in force. Even the road to the Buddhist temple was cordoned off, and, when the trishaw turned down a side road, there were soldiers blocking their way. She guessed there might have been a grenade attack, and her heart lurched, for immediately she thought of Tha'm's excited anticipation of a mission. Let her be safe, she prayed. Her comrades in the north invaded towns, but she and Tha'm had to thrust at the heart of the enemy. Fowler showed no interest in the troops in the streets but ordered the trishaw driver to skirt round the blocked roads. They turned away from a huge armored vehicle bearing down on them. She noted that it was new, another sign that the French were being supplied with the best of up-to-date equipment. She thought the tank was the new sort called a Chaffee, and, as she tried to memorize its features, Fowler spoke insistently at her. "I like that fellow," he said, unconvincingly. She knew that if she agreed, his jealousy would be confirmed and he'd become more watchful, but she could give no reason for expressing dislike for a mild mannered rose among so many thorns. She settled for, "He's quiet," though, as she spoke, she realized her description sounded less benign than she had intended.

The Chalet loomed up. Drunken French officers were reeling out of the doors, and two civilian Europeans were fighting over a girl in a tight pink dress, pulling her between them like diners dividing a morsel of duck. Fowler shouted in her ear. "Go straight in and get us a table. I better look after Pyle." She watched him turn the corner before scanning the street, looking for some contact, maybe Tha'm herself, safe and well. But there was no one she knew, and she couldn't risk going back towards the French barricades, dressed for the night club. She lingered, hoping to hear snatches of information, but the westerners outside the Chalet spoke only of bets, girls, and opium. The officers hung over her, asking her to join them inside until the doorman told her to move on. She answered haughtily, "*Je suis avec un groupe Américain qui arrivera bientôt,*" and he let her in. *American* was now opening doors.

Inside, an orchestra was playing, and a woman in a fish-like dress was singing that she wouldn't dance and no one should make her. Phuong went towards the dance floor, ignored an invitation from two French officers to join them, and found an unoccupied table. As she sat down, Lan was beside her.

Phuong spoke softly. "What's happening in Cholon? The streets are closed. I counted four armored cars. Do you know of a mission?"

"It was disaster!" Lan looked towards the entrance. "Who's that with Fowlair?" She moved towards the crowded bar and was gone before Fowler and Pyle arrived at the table. To Fowler's amusement, Pyle was speaking in dreadful French, apologizing intensely for keeping her waiting. He seemed to be distressed by more than his unpunctuality, and she guessed that he was shocked by so many girls for sale in the brothel. And so cheaply— each could be bought for less than the cost of a drink in the Continental. They were casualties of war even more than her, but she could not shake off her concerns about Tha'm. If Lan knew of the mission, then it was one by their unit. Could she risk going to find Lan to learn more?

Pyle was asking her to dance. She would have to touch him, let him close enough to smell his skin. She suppressed a shudder and carefully looked at Fowler for permission. He shrugged. She was not taken in by his apparent indifference. Pyle followed her onto the dance floor, hesitating before putting his left arm round her waist and then withdrawing it. He smelt as other foreigners did, not of Scotch like Fowler, but still of something indefinably alien. She let him take her right hand and raise it into the air. He returned his arm to her waist. It was as if he was trying to replicate for the first time a diagram he had once seen of how to hold a dance partner. Wide-eyed, like a child trying to recall a difficult lesson, he nodded his head in an attempt to catch the rhythm of the music. A space as large as a person lay between them, so she had no way of knowing how he was going to move. Just after the second beat, he flung his right leg forward. Hastily she drew back her left leg and tried to anticipate the next jerky movement. She guessed he was doing a leaden version of a waltz, though the orchestra was playing a quick step. How foolish he was, and how she hated the smell of sensuous appropriation he exuded! Was he deaf to the rhythm? He trod his way around the floor, and she skipped backwards as smoothly as she could. When they turned a corner by Fowler's table, she saw his lugubrious gaze upon them.

The next time they approached his table, she saw that Lan had joined him. She wished the song would end so that she could return to them and find some way of learning from Lan about the night's failed mission. In her moment of distraction, Pyle's heavy shoe bore down on her left foot. She winced and let go of his hand. He blushed. "*Désolé. Je ne suis pas un danseur accompli.*"

Vous n'êtes pas de sorte de danseur, she thought, unable to smile. He took her hand again, and they ploughed on round the room. Lan was talking, and Fowler was pretending to listen while still watching her and Pyle.

When the music stopped, she tried an old trick. "That is my sister with Mr Fowlair," she said quickly in Vietnamese. Pyle turned towards their table. There was a pause before he turned back, trying to mask his mistake. She gazed at him, thinking, yes, I have caught you out. You are more knowledgeable than you pretend.

His face resumed its diffident expression. "*Vous comme... no, peux je,* oh hang it, my French is lousy. Miss Phuong, would you like another dance?"

"I think maybe the cabaret will begin soon," she said, indicating the men in garish women's dress who were standing waiting by the side of the stage. Pyle followed her gaze, taking in the bouffoned hair, rouged cheeks, and flamboyant dresses. One of the troupe was gyrating

The Quiet Soldier

his hips, bumping against the saxophonist, who was blowing deep, dirty notes. Finishing, the dancer kissed the saxophonist full on the lips, as the orchestra cheered him on. Pyle looked shocked. She saw him clench his fists, then relax his hands and try to laugh, "I guess we don't have that kind of entertainment in Boston." She wondered where his disgust came from when she enjoyed their simple foolish performances. It reminded her of the entertainers who'd come to Cu Chi when silliness was allowed.

She limped back to the table where Fowler and Lan were talking, curiously, about sewing machines. Pyle held her chair as she sat down. Her foot was throbbing. Fowler introduced Miss Hei, and Pyle shook her hand vigorously. He blushed, too, perhaps reminded of his blunder in responding to Vietnamese. Lan turned her attention to him. They learned more in one conversation about the past of the younger man than they had in a year about the older. Whether it was true or false was another matter. Alden Pyle was apparently from a city called Boston, and, from what he said, it seemed that he was from the intelligentsia. It all sounded very mild, very comfortable, very nice, but she thought, as she kept her gaze down, you could still be a soldier now, as I am.

Lan's heavy hand hit her knee. Her sister was glowering, and her look told her to pay more attention to the young American. Pyle complimented her on her prettiness, and Fowler replied sarcastically, "Even the most beautiful girl in Saigon must eat." He ordered for her, requesting a plate of the strange raw meat that the Chalet served.

Lan was trying to ingratiate herself with the new American. Though she was unable to conceal entirely her disdain for foreigners, her apparent preference for Pyle riled Fowler, and he was drinking quickly to fuel his words with spite. As he tried to get a waiter's attention, Phuong tugged at Lan's sleeve beneath the table but was shrugged off. Lan was saying, "My sister is very, very loyal." And Phuong thought, when Lan talks of loyalty, unpleasantness follows. Lan and Pyle began talking about families. *Your child would be less than dust.* Pyle said he had no brothers or sisters.

Lan countered proudly with, "Our father was of a very good family. He was a mandarin from Hue." Having got a waiter's attention, Fowler began ordering even more food for them all. Maliciously, Lan waited until he'd completed the order before saying she had to leave.

As soon as she had gone, Pyle began to speak in glowing terms about her, which irritated Fowler further. So often she had assuaged his annoyance, but now she could not resist pushing him further, and still she wondered whether the American meant what he said. "My sister is very accomplished," she told him. "Her English is very better than mine. She types very fast. Many words every minute." As if she could no longer continue in English, she switched to French and told the story of Miss Hei's life—the cover story her sister had assumed since arriving in Saigon. Though his speech was becoming slurred, Fowler translated accurately enough and the American said promptly and with apparent enthusiasm, "I wish we had more like her in the Economic Mission."

So do we, thought Phuong, marveling that he should take the bait. Maybe she was mistaken about him. Surely no covert operator would fall for such a trick, unless he saw what she was doing and was laying a trap of his own. "I will speak to her. She would like to work for the Americans."

Still the cabaret had not started. The orchestra played on, and she was obliged to dance with Pyle again. On the dance floor with him hugging her at arm's length and stomping about, she wondered how Lan, with her loathing of foreign devils, would handle such people daily.

When the music stopped, he escorted her back to the table and excused himself. Fowler had a line of empty glasses in front of him, and he stared accusingly at her as she resumed her seat. At last the Chalet's entertainers were about to begin. Her heart was heavy with concern for Tha'm; she yearned to laugh again and looked towards the stage, ready for innocent antics.

In the shadows, as the lights dimmed, she saw Alden Pyle close to the side of the stage where the entertainers were still waiting. The one who'd kissed the saxophonist laid his hand on Pyle's thigh and said something she could not hear. The smile on the man's face faded as Pyle cut him down with a blow to the stomach. He keeled over and barely touched the ground before two of the company swiftly dragged him behind the stage curtains.

The speed of Pyle's response made Phuong feel short of breath. My God, she thought, he can turn in an instant, without warning. Quiet, but more dangerous than the noisy bastards—deadly when he chooses.

Blithe music started up. The remaining entertainers danced onto the stage, their arms linked, the tightness of their smiles revealing their shock at Pyle's assault. Phuong watched as he wiped his knuckles, straightened his jacket, and walked slowly back to their table. His voice was steady as he said to Fowler, "Let's go. This isn't a bit suitable for *her*." He did not address a word to her but had appropriated her as swiftly as he had dealt the entertainer a blow. Alden Pyle believed he knew what was right. She had never been so frightened.

CHAPTER 23

The basis for guerrilla discipline must be individual conscience. With guerrillas, a discipline of coercion is ineffective.
—Mao Zedong

It was more difficult to leave Fowler when he was drunk than when opium sent him into deep, dream-filled sleep, but she was determined to go to the Quai Mytho to discover what had happened in Cholon that evening. He stayed awake until she got into bed beside him and then threw a proprietary arm across her; she lay under its weight wondering how soon she dare move. A few muffled voices came from the corridor; she would not get away without being seen. Late night revelers leaving the bars and casinos were the danger. She'd be safer in peasant clothes.

At last, with a snort, Fowler turned away. She slipped from the bed and drew the pyjamas and her knife from her box under the bed. Dressing quickly, she unlocked the door and left. Darkness was her ally. She kept close to buildings and hid when she heard anyone approaching. Hien could be close at hand, but even if she sought him out, what could she say?

When she arrived in the street of the Chous' house, she watched from the corner to ensure there was no sign of a Sûreté raid. All seemed quiet. Only a faint light from an upstairs window indicated that the household was still awake. Finally, she knocked, and the door opened. She slipped inside to see the young boy Chinh wide-eyed with shock. "What's wrong?" He did not answer but let the door swing open as if he lacked the strength to stop it. She rushed up the stairs. Her heart was beating fast even before a figure met her on the landing. "You," she breathed. She could not speak his name aloud, though she had dreamed of him for years as Bui Hien. *Nice, kind, gentle* Hien, who had won her with a simple tender question *How can I help you?*

"I saw you yesterday. I recognized you," was all she could manage.

The Quiet Soldier

His smile was as she had seen in her dreams since that day in the market of Ba Ra. "Well done. You are sharp. They say that about you. But now you must be strong..."

She gasped and followed him into the attic room which was as full as ever—some lay in hammocks, others on the floor, talking softly in night voices. A hissing lantern hung above a corner of the room concealed by a battered screen. At this time of night, only birth and death warranted the use of kerosene. Conscious of Bui Hien by her side, she pushed by the screen and saw Heng, Mrs Chou, and a man she did not know looking down at a body on a blood-soaked mattress. She cried out at the sight of Tha'm.

Her friend groaned as the man bending over her dug at an open wound below her ribs. Phuong recognized the Chinese doctor who sold herbal remedies from a stall by the rice mills. Tha'm's body was covered in shrapnel wounds, and her eyes were closed and swollen. Muttering, she tried to reach upwards, and Mrs Chou restrained her. Phuong saw that Tha'm's right hand hung backwards against her arm. As she gasped, Bui Hien held her, comforting her softly.

"We shouldn't wait any longer," the doctor said. "We'll do it."

"Do what?" asked Phuong.

Heng said matter-of-factly, "The hand will have to be removed."

"Can't it be saved? If we take her to a hospital?" she asked.

"They'll arrest her. Half the Sûreté is looking for her as it is." He pushed his hair back from his brow. "There are no options, Phuong. She's lucky to have got back here."

A crate and a chair, the heaviest pieces they had, were already in place by the patient. Mrs Chou, rope by her side, muttered as she struggled to sit Tha'm up so that she could bind her. "I'll do that," said Phuong. She spoke to her friend gently, raising her up and lashing her with the rope. She tied one end round the crate and the other round a chair leg. Tha'm lay down, and the doctor pierced her skull with acupuncture needles. Then Mrs Chou brought a second lamp. She sat on the trunk and held it aloft. Phuong placed her arms on Tha'm's uninjured side as the doctor wiped his knife. As soon as he touched the hand, Tha'm's eyes opened, and she shook, flinging Phuong off her.

"You must hold her," said the doctor and waited for Phuong to take hold again before cutting the wrist. Sweat poured from Tha'm's forehead.

She screamed out once before Heng gagged her. She fought them for a few minutes until she sank back. "Good, she's fainted," said the doctor, peevishly. Phuong stayed kneeling by Tha'm's side. Mrs Chou and Heng removed the rope. Then Heng put his hands on her shoulders to draw her away, and she hit him one hard blow before Bui Hien restrained her. She reached for her knife, and Heng gripped her wrist and shook the weapon to the floor. He emitted a full-fanged laugh then turned away.

Those on the other side of the screen heard the clatter and Heng's laugh, but no one said anything when she walked out, dazed, with Bui Hien beside her. Uoc, with her baby on her hip, put a comforting arm around her while Ly brought her tea. They sat round, whispering, as one lamp and then the other was extinguished. Bui Hien joined in the chatter as if he'd always been part of their little army. No one commented on his arrival any more than, all those years before, they had commented on hers. She should be getting back to Fowler, but even if Heng ordered her directly, she wouldn't go. She needed her own; she needed Bui Hien; she could not return to *la solitude* yet. They sat in the darkness and talked about the mission that had cost Tha'm her hand. Her orders had been to throw a grenade into the Grand Monde. Nobody understood the politics of it, unless Heng did and he wasn't explaining. All they knew was that the Binh Xuyen had withdrawn their protection from the casino and the Party was assisting them. Tha'm had rolled a grenade into the crowded bar but been blocked from leaving and been blown up by her own grenade. In the confusion that followed, a sympathetic trishaw driver had dragged her away.

The armored cars out on the streets that evening had been Tha'm's doing. Had Lan known what had occurred in Cholon when she had met them at the Chalet?

The doctor stood before her. "I need alcohol for a poultice. Can you get it?"

She nodded. She'd have to return to his apartment for that. The blood on her clothes was still damp. Maybe she should clean up. If Fowler had woken, found her missing and questioned her on her return, she'd have to weave the blood stains into her story, maybe say she'd helped a friend give birth. She went to check Tha'm, feeling the warmth of Bui Hien beside her. The doctor had given Tha'm a sleeping draught, and Mrs Chou sat by her side. "Don't worry too much," Bui Hien whispered, "she's strong. Others have survived worse. I have seen it with my own eyes."

The Quiet Soldier

She wanted to leave with those words in her heart without speaking to Heng, for the rage that said it was his fault had not abated. She wouldn't say sorry for hitting him, but he had her knife, and she needed that. Bui Hien did not follow her as she approached Heng's hammock. His eyes opened, and he rolled out of the hammock to ask abruptly, "The doctor asked you about the alcohol?"

"I'll bring it as soon as I can." She avoided looking at his reddened cheek.

He said angrily, "Tha'm was given a mission she wanted. She is a soldier through and through."

"Give me my knife."

She took it without a word when he drew it from his tunic by the blade and handed it to her. She sheathed the knife and walked out alone but heard the steps behind her. It was Bui Hien. He said softly, "Let me accompany you."

She tried to shake her head, to stay strong, but his tone was so sympathetic. She said falteringly, "I must go back, go back to a foreigner. My orders are..."

His hand briefly touched hers, the hand that no longer seemed a hand to wield a knife. "I know. I understand," he said gently. He knew where she slept, that she was Fowler's mistress. Crisply, he added, "We must all obey our orders, whatever they are." Was it possible that he understood her sacrifice?

She said no more but basked in his presence as they left the building together, shoulder touching shoulder. They walked together through the deserted streets. They did not hurry, and few words were spoken. These moments would be my forever, she thought, if I could make them so. "Every parting from you is like a little eternity," the woman in *Waterloo Bridge* said to her soldier. The soldier had wanted to marry her even when he discovered she prostituted herself, such was his love. But she could not dishonor him in that way. Once, Bui Hien's shoulder brushed against hers; his touch filled her with longing, a longing she had never known with any of the men whom she'd slept with. Dawn came as they approached the apartment. "Don't come any further," she said. Obediently, he stopped and watched her turn the corner into the rue Catinat.

The stairs were empty. Fowler was asleep when she carefully opened the door, so she went towards the bookcase where he kept his Scotch. He rolled over and asked drowsily, "Where've you been?"

She stripped off her clothes, rolled them in a bundle with her knife and put them under the bed. He was awake now, and, when she climbed in with him, he wrapped his legs around hers. She knew better than to resist. She let it happen quickly and silently. When he'd finished, he said. "You're concerned, aren't you, about my traveling north? I won't go if you're worried."

"You must do your work."

"It's not like my other visits, when they took us up in a plane. I'll be on my own this time. It will be dangerous."

He wanted to worry her so he could use her concern as an excuse to avoid going. He must go, she thought, to bring back information and so I can help Tha'm—and see Bui Hien. "That other man, the quiet American, he said he was going?"

"I doubt if he meant it. After all, he's not a journalist. Why would the Economic Mission be interested in a battle in the north?"

Exactly, she thought, as Fowler raised himself on one arm and looked down on her. The flesh on his cheeks drooped like a cockerel's wattle. "Phuong, I have to tell you something that will upset you. I love you, and you've transformed my life. There's no easy way to say this—I'm married."

The irrelevance of his statement struck her as funny; she wanted to laugh as Heng had laughed when she hit him. She struggled to look interested, to seem *surprised*.

"I can see I've shocked you," he said humbly, but with that little touch of triumph that he'd displayed after he'd "seduced" her. "What I'm trying to say is that I want us to be together always, for the rest of my life. I would marry you if I could."

She wondered why he would make so unnecessary a declaration. Wasn't she in his bed? What more could he want from her? She turned away as he spoke on and on about his need for her. He'd begin to die, he said, if she left him for someone who was free to marry her. She was glad to have an excuse for tears. She let the tears flow, crying for Tha'm and for herself because she had found Bui Hien too late.

CHAPTER 24

I'm nobody's fool, least of all yours.
—*All About Eve*

The next day, Fowler was on a plane for the north. She was free to take his bottle of Scotch to the Quai Mytho. Tha'm's muscles had tightened, and she was shivering, sure signs of fever, so Phuong tried to cool her with water as Mrs Chou prepared a poultice for the stub using the alcohol and chewed rice. Patrols searching for the bomber had resumed at daybreak. Only a few people remained in the room; most had scattered before dawn. They all knew that if a raid came, the weak would be sacrificed and that Tha'm, unable to move, would certainly be one of them. The last to leave would pull the pin from a grenade and put it under her body so that she blew up whoever touched her. As she sat at her friend's side, cooling her brow with a wet cloth, Phuong dared to ask, "Where is Bui Hien?"

"Who? I know no one of that name," snapped Mrs Chou. After a while, she left Tha'm's side, and Mr Chou came in. "You must go now, Phuong."

"Let me look after Tha'm." She wanted to be with her friend, even if a raid was to come. She wanted to say, *let it end for me and Tha'm here together*, but had she spoken, she knew Mr Chou would forbid such waste.

Even Heng deferred to Mr Chou on occasion and now, with a mandarin wave of his hand and a sharp snap of his fingers, he urged her to stand. "No. We each have our tasks. You must go." She would have argued with Heng, but Mr Chou was a different matter. She rose, and he shooed her past the screen, muttering. She cast a look back as he drew open the door and shut it firmly behind her.

With Fowler away, she was free to go where she pleased. She went to the fish shop off the rue Catinat. The old woman was there with a stall of live eels in front of her. Phuong lingered longer than was safe and, finally,

Bui Hien emerged from the alley. She dodged between the cars and cycles towards him. She knew better than to call his name, but she could not keep her face expressionless as she went up to him. Their fingers briefly touched before he led the way into the alley. "How is your friend?" he asked, not *our comrade* but *your friend*. She'd love him for that alone.

"She has a fever, but that is to be expected."

"What a tragedy. Such a brave girl! A heroine."

Tears ran down Phuong's cheeks. "She still bleeds here, and here. Can't we get her into a hospital?"

"Such injuries cannot be disguised as an accident. She would be arrested," he said gently. "Such is our struggle. We won't give up."

She didn't resent his *us* as she did Heng's, wanting to be on his side, feeling its righteousness. She was about to let him take her hand when a shadow appeared at the entrance to the alley. Both Bui Hien and Phuong stepped back, ready to run, but it was only the old man who worked on the fish stall shambling into view with a crate of fish. Even as he eased past, he ignored them both. When he had gone, Bui Hien asked kindly, "And what of you?"

She could not utter Fowler's name nor allude to his existence, except to say, "The Quai Mytho is unsafe for now, and there is no one I should be... that is, I have no duties."

"Me too," he said with a smile.

Suddenly, she was asking, "Have you ever been to a western cinema? Would you like to see a Hollywood film?" He agreed eagerly, and happiness soared. It was the first time she had invited a man to go anywhere with her and meant it. She had to wait for him to "go and change." When he returned, he was wearing western clothes—far shabbier than those Nam and Long had worn in their Sorbonne days, even shabbier than Fowler's, but good enough to get him into a Saigon cinema.

Bui Hien made no mistakes as he bought two tickets at the Majestic, and the French cashier let them through with a scowl. The afternoon performance had attracted few customers—a couple kissing at the back of the cinema, three French officers together, and a bulky westerner in the front row, whose haircut identified him as a western civilian. As the lights went down, her awareness of Bui Hien beside her was intense. The shuffling sounds of others as they made themselves comfortable to watch the film could not diminish her awareness of being alone in the dark with the man she loved. If only her first caress lay ahead of her. Her throat dried. She'd lied to Tha'm; western films weren't just different from the primitive play-acting of village theatre, they were better. These films were as powerful as opium. Watching the screen, she could believe herself *perfection* again, a young girl waiting for love.

The film was about a woman. Men circled her adoringly, but in vain. She seemed even older than Lan, yet she still had great power to attract men. She was pampered and uncomplaining. She gave orders. She was bold and dramatic, giving wonderful performances in the theater. Then along came a younger woman, quiet and respectful. She had sought out the older woman, like a disciple seeking the Master.

Phuong stole a look at Bui Hien, her heart constricting at his boyish absorption. So this must be what it is like to enjoy a lover's company. As if he's read her thoughts, Bui Hien turned and whispered, "It's a beautiful film. I admire the woman, but she is not beautiful like our women." His breath on her cheek was intoxicating.

Suddenly, she heard a commotion. One of the French officers had approached the couple kissing at the back and asked the woman, "*Combien chargez-vous?*"

Her companion, a French civilian, shouted, "*Échappez-vous!*" which brought the other officers to their comrade's aid.

Phuong put her hand on the hilt of her knife, but Bui Hien stilled her. "This is not our fight," he whispered, as the soldiers surrounded the civilian and the woman screamed. "Come on, let's get out of here." He took her hand.

They could not get out through the main entrance so headed down towards the fire exit. As they did so, Phuong came face to face with the westerner who'd been sitting in the front row. It was Bill Granger. He barged past, shouting, "Here, damned Froggies, what're you up to with that dame?"

The fire exit was shut. Bui Hien pulled at the bar of the door, but it remained shut. Behind her, Phuong heard women's screams and the scuffling sounds of fighting. An arm fell on her shoulder as Bui Hien kicked at the door. It burst open, and they ran out into the sunlit the street. When they came to an alley, they ran down that, skidding on a small heap of vegetable peelings outside an open door. Inside, a man was throwing pieces into a steaming cauldron. He raised a cleaver, scowling, "Don't bring your trouble here!" Panting, Phuong made an apology, and she and Bui Hien eased past the row of ovens. They walked through the restaurant onto the open street, then ran.

Finally, Bui Hien stopped, leaned down with his hands on his knees and joked, "I'm out of breath! Watching Hollywood films is too much excitement for me!"

Phuong laughed too, thinking, even this life could be fun with him beside me, but then her smile faded when he asked, "That American. Have you seen him before?"

She nodded.

"Who is he?"

"His name is Bill Granger. He is a journalist."

"I think he recognized you. You'd better have a story ready. And we'd better say goodbye here," said Bui Hien, giving one last smile before he left her.

As she wandered away, loneliness flooded her and something else—an uneasiness she sought to locate. Returning to Fowler's empty apartment, she lay on her back on the floorboards, thinking through what had happened, as Van had first trained her to do. Was it her fears for Tha'm? No, the shock of her injuries was profound, but her friend was resilient and would survive if well tended. Granger? Yes, but at least he hardly knew one Vietnamese from another. She'd deny being at the cinema. Fowler and Granger disliked each other already. Granger called Fowler *a Limey*—whatever that meant, it was no compliment. She thought again of the hours spent with Bui Hien. His smile, his gentleness, his sweet breath on her face were memories to cherish. Then she thought of his words, *You'd better have a story ready*. Of course he was right; hadn't she already devised a story? But still, from his lips, those words jarred. It was the sort of thing that Heng said.

CHAPTER 25

Without humanity and justice,
it is impossible
to employ spies.
—Sun-Tzu

The next evening, the smells of cooking drew her onto the landing where the women were chatting over the steaming pots. She thrust her open hand full of piastres towards them. One of them took the coins and another filled a bowl with rice. She bowed in thanks and squatted down, taking mouthful after mouthful. When she had scooped the last grain from the bowl and licked it from her finger, the woman who'd taken the coins said, "Left you, has he? We thought you ate your fill in foreigners' haunts."

"The way of war is a way of deception, Mother," said Phuong softly, daring to speak this way because Tha'm had told her the old women were good sorts and her friend would never say such a thing unless their loyalty to the Party was sound. With Fowler about, she could not speak to them, but now, with Heng's family dispersed, she longed for some company of her own kind. They liked her answer and she stayed sitting with them. The old woman who'd taken the piastres was, she decided, like Mrs Chou, sarcastic but good-hearted. They were her neighbors and the thought came to her that if Fowler was killed in Phat Diem, she could live in the apartment alone and join them every evening, a good Vietnamese housewife. Maybe, after a time of renewal, a fresh spring, Bui Hien would join her and they would be a respectable couple.

The next day, she went to the fish stall and waited for hours, but Bui Hien did not come. She knew she would not be welcome at the Chous until the Sûreté stopped searching for Tha'm. She was impatient for a message to say she could tend her friend again. It was curious to have so little to do. Not since childhood had days of idleness and freedom stretched before her. She was grateful that the women welcomed her onto the landing. One evening, four days after Fowler's departure for the war, she smelt gynura and went out on the landing to share their soup. They tried to refuse money now, but she forced it on them; it was Fowler's, after all. The gynura's pungent aroma brought back those days in the garden at Cu Chi when servants placed dishes under the canopy. Talk then had seemed to her idle and harmless, her father's protection absolute and Lan's affection staunch as a mother's. She crouched with the women and took the bowl offered to her, with thanks. They seemed pleased that she had joined them, proud even. They let her eat, the girl in an ao dai squatting beside them who was the whore of the old European upstairs.

The soup was bitter; too much gynura and not enough salt to her taste. She drained the bowl and handed it back to the woman who'd given it to her. "Delicious, Mother," she said.

"He still away?" one of them asked, *he* said with a flick of the head.

She turned and spat onto the broken tiles. "Still gone. When he gets back—if he gets back, he'll want to know where I've spent my time." The old women shuffled closer, smiling at her response. One, toothless, with a scar from ear to nose, advised, "Men don't listen. Give him a smile and talk. It's silence that gives you away." Her companions nodded in agreement. She stayed with them on the stairs until the night came, gossiping. Their chatter stopped when a figure in a canary yellow ao dai appeared at the bottom of the stairs. It was Lan, who had never been near the apartment before. With foreboding, Phuong led her sister up the stairs, conscious of the women's curiosity.

Lan stood in the middle of the living room surveying the apartment with distaste. "It's as I thought," she said and sat on the hard-backed chair by the window. She sighed, looking out into the darkness outside. Phuong wondered whether she had come alone or whether others waited outside. Did Lan bring orders, or was this a sisterly visit? She recalled the bitter disappointment when she reunited with Lan. Where was the Lan she had sought? With reminiscences of Cu Chi and their family fresh in her mind, she dared to say humbly, "Lan, tell me what happened to you after you fled our home. Recently, you spoke of children. What did you mean?" She saw her sister stiffen. "Please," she begged, "let me know your sacrifice."

Lan, with beautiful features that had turned to stone, asked, "What shall we gain? These are matters of great delicacy that touch another's dignity. The prison at Ba Ra is a place of terrible tortures."

"Ba Ra?" Only the other night Phuong had had a nightmare about the place, Kaneko's grisly flat face looming over her. She'd cried out, relieved that Fowler was not there to ask, "Le cauchemar?" Now she divined her sister's meaning. She was protecting Ngo Quang Long by keeping silent. "You have had no children—nor any chance of them."

"My husband was not the same man when he escaped from that place," said Lan, but then could say no more. Lan's reticence was born of loyalty. Phuong moved to her and felt her sister's tears as she held her. Lan's arms were around her for the first time since she left Cu Chi on the night of the Sûreté raid—a sister's embrace, second only to a mother's.

Finally, Lan drew away, wiping her tears, as Annamite women have done for centuries, on the silken slip of her ao dai. "Tomorrow, come to the shop," she said. "The Committee has orders for you."

"All of them?" exclaimed Phuong. "What is it? Why do they all want to see me?" A chilling thought struck her. "Is Tha'm still alive?"

But Lan's answer was colder still. "Don't be foolish. We have more concerns than one incompetent soldier."

That night, Phuong lay awake on the bare floorboards wondering what orders she was to be given. She went at first light but then waited along the street from the bicycle shop. The old man on guard was careless; he did not spot her, and she watched the only entrance without being challenged. Three of the Committee she knew—Heng her controller, Long, and Lan, but she had never seen the others. Now she wanted to observe them before they gave her orders that merited a full meeting. She spotted them as soon as they entered the street. They were in western suits but poorly disguised, for their intractable expressions identified them as central commanders. She wished she could tell them how clearly they stood out. They had trained her to watch herself at all times, but they were careless to the point of—she remembered Lan's description of Tha'm yesterday—incompetence. Their clothes were dust-laden, and they carried provisions. Obviously, they had traveled into the city and were already tired. That would make them irritable. I must be careful, she thought. These men will use me with less compunction than would Heng. She was about to go into the bicycle shop when another man turned into the road. It was Bui Hien, and for a second her heart rebelled with delight.

But as she watched him approach the bicycle shop with trained caution, her heart jumped again as a dark thought—why was he visiting the Committee? You'd better have a story ready, he had said to her—words of a friend or a political cadre?

She saw him give the signal to the old man on look-out and noted the respectful expression on the old man's face as Bui Hien moved inside. She lurched forward and, when the old man tried to stop her, she waved him away. "You should have given the password," he complained, but she stepped by him, following Bui Hien into the dark room where she'd been reunited with Lan months before. He was already ascending the steep, narrow stairs.

He must hear me following, she thought, but Bui Hien did not turn. Heng, Long, and Lan were ranged with the men in suits on the far side of a table, and Bui Hien scraped the final chair across the floorboards to sit by Long the chairman. She stared at the line of cadres; it was impossible not to see that he belonged to the committee.

"Ah, Phuong, punctual as ever," said Heng, cutting through the leaden silence. She looked at Bui Hien, waiting for a hint of the smile that she loved, but his expression was as impenetrable as those of the central committee.

"Phuong?" prompted Heng. He must have asked her a question but she'd missed it. "I said, tell us all you know of this new American. His name is Pyle?"

How may I help you? Bui Hien's first words to her years ago in Ba Ra. If only now he would show some sign that he wanted to help her! She waited dumbly so Lan, scowling, filled the silence. "Alden Pyle. He says he comes from Boston where his father is a professor. He claims to work for an American organization called the Economic Mission. He talks of 'aid' but intends control. And he's interested in the war in the north. He's probably in Phat Diem now."

"Is he another journalist?" suggested one of the strangers. "Younger reporters venture into combat areas. They like to be heroes."

"Phuong?" encouraged Heng, but still she could not begin. Finally, she found the resolve to look at Bui Hien and, in the manner of a soldier giving

The Quiet Soldier

her report, she said crisply, "Alden Pyle speaks Vietnamese and pretends he doesn't. He's quiet and watchful, not like the noisy bastards of the press corps. He has offered to give comrade Lan a job at the American Embassy, because she can type and do shorthand." She paused, and then added, still looking directly at Bui Hien, "Pyle acts the gentleman but he can be swift and brutal." Bui Hien shifted uneasily.

One of the strangers had laughed a little when she talked of bastards. Now he leaned forward. "He speaks Vietnamese? You're sure?"

She shrugged and said insolently. "Believe me or not, I don't care."

"Sister, you forget yourself," admonished Lan, as the strangers' expressions hardened. Yesterday and its tenderness were gone, and there was no sign from Bui Hien that he would help her, whatever trouble she caused herself.

"If he's American Secret Service, surely he wouldn't be so naive as to offer the sister of someone he had just met a job in the embassy?" Bui Hien spoke. His tone was less gentle than that of her cherished memories. He is unmoved, she thought, as I am by Fowler's distress. He is implacable; he is a soldier. Maybe the committee decided that I should be kept under surveillance, and one of their own was best suited to do it because of my foolish weakness for him. My feelings have been fed into the fire of Struggle. I should have realized. Of course there are others like Long.

At that moment, her brother-in-law rose stiffly from his chair, as if his injuries were giving him pain. He leaned with one shoulder up against the bare wall, saying thoughtfully, "Maybe Alden Pyle is so absorbed with his own plans that he misses those of others."

Lan said, "He's smitten with Phuong. That's why he makes this offer of a job to me."

"You must take the job, of course," said one of the central controllers deferentially, "but we need to follow him more closely. Comrade Phuong must become his mistress."

"No! I am a soldier too!" she shouted.

"A soldier obeys orders," said Lan, adding bitterly, "this is how you can be useful."

She waited for Bui Hien to speak, but already hope had faded that he would oppose further degradation for her. "Lure with bait; Strike with chaos," he said calmly.

I, then, am the bait, she thought. She ran from the room, hearing shouts of command to stop as she did so, but she jumped down the stairs. She heard someone following and, as a hand fell on her shoulder, she hoped to see it was Bui Hien. One remorseful phrase would be enough to win her back, but it was Heng. He said ruefully, "Little sister, you really are making this hard on yourself. Do what we tell you. Have things really been so bad? You've got what you wanted—you have your family again. That's more than most of us."

"You said that love is agony," she recalled, remembering bargaining with him in a damp tunnel to be told Bui Hien's name. She had been triumphant when, in Ba Ra, she realized Long was still alive. With Long and Lan restored to her, she'd thought happiness would rise again, like the phoenix. Now, she knew better.

"Actually, Phuong, I said love is a waste of energy."

CHAPTER 26

Eyes opened wide in defiance, gazing contemptuously at a thousand giants.
—Communist Party maxim

    For two days and nights, they left her alone. She stayed in the apartment building, knowing that if Fowler did not return, the others—her comrades—would drag her out. The knock came; it was Lan. "Come with me."

"I'm sick."

"Come down to the milk bar. Someone has been waiting to see you." Lan spoke so cajolingly that hope came to Phuong that she would find Bui Hien waiting to apologize. Her older sister had a soft heart after all. But, as they were across from the milk bar, she saw Alden Pyle sitting expectantly at one of the tables. A book and two milkshakes lay on the table in front of him.

"No!" said Phuong. Lan grabbed her arm. "Listen! He's more important than your journalist."

Phuong shook her off. "*My* journalist? Bitch!"

She walked quickly away but Lan kept pace with her. She tried to get back to the apartment but, as she reached a side street, Lan signalled and a trishaw driver pulled up next to them, pinioned Phuong's arms, and lifted her into the vehicle. Lan restrained her as she tried to get out. "Your orders are..."

"Fuck my orders. I'm done taking orders." The trishaw traveled at speed through the traffic as Phuong struggled with her sister. Lan was weaker than her, and Phuong pushed her away. She was ready to jump when Lan said urgently, "Tha'm! You want the best for her, don't you?"

Phuong sunk back in the chair. She felt dizzy. "What's this got to do with her? How is she?"

"I'll tell you when we're out of the streets." Lan righted herself and smoothed her dress. "Such a fuss. You are still a child."

"A useful child. A dishonored child." They rode in silence from then on, until the trishaw stopped at a building in the Boulevard Cong Phuong in the Cholon district. They dismounted, and Phuong asked, "Is Tha'm here? If you've hurt her..."

"Again, such childishness! Do you think all we have to concern ourselves with is one injured soldier? Think how many are dying in the north."

"You can always justify your indifference, can't you, with that argument? Somewhere, there are more calls for help, but I will answer my friend's cry, Sister."

"Then take the consequences. I won't protect you."

"I'm asking you about Tha'm."

"She is showing signs of recovery. If she gains strength, she could be taken to a safe place outside the city, but that will only happen when you've followed your orders."

Phuong felt she was playing chess against the masters who had taught her. She made the only move she could see. "I will become Alden Pyle's mistress when I know Tha'm is safe and well. She must receive the best medicines—what the westerners give their own. That is my price."

"Sister," said Lan, "You have no price."

After Bui Hien's betrayal, her sister's words scarcely hurt at all. Phuong managed to say steadily, "I demand to see Tha'm now. You need me. Alden Pyle wants *me*. Not you or any of these women about here." She watched her sister's face, saw her calculating.

Finally, Lan said, "We must speak to Long." She gave an order to the trishaw driver, and he turned in the direction of the shop. As they reached the street, Phuong saw that the look-out had been replaced. There was a younger man now sitting astride an upturned bicycle. He spun the wheel, as if intent on the repair, but noted the trishaw and its occupants immediately. He signaled to another man who came up behind them. As they alighted, he stood behind her, as if expecting her to run, but at a word from Lan, allowed them in.

Through the door, Phuong pushed her away and ran up the narrow stairs. Seated at the table, Long looked absorbed in the papers in front of him, like a scholar, detached from the world. But he turned sharply as she came in. "What's happening about Tha'm?" she shouted.

The Quiet Soldier

"Little sister," he began. Lan had followed up the stairs, her eyes were wide with astonishment as Phuong shouted him down.

"Don't *little sister* me, just tell me—is Tha'm being cared for?"

He sighed. The gentleness that she loved was still there, she saw, but she recognized now that it would benefit none of them; there was too much guile, born of commitment to his cause. She had made the same mistake with two men. He said, "Yes. You can visit her if..."

"Agreed. Tha'm survives, and I do what you want." Her head sank—it was no bow of thanks, but relief. As she looked up, she tried to make her question matter-of-fact. "When can I see her?"

"When you choose." He made *choose* sound like a western disease. "The comrade who let you in will take you to her." Then he turned back towards his papers and picked up his pen, as if to say that she was only, after all, such a small part of his plans.

She forced the words out haltingly. "Why did you not trust me? Why send Bui Hien to spy? You knew how I would feel..." She faltered. "I did many terrible things to find you. It was you I sought." He did not look up from his papers.

Her guide went by the name of Qua^n. His speech was rough, and he walked with a swagger that made her suspect he was Binh Xuyen, more used to the brothels and opium houses of Cholon than any soldiering. His blatant coarseness, which would once have appalled her, now came as a refreshing change. Every woman would know what he was. You'd get what you saw. Maybe when she had some minutes to spare, she'd have sex with him, to reward his honesty. He'd be loyal to the Party and suffer his own losses without complaint. Qua^n led her to a location close to the Chous, still in the Quai Mytho, in view of the red-tiled roof where she and Tha'm used to sleep. Inside, she found a few of Heng's army who had escaped the Sûreté raids by moving less than half a mile from their old location.

Tha'm was awake, sitting on a mattress in a corner of the room. Phuong began to cry, and Tha'm joined her. It was the first time she'd seen her friend's tears. They wept together, foreheads touching. Finally, each drew back. Tha'm's face and body were clear of the minor shrapnel wounds. She raised the arm that ended without a hand. "It will heal. I had a fever and the Chinese doctor said I must wait..."

"Tonight we will steal medicines from the army hospital." She looked towards the door where Qua^n stood watching. He grinned in agreement. "They're more powerful. Penicillin. I would have come to see you..."

"I know, I know. Safety." Tha'm's voice had weakened, and she said falteringly, "I'll fight again, when I'm stronger." She closed her eyes. Phuong let her sleep.

She returned alone to Fowler's apartment. She knew every inch of it, knew the places that escaped Fowler's scrutiny and the places where his secrets were concealed. She picked up the book that hid his wife's embittered letter and settled into the threadbare armchair that faced the window. The letter was there, brittle like its contents. *Perhaps you feel that money fulfils your obligation to a wife you no longer love.* Idly, she scratched at the surface, scoring the paper where *Helen* had signed her name. What a foolish woman she must be. She had felt sorry for her once, but after Bui Hien, sympathy was dying. Maybe she'd live long enough to care for no one. She started to bite her nails. It soothed her to gnaw away at the jagged edges. She thought with dread of Pyle. He was still an enigma to her. He had danced with her, stepped heavily on her foot and had somehow decided that he "loved and respected" her, this brutal, sentimental man.

Her nails continued to tear at the paper, as if the answers to her problems were somewhere beneath. She screwed the paper into a ball, and then wished she hadn't. The book fell from her lap as she jumped up and went to the table with the crumpled paper in her hand. She tried to smooth it out, but it tore into pieces. If Fowler walked in now, he'd see her trying to flatten out his wife's letter and what would he make of that? She ripped it until the pieces were too tiny to hold, went to the open window and threw them all, as if releasing a bird into flight. As they fluttered to the ground, she wondered what she would have to say if Fowler turned into the rue Catinat at that moment and saw them falling, like blossom from a tree. How tempting it would be to tell him the truth, to show him every occasion where he had imagined himself to be in control when it had been otherwise: Remember when we met? I was ordered to meet you. How you wooed me? Nothing you said or did made any difference. How you took your opportunity when my sister was ill to seduce me? She was not ill. She is a political cadre, and her absence was part of the plan. Dangerously, she wanted to hurt him, to claw at his pride as she had done Helen's letter.

She knew she would not sleep, so she bent down to the book she'd dropped. It wasn't one of those she tried to read when she'd first come to the apartment. "You can learn a lot about a man by the books on his shelves," Heng had taught. This one was called *Journey without Maps*. She leafed through the pages until it fell open at the place where the letter had been hidden. She read a passage:

Where the English map is content to leave a blank space, the American with large letters fills it with the word "Cannibals." It has no use for dotted lines and confessions of ignorance; it is so inaccurate that it would be useless, perhaps even dangerous, to follow it.

That was it. She closed the book slowly and replaced it carefully where she had found it. Her fear of Pyle was confirmed. He was a man of certainties who had no use for dotted lines. She feared and hated him, now she knew she was to be his mistress. She hated him more than she had ever hated Fowler.

CHAPTER 27

Sometimes she seemed invisible like peace.
—Graham Greene, spoken by Thomas Fowler in *The Quiet American*

She would have to meet Pyle and allow herself to be persuaded to go with him. She'd told Qua^n, "Tonight I will go to the Chalet. Tell my sister." *Miss Hei will be my chaperone*, she'd wanted to add sarcastically, but he wouldn't have understood.

That evening, she waited for Lan outside the night club. A group of Americans arrived, shouting to each other as the trishaws stopped, and they flung coins at the drivers, but Pyle was not among them. One looked like Granger, and she drew back. Eventually, Lan arrived, severe in an ochre-colored *ao dai*.

When they were seated at a table, close to the orchestra, Lan said, "I sent a message to Mr Pyle to say that we would be here tonight, but he may not have received it. He has been away. You should have acted more quickly."

"Pyle must believe he takes the initiative," snapped Phuong. A French officer approached their table and, with great formality, asked her to dance. Lan refused for her, and then an American in civilian clothes, but with a harsh, military haircut, offered to buy them both a drink. Lan waved him away without a word.

They drank their fruit juices slowly and repelled the attention of other men, until finally it became clear that Pyle was not going to come. "Perhaps he is away. He has not been at the embassy again today. What is he doing? There's a rumor he's importing plastic explosives."

"So what?" She smoothed her dance dress, pink with filigree sleeves, an *exquisite gown*. The singer sang, *Baby face, you've got the cutest little baby face; there is no other one to take your place.* "We know his government is supplying planes, armored cars, and bombs to the French. Go down to the riverfront and see the planes disembarking. So why does it matter if one more American is importing explosives?" She turned to Lan. "You've said it yourself, the enemy are fighting a rich man's war."

"Pyle is not supplying the French. He is engaged in a covert operation. He wants to arm 'a third force' that is neither us nor our old colonial masters. What exactly he wants them to do with the plastic explosives, we don't know. And it's your job to find out." Lan strode away and Phuong followed.

Days passed, and Fowler came back before she could find Pyle. She'd just lit the lamps when he walked in, the shadows accentuating the dip of his jaw, the lines around his eyes. "Four hours on that bloody plane!" he complained. He looked into the bedroom and moved around the room as if checking for signs of company. "Have you missed me?" he asked, dust rising as he sank into the old armchair.

"Of course."

"How have you spent your time?"

"My sister and I enjoy being together."

"Where have you been?"

She sat on his lap, smelt his skin, looked into his anxious ice-blue eyes, and forced herself to fold her arms around him and nestle close to his neck. "Was it dangerous? Was there fighting?"

"There was a great deal." He pulled her round to kiss her on the lips and then stroked her arm. She felt his heart beating against her as he said plaintively, "I don't know what I'd do if I didn't have you to come home to." He grabbed her hand. "You've started to bite your nails. Tell me, Phuong, do you want a younger man?"

She rose, trying to keep her step and voice light. "You are not old." He recognized her evasions, but she would not say *I love you.* After the kiss, she was ready to smear herself with Mrs Chou's ointment, but he was tired; he wanted opium, not her.

When he had smoked one pipe, he began to talk about his trip. "I went out with a patrol. They killed a mother and child, civilians—just a careless accident, and two people are dead. War, it's so indiscriminate. The French are losing. It's alright for Granger to goad them..."

"Granger? He was in Phat Diem?"

"What? No, he was at a press conference in Hanoi. He wouldn't risk his neck in a battle zone, but the enemy is within fifty miles of the city."

"What did Granger say?"

"Is that pipe ready? You know, there was a moment when I was ready for death..."

Yes, yes, she wanted to say, but what about Granger? Did he recognize me at the Majestic? Her hand shook as she released the opium and turned the bowl over the flame. The vapor filled the room. Soon, Fowler would be confronting the devils of his dreams, but now he was still looking at her, noting every movement. Had he questioned her about her whereabouts because Granger had said he'd seen her with a Vietnamese man? He went on, "Sometimes, I yearn for the permanence of death. I've always been afraid, you see, of losing what I love." He spoke as if he knew she was about to leave him. He waved his hand as he talked. She saw the thick, blue veins of age and thought, what indulgence, to yearn for death. Her countrymen had death visited upon them, by this war and famine. His eyes flickered and closed. She thought, you will live to a great age, and you will go on talking of your desire for death.

She searched his pockets and found a telegram. It was from his employers, the newspaper, who were transferring him to London. The job sounded like advancement, yet he had shown no signs of pleasure. Clearly, he wanted to stay. She folded the telegram and returned it to his pocket.

When he woke, she told him about the curious plastics that Pyle was importing. She didn't have to weigh his reaction. "That's bloody York Harding's influence," he cursed.

"Who?"

"A writer, an American that Pyle gets his ideas from—and what ideas! Harding wrote *The Role of the West* after visiting this country for all of a fortnight. So now Pyle's got it into his head that what this country needs is a 'third force'— one that's neither communist nor colonial! By God, he'll cause some harm. He's watched too many westerns, thinks he's bringing the Law to Dodge City."

She memorized his words. So Pyle was going to build up a third force to fight against the Vietminh. Well, he had enough madmen to choose from. She nearly missed what Fowler said next. "*Comment?*" she asked.

The Quiet Soldier

"I said he's coming round for drinks." She'd never known him to invite anyone to the apartment. She saw him waiting for her response. The promise with Long had been made. This was a golden opportunity, yet she balked at the thought of spending the night in the American's embrace.

"This evening I must go and see my sister," she lied. She had to have time to think. Fowler seemed pleased that she was going. Having left, she listened outside the door, hearing the tap tap tap of his typewriter. Then she waited in a doorway and watched as Pyle strode along the rue Catinat. He wore a brightly colored shirt of the sort holiday-makers wore; it was a disguise as inept as the commanders' linen suits. A large black dog kept pace with him, trotting into the building beside him.

Lan was the last person she wanted to see. Her advice would be clear—go back and charm the American. Phuong lingered on the bridge on which she and Tha'm had once idled. The sampans drifted in the water below, and junks full of vegetables headed for the quay. In *Waterloo Bridge*, the soldier's love for the woman remained steadfast. Even though she had been defiled, he still wanted to marry her, but there was no such love in Vietnam, at least not for her. She had deceived with charm and been deceived in her turn. She was losing no more than what was already lost by becoming Pyle's mistress.

She retraced her steps to the apartment and heard English being spoken inside. The door was open, but she couldn't hear what they were saying, only that Fowler was tense, sarcastic, and Pyle more controlled. "There she is," he said, even before she walked into view—he could recognize her step. She eased past the dog standing guard in the doorway and waited. Abruptly, Fowler told her to sit down.

She sat in his armchair while Pyle stood over her. He apologized in bad French for his bad French. Like an irritated school master, Fowler said, "I will translate for you."

Pyle began. "Phuong, I want to tell you, oh heck that's not right. Phuong, ever since I first saw you, I have loved you."

Scathingly, Fowler translated. "Phuong, *je veux vous dire, oh estacade à claire-voie qui n'est pas exacte.*"

"I don't want you to think that it's because you're beautiful."

"*Je ne veux pas que vous pensiez...*"

146

"Not that you aren't beautiful! I mean, you are beautiful, but I was brought up to value the person within, not just outer beauty."

Fowler's translation continued. She sat impassively as the absurd words were addressed to her twice.

"Tell her I want to marry her," instructed Pyle. The dog sniffed about her as the men began to quarrel. Fowler was animated now, while Pyle was no longer quiet, urging his youth, his affluence, and his respectability as reasons why she should marry him. She wanted to run from the room, but who could she run to who would not command her to say yes?

"Well, Phuong, are you going to leave me for him? He'll marry you. I can't. You know why." Fowler kicked at the dog, who yelped.

Their great gift—marriage. She stalled by asking, "Are you going away?" His hand went involuntarily to a pocket—no doubt the telegram summoning him back to London was there.

"No." His lie made her feel better; none of them spoke the truth.

She started to say, "I must consider this," but Pyle talked over her. His great hands kept count as he listed the reasons why she should marry him. "First, I can offer you a good home... Second, I'm a relatively young man and can give you children."

Who will be as dust. Fowler's translations became erratic, then ceased, as if the tussle was solely between him and Pyle. Finally, with the dog panting beside him, Pyle addressed her directly. "Come away with me now. *Avec moi*." The French term was ugly in his mouth.

Yes, she should say yes. She had agreed with Long that it was to be so. Bui Hien would approve, Lan too. "No," she said, "no." Pyle repeated the word as if it were new to him. She was one of his certainties. She thought of Tha'm lying wounded and helpless while these men fought over her like dogs over a tasty piece of meat. At her *no*, she'd heard Fowler sigh. He smiled, not so much magnanimous in victory, as triumphant. He offered Pyle another Scotch, though one lay untouched on the table beside him. Pyle refused, and the dog growled threateningly at Fowler. Pyle looked shaken. He picked up the Scotch and took it down in one gulp.

What have I done, she thought. What will my broken promise cost? Qua^n was breaking into a military hospital on the strength of her yes, and she'd said no. She nestled into the chair, wishing herself invisible.

The Quiet Soldier

As Pyle's heavy footsteps echoed down the stairs, Fowler let the door swing shut. She heard the click of the lock and waited. A tiny slither of Helen's letter was, she saw, stuck to the leg of the table. Finally, she offered him opium, and he said that he needed to write a letter first. Pyle's proposal lay between them as a silence, not of disbelief, but of exclusion, as if what had happened was not about her. Fowler began writing with a pen, so she guessed his letter was not to his editor. When he was finished, she gave him his pipe then talked about Pyle. Then he told her that he had written to his wife to ask for a divorce.

She tried to smile, to look as if this was a wonderful thing that he had done. The *no* to Pyle had risen, as if from her soul. She was risking Tha'm's recovery and her own life, but the word had been irresistible. She wanted to say to the two men, you are both offering me misery. To be your second wife, one of your countless mistresses, or his wife, his mistress— if it weren't for Tha'm I would choose neither. You talk of taking me to countries you have readily left. I have little here, but if we go, I shall be an outsider who understands nothing. I shall care for nothing. London, Waterloo Bridge, double-decker buses; skyscrapers, the Statue of Liberty, Boston are as sand to me. I yearn for the tunnels of Cu Chi.

CHAPTER 28

There is nothing picturesque in treachery and distrust.
—Graham Greene, spoken by Thomas Fowler in *The Quiet American*

"I'm driving to Tanyin today," he said. She sat still, idly flicking through a copy of *Vogue*, forcing her eyes to stay on the magazine. "I need to return before nightfall. The enemy is active on that road when it's dark," he said.

Of course he wanted to wring some concern from her, but she could not squeeze the words out, and he left disappointed. She knew him, his strengths and weaknesses, and could handle him. A saying of her aunt's came back to her—*to lift autumn fur is no strength*—Pyle, young and CIA trained, would be tougher. She bit her nails, thinking of what lay ahead. The rougher her nails became, the more she caught them on her silk garments. Pulled threads sprung out like spikes. Sometimes, when she should have been alert and watchful, she'd find herself thrumming the fabric of her dress as Tha'm's injuries filled her mind.

With Fowler away until late, she was free to go to the house where Tha'm was being tended. But if she showed her face, they'd ask about Pyle. The need to see Tha'm overcame her fears; she'd prevaricate somehow, but she must ensure Tha'm had penicillin.

She found her friend progressing. Qua^n had stolen the medicine, which was driving infection from Tha'm's wounds. She was more coherent, more the old Tha'm, but she held her side, as if concerned that the wound would re-open, and she was bandaged tightly.

"Does it hurt still?" asked Phuong. An amputated limb could ache as if it was still attached, like the pain of a destroyed home or a lost existence.

Tha'm shook her head. "Not much. It's the grenade going off that I still think about. I want to do my bit to drive the colonialists out." Even this remnant of Tha'm was a soldier.

The Quiet Soldier

Now she sank onto her straw mattress. "I get tired quickly," she said, closing her eyes.

"I wonder if we're near the end," said Phuong. Tha'm had earned the right to complain of weariness, but she felt it too, not the exhaustion of a long day, but as of a lifetime's struggle. She felt as old as Mrs Chou, as if the war had taken her from childhood to age with only suffering between. "Will we have victory soon? Fowlair is sure the French are losing, even in the north where they fight pitch battles."

"I'd love to see us shooting down their planes," said Tha'm, opening her eyes and trying to raise her hand to form a fist.

"You better go now," Uoc said tetchily to Phuong. She'd had to leave her baby behind in the attic room in order to nurse Tha'm, and she was nervy. Qua^n had a welcome message from Lan. "She says the American is in Tanyin. He is likely to be away some days." Phuong smiled with relief. And with Fowler in the Caodai stronghold too, there was a chance she'd learn who Pyle was grooming to be the leader of his third force. They were a duplicitous lot and always breaking into factions. He'd have his choice of madmen.

He did not return that night as he had said he would. In the morning, he still had not appeared. Maybe he'd been blown up by a Vietminh night patrol. The road was lethal after darkness fell. The French could only retain control during the hours of light; the puppet soldiers they positioned in the watchtowers along the roadside would quickly surrender when threatened. Days passed and still he did not return, so she kept to the apartment, fearing any moment that a message would come that Pyle was back in Saigon and that she should seek him out.

As she waited, a letter came from England. She saw the delicate writing on the envelope and knew it was a woman's hand—Helen replying to Fowler's request for a divorce. Then a telegram arrived. She opened it. His paper wanted him to write an article about de Lattre. "Explain how French commander's departure affects the political balance." What a fuss about one dying Frenchman.

She was free to go daily to check on Tha'm's progress, with neither Pyle nor Fowler in Saigon. Then, late one afternoon, she heard a shout from the women that the old fart was on his way up the stairs. She had time to compose her face, so that, when he opened the door, she could rush to him with, "I've missed you!"

He had a limp like Long's and a story to tell of ambush on the road back from Tanyin. So it was as she'd guessed, his car had run out of petrol, which had been siphoned off, no doubt, by the thieving Caodaists. She wondered what he'd done to offend them. Perhaps they sensed his contempt for their *Technicolor* cathedral and delusions of grandeur.

His leg was splinted, and he walked with the aid of a stick. He immediately began questioning her about what she had done in his absence. "I've been to the cinema many times with my sister. Oh, we have watched many films. My favorite was one called *The Mystery of the Girl with Pink Shoes.* Her name was Corinne, and she was in love with a postmaster. Oh, how they laughed and sang! Though of course there was much to concern them. The postmaster climbed up a tree to enter the house through a window, but was stopped by—I think he was the mayor, but he might have been her father. Then Mme de Lattre came in and told Corinne that she must wear a magnificent gown covered in feathers and visit, not the mandarin, but someone like a mandarin..."

He had ceased to listen, which was just as well; stories are as difficult as lies. He moved around the room looking for something, picking up pieces of paper and discarding them. "Phuong, do you love me?"

"It was a very funny film," she said. She suspected he was searching for Helen's reply, so she disappointed him by giving him the telegram instead. He took it eagerly. As he scanned the words, his excitement died. A request for four hundred words about de Lattre was not what he was hoping for. Then it occurred to him to ask why she had opened the telegram and how she had read the English. "I took it to my sister." He'd never wondered why Miss Hei knew a language that she did not, cherishing her ignorance.

"If it had been bad news, would you have left me, Phuong?" She could have laughed at the idea that his pieces of paper mattered. She offered him some opium before she told him about the letter, which she placed in her scarf drawer. She held it delicately, as if it contained her future. He asked, suspiciously, "Did you open that too? Make me a brandy and soda." He stopped reading to pour a second brandy himself. He drank a third and a fourth without soda and a fifth slopped over the brim of the glass. His face was flushed, his nose inflamed, and when she again offered him opium, he looked up with ice-blue despair. "Anything, anything." Helen had refused.

The Quiet Soldier

Knowing the answer, she dared the question, "Will she let you marry me?"

"I don't know yet. She has not made up her mind. There's still hope."

Below, in the rue Catinat, she saw a familiar trishaw driver looking up. He signaled. She had been summoned—but for what? Her duty surely was to stay with Fowler and induce him to talk about Pyle and the third force. She quickened her preparation of the opium pipe.

"Since I was a boy and Wheeler betrayed me, I've yearned for death...," he said, not for the first time, as he lay back on the bed smoking. His familiar claim of exceptional human suffering went on and on. The despair, the woman in a red dressing gown brushing her hair, betrayals, goodbyes, the child unmentioned, the pain only his. She was scarcely listening when he said, "I nearly died coming back from Tanyin. Finished, it could have been finished. I didn't ask Pyle to save me."

"Pyle, he *saved* you?" she asked quickly.

"I've no savings. I can't outbid Pyle."

"Who did Pyle go to see?" she asked.

The mixture of alcohol and opium was making him groggy, but she heard the name Thé. "General Thé, once a Cao Dai commander, now a law unto himself," Fowler said. "Hell, if Pyle gives Thé explosives, there'll be carnage." His eyes flickered and shut. She went out into the street and got into the trishaw. It raced through the streets towards Cholon. In the early evening, the traders were at their busiest, and the sampans were still out on the river.

The driver left her in the Quai Mytho outside the Chous. The ground floor room that the old couple had occupied was empty, the door swinging open. Phuong made her way up the familiar staircase. In the room where she'd lived when first arriving in Saigon, she found many of her comrades. Chinh was there, unperturbed but vigilant, a soldier now. Uoc nursed her baby daughter. Ly sat by her side with her son, stirring a pot of steaming rice. Ly's husband was there too, a regular back from the north, a fortunate man indeed to be allowed leave to see his first-born son. No Tha'm though. "She is safer away from here," Ly said. "They've given up the searches, but with one hand..."

Ly stopped chattering as Heng entered the room. Phuong went to him. It was comforting to see and hear the casual child care, cooking, and mah yongg again; it was life undefeated. Heng asked, "Is Fowler back? What have you found out?"

"Where's Tha'm?"

"You're still bargaining? She's not well enough to move yet. When she is, we may get her out of the city, maybe to the Rung Sat."

"I don't trust the Binh Xuyen. They're nothing but gangsters."

"Come on, Phuong, enough of this. Pyle is back in Saigon."

"Thé is his third force," she said. "General Thé, he calls himself now. The American is supplying him with the explosives."

Heng wiped his brow. "Pyle's a fool if he thinks he'll control that Caodai turncoat! What a bunch. One minute they're our allies, the next back with the French."

"I have an idea. Fowler must be shown the explosives. He'll write about it for his paper. He could expose Thé and Pyle for what they are."

"Westerners want to read only of communist atrocities," said Heng bitterly.

"Play Fowler right, and he'll be a weapon in our hands," she urged him. "Let me go back to him—for a few days."

Heng sighed. "Be careful, Phuong. You are making powerful enemies."

When she returned to the apartment, she found Fowler writing a letter. He jabbed his pen into the paper and ink flowed. "Where have you been? I woke and you weren't here."

"I told you before you fell asleep. I arranged to see my sister."

"Just her? Or was he there? You're a commodity to your sister, you know that, don't you? She'll sell you to the highest bidder." He turned back to his letter. When he finished, he handed her the envelope. "Post this for me."

It was addressed to Pyle. "I'll take it to the Legation. It would save a stamp."

He looked angry at this. "I would rather you posted it."

"Yes." She had to say yes again, when he drew her towards the bed, but the opium had finally enervated him, and he fell away from her, complaining, "You want a younger man."

CHAPTER 29

Is the enemy strong? One avoids him. Is he weak? One attacks.
—Vo Nguyen Giap, Vietminh military commander

As soon as he'd limped away from the apartment in the morning, she steamed open the envelope. Fowler's letter was a disappointment. He thanked Pyle for saving his life, made a bitter allusion to his own aging bones, and then lied about his wife giving him a divorce. He'd written to the American, "So you don't need to worry any more about Phuong."

Was that what Pyle was doing—worrying about her, at the same time as amassing explosives and handing them to her enemies? She resealed it and went down to the rue Catinat, past the Notre-Dame Basilica to the post office.

She was queuing when she knew that she was being watched. The post office was the size of a cathedral, with a marbled floor and great vaulted ceiling. Its ridiculous grandiosity had misled her into walking in without checking for a way of escape. Vast though it was, there was only one doorway; there was no other way out. She did not turn to look at her tracker. She waited in the queue as it slowly moved forward towards the counter. She was safe among so many people. When it was her turn at the counter, she looked hard at the reflection in the glass panel. She saw the image of a man who was leaning against one of the dusky-pink pillars, in peasant clothes. She saw him casually reach for a cigarette.

"Mademoiselle, what do you want?" demanded the counter assistant, switching to Vietnamese to ask for the second time, but Phuong swung away, the letter still in her hand.

It was Bui Hien. She walked directly to him and had the satisfaction of seeing his shock at her approach. "How did you know it was me?"

She ignored the question but thrust the letter at him. "Here, if you want it, read it. But if I'm under surveillance, use someone more *efficient* than yourself."

When she returned to the apartment, there was a note. "Will be late home. Eat without me. I'm meeting a contact in the Quai Mytho. Thomas." Cold triumph filled her at the mention of the Quai Mytho. So Heng had done what she suggested and contacted Fowler. He'd show him the American-manufactured explosives. Heng was bold enough to enjoy doing that, leading Fowler by the nose. She could see him now, dressed in his linen suit, pointing out the chain of evidence to *The Times* correspondent.

Footsteps sounded unevenly on the stairs, so the old women's shouted warnings that Fowler was back were unnecessary. One screamed out that the next time he was injured she hoped the old lecher broke more than his ankle. The tapping of his stick came closer. As he opened the door, he found her behind a copy of *Vogue*.

"Ah, Phuong, you're here."

She drew the magazine aside. "Yes, I am here." She prepared to account for her time. He was alert, revived. She smelt no alcohol as he brushed her forehead with a kiss, so he had not stopped at a bar, but come back straight from the Quai Mytho. He was more dangerous sober; the sharp edge of his cynical intelligence would cut her then, if she were not careful.

He wanted to talk. He was like the Fowler she had first met, invigorated by some scheme. What he had learned in the Quai Mytho had excited him. "No wonder the natives call this place the city of tigers," he said to her. "The Sûreté don't know the half of what's going on! My God, no wonder the French are losing this war! I've met a fellow today who's probably Vietminh—you know who they are, don't you? My assistant Domingues put me on to him. He's operating right here under the noses of the authorities."

Her eyes widened. "Should you report such people?" she asked. The Chous, Heng, Chinh, Uoc, and Ly could all be swallowed up by a Saigon prison if he reported their location. Bui Hien too. Let him try to be charming there.

"What for?" he asked sharply. "I have no politics."

She wished she had such a luxury. She had put Fowler in touch with Heng; it was as explosive a mix as the plastics that Pyle imported. That night, she awoke from a dream where Pyle was burying Tha'm alive, saying as he did so, *this isn't at all suitable for her*. She screamed out as Tha'm's head disappeared under the earth, and Fowler woke, asking drowsily, "*Le cauchemar?*" She moved away from him without answering, her naked body wet with sweat. Tomorrow, she would make sure that Tha'm was still safe.

The next day, she went, but the heavy oak door would not open. Then Qua^n's head appeared. "Fuck off."

"What!"

"You heard me. These are orders—return to the Catinat. The American is there, waiting."

She heaved her shoulder at the door. "Let me see Tha'm."

"Have you spent so much time in bed with foreigners that you've forgotten Vietnamese? Get on with it."

Cursing him, she turned and ran towards the bicycle shop. She took no detours and spared no time to check whether she was being followed. She was out of breath when she reached the shop and stopped, panting outside. The door was closed. She'd never seen it shut and padlocked before. She beat on it with her fists, shouting, "Sister!" But no one answered. Even then, she could not stop, and she hammered on the door until her fists were bruised from the effort. Finally, she turned away and walked slowly towards the city centre and the rue Catinat.

There, pacing outside the apartment building as Qua^n had said, was Pyle. "Phuong!" he called out as he saw her. "What are you dressed like that for? You look like a peasant."

She laughed bitterly, "How can that be? Hasn't my sister told you many times that our father was a mandarin in Hue?"

He drew his hands through his stubbled hair and looked about wildly. There was a moment when she expected some confession. He was going to tell her that he imported plastic explosives and what Thé was to use them for. When he spoke, his words baffled her with their irrelevance. "I've learned something," he said. "I'm sorry to tell you this, but Fowler's lying to you. His wife has denied him a divorce. He'll be gone soon, Phuong, leaving you high and dry!"

A sigh escaped her. "*Comment?*" she replied, measuring her pace as she walked into the building with him moving frantically round her.

"Darn it. You don't understand..." He followed her up the stairs and the old women on the landing watched as he bounded ahead, then stood above her, repeating what he had said. She understood alright. Lan had shown him Helen's letter to force her hand. Time had run out. She had to leave Fowler immediately and move in with Pyle.

As she and Pyle moved past the women, one of them said, "The old one's in," and she noted again that Pyle could not disguise that he understood Vietnamese. He was striding up the stairs, intent on his task, fired up with indignation. When they reached the apartment door, he knocked loudly, and she heard the excited chatter of the old women again.

"Darn it, I wish my French was better. You don't understand—I'm looking after your interests! You've no idea what's been going on. Thomas, I know you're in there." Still the door did not open.

It was the day of closed doors. He put his hands on her shoulders. She itched to pull her knife, to set back his third force in the simplest way possible, by killing its creator. He drew his face closer to hers.

The door opened. A heavy-lidded Fowler took in the sight of their touching bodies. He was icily polite as he let Pyle in. The American refused to sit down or take a coffee, ready with his accusations. He was furious and made even more so by the way Fowler answered him. "Couldn't you have won without lying?" he asked, which Fowler brushed off with, "No. This is European duplicity, Pyle. We have to make up for our lack of supplies."

She waited for him to say more about supplies, sitting immobile and upright in the chair, but all they seemed to want to do was bicker over her. As she'd guessed, Pyle had learned of Fowler's lies from Lan. She tried to rehearse her explanation of why she'd taken Helen's letter to her sister. I was so proud, so proud. I was so proud. As they both seemed to believe she wanted to marry one of them, they might think she'd flaunt the letter like a prize. Pyle ignored Fowler's jibe about supplies, intent on blaming him for lying about the divorce. Fowler defended himself by beginning a lecture on what she was like. From the very beginning, he'd shown flashes of insight.

"She's no child. She's tougher than you'll ever be."

How shocked they'd both be if she'd interrupted to say he's right, you know. The worst has already happened to me. And choosing between the two of you is deciding between two different poisons. But I don't have the choice; I'm under orders, and only one door is open to me.

Pyle was no longer a quiet American. He shouted and paced about, pointing an accusing finger at Fowler, who answered with claims of experience. He said she'd survive them both, speaking of her as if she were a rock or stone. She picked up a *Vogue* and hid behind it as the argument grew more heated. "She'll suffer from childbirth and hunger and cold..." Fowler stood by the side of her chair, his penetrating blue eyes gazing at her as he spoke.

She flicked the pages of the magazine, pretending indifference to him and the furious, strident American. "Phuong! He's cheated you!" Pyle shouted. That was her moment to get up and walk out with him, as ordered. Tomorrow, she thought. One more night without his hands touching me, and I'll do it. She looked up and said mildly, "*Je ne comprends pas,*" and both men seemed to believe her.

CHAPTER 30

The Quiet American affected me disagreeably. I like to think that good intentions had value. In this book good intentions accomplished nothing.
—Tobias Wolff

She packed the cloth bag that she'd used when she'd moved in with Fowler, taking the possessions he thought she valued. He would find her and her clothes missing when he returned from his office that evening. She reached no further than a side street adjoining the rue Catinat when she found it blocked by armed policemen pushing back a crowd. "What's happening?" she asked a man at a flower stall, but his face clouded over, and he turned away. When she spoke in French to a European, he tried to take her arm, and she had to shake him off. She turned back as another armored vehicle sped from the direction of the Sûreté Headquarters. It drew abruptly to a halt further along the road. Policemen ran from the vehicle into a crop of bicycles and started sifting through them.

"What are they looking for?" asked an old woman who had shuffled up to Phuong. "They won't let me through. I've got to get to work…" Her complaints were drowned out by the sound of one of the bicycles blasting alight. Phuong was flung off her feet, and then shrapnel rained down. She covered her head, which felt as if it too might explode, the noise of the blast between her ears. Something soft fell against her—a child with a deep gash in its cheek screamed and clung to her, as if she were his mother. She got to her feet and let the child hold her as she sought refuge behind the old man's flower stall. A second blast came then and pieces of metal landed and bounced off the wooden roof. Even the child's screams seemed far away as a third explosion flung more pieces of metal into the air. She protected the child's head with her hand, trying to find words of comfort, but her mouth was too dry. Crushed flowers lay all around them. A wheel

The Quiet Soldier

buckled as it bounced off the stall roof, landing in front of them, and her screech matched the child's. They clung, shaking in equal terror, and she tried to brace herself for another explosion. Thick smoke hung in the air, but no further blast came. Finally, she heard a policeman shouting in fierce Vietnamese. Amidst the smoke she saw policemen hastily grabbing the bicycles that remained round a fountain and throwing them in. Water hissed and steamed from the smothered explosive devices.

She choked on the smoke as the noise died away and the cries of the injured increased. The police struck out with their batons, forcing those who could move to retreat. Phuong backed away too, trying to sooth the child who was calling out for his mother. When the police got into their vehicles and drove away, the people returned, some searching for their possessions, some to help the injured. Phuong's ears ached and, even with people, her own people all around her, she felt strangely distant. She had no idea which direction she should move in. The street itself seemed unfamiliar. Then a young woman, arms outstretched, came towards her and pulled the crying child from her arms, muttering. Phuong could not hear a word, but the mother's expression was dark with blame. The world seemed remote. She looked around and recognized where she had come from and remembered that she was meant to be going to find Pyle. She began to shake as she realized that she'd just experienced Pyle's explosives at work. He meant to use them on the streets of Saigon.

Her arm was wrenched before she even knew someone was addressing her. "Hey! I thought as much. You're the dame who was in the Majestic. Whoa, ain't you Fowler's tail?"

She shook Granger off and weaved through the crowd into a side street. When she knew he wasn't following, she leaned against a wall to rest and think. Where should she go now? Her tunic was speckled with the child's blood, and pulped oleander stained her trousers. She'd lost her bag too; she couldn't even remember where. If she went to the Quai Mytho to clean up, the door would be barred to her again. The committee would soon hear of the bicycle bombs and realize they were made with Pyle's explosives. They'd blame her for not finding out what he was up to sooner.

There was only one hope for her, and that was to find the American and become his mistress immediately. After the bicycle bombs, the committee would be even keener to gather intelligence on Pyle, and that might keep her safe for a while.

She walked slowly towards the American Embassy, every step an effort. The smells and sounds of the explosions lingered. Bombing tore flesh and bone; she wished it had torn hers before she realized Hien's role. Now she was to be the mistress of the man responsible for the bombs. Pyle. When drunk, Fowler joked that the name "had connotations." She didn't understand what they were but was sure they were unpleasant. She must sleep with Pyle, who spoke of himself as her savior. She would have to wait for him outside the embassy grounds, because an ordinary Vietnamese would not be permitted to enter. Lan would be inside, typing efficiently at a desk. Maybe she would look out and see her waiting, or come out and find her there, so she could say, *you were right all along, sister*. The personal must give way to the political. There's nothing else left for me now.

★

"You're safe with me now, Phuong," Pyle said, as they lay in his bed later that afternoon. "*I* won't lie to you." Between kisses, he breathed promises about taking her away. "Mom and Dad are wonderful, just a little old-fashioned, that's all. They'll come round. Wait 'til you see Boston. It's got so much history. I can't wait to get you home." He performed the sex act with mechanical clumsiness reminiscent of his atrocious dancing; he knew where, but not how. He'd muttered above her about *trying something else*, then come crashing down on her again, while she closed her eyes and waited for it to end.

Afterwards, she lay in his yielding bed, shuddering, as darkness fell outside, thinking of Hien. What a fool she had been to think he cared for her. He was simply the soldier she should have been all along, she thought, as Pyle breathed stentoriously beside her. She wanted to smash his skull, to grind the pieces to pulp, to say, *but you're not safe with me*.

When he left for work the next day, she waited. Maybe she was watched still and the committee would send a messenger. While she waited, she examined the books on his shelves. He had many on politics and one called *The Physiology of Marriage*. She'd tried to read *The Advance of*

The Quiet Soldier

Red China, but the language was too difficult, and the diagrams in *The Physiology of Marriage* was the appalling story of all she'd had to do with men since Ba Ra.

When the knock came at the door, it was Qua^n telling her to go to the milk bar. There she found Lan. Neither smiled, and Phuong thought, now we are both like stone. Lan said, "Fowler came to the Legation this morning. He barged his way in—that's what a European face can do. He was furious, shouting, 'Pyle's taken my girl!' Oh yes, he certainly forgot his reserve. The American that calls me *Hi there*—Joe his name is—reminded him that Pyle saved his life. He didn't like that. Then he went to the lavatory and cried. Big sobs. I listened outside."

Phuong would not comment on the old man's pain but asked, "So, is Tha'm well enough to move?"

"Do not think your disobedience has been forgotten. When and where are the rest of the plastic explosives to be used? You know we're being blamed for that display yesterday? That could have been avoided if you'd done what you were asked."

Phuong resisted goading her, as she'd done when they'd gone out to night clubs to find Pyle; it would only enflame her temper, and Tha'm might suffer as a result. So, as they sat like loving sisters with heads close, drinking sweet pink milk through straws, she listened in silence as Lan spoke of her errors. Yet even as she felt Lan's warm breath on her cheek, her voice seemed far away. She heard thudding in her ears as she remembered shrapnel raining down and the child with the cut cheek clinging to her, so that Lan's words of command were like a distant mosquito hum.

CHAPTER 31

*Live spies
are those who return
with information.*
—Sun-Tzu

It was a week before Lan told her she was again permitted to go to the Chous, giving some hope that the committee valued the intelligence she was gathering from Pyle enough to overlook her past stubbornness, at least for a while. When she got there, the door was open, and she bounded up the stairs to the attic room where she found Tha'm giving a display like a *Cheo* performer. They'd cleared the pots and the pans away from the center of the room so that she could show off her one-armed skills with knife and punji. She was thinner than ever and her body caved on one side, but she was laughing for the first time since her accident as Phuong joined her audience. Uoc clapped her baby's hands together in appreciation as Tha'm cut and parried and Chinh looked on admiringly.

I am one of them again, thought Phuong. Will my disobedience be forgotten, or are they waiting to bar the door to me again when I've been bled dry? "Come on," she said to Tha'm as her friend finished her display, "let's go up to our roof." She helped Tha'm up the narrow stairs. They linked arms and watched the dark, snaking river until Phuong felt that her friend could no longer stand. She helped her down to rest against a rusty kettle drum and then whispered urgently, "Listen, Tha'm, you're getting stronger. When you feel able, you should leave here—by yourself. Just walk out the door one day and don't come back."

Tha'm pushed her away. "They said you'd gone odd. Why should I leave my comrades? I'm going to fight again, you'll see. I can still use my dagger."

The Quiet Soldier

"You think they'll let you? You botched your last mission," snapped Phuong in exasperation. "Forget everything you did before, they just remember mistakes. I'm telling you. Don't trust them—not Heng and certainly not Lan!"

Tha'm looked at her in bafflement. "That's your sister you're talking about. She clings to the pole, doesn't she? I mean, going into the American Embassy every day and talking to them as if they're... well, like us. I couldn't do it."

"She *types*! But she's implacable and ruthless. You don't mean a thing to her."

"You're jealous of her. You want to be the wife, not the sister-in-law, that's why you're saying these things!"

Before Phuong could answer, Chinh appeared in the hatch-way. "You're wanted downstairs," he said.

"Fuck off," she said, but there was nothing more to say to Tha'm, who'd shut her eyes and was either asleep or pretending, so reluctantly Phuong descended and found Heng pacing impatiently.

"Pyle's imported ten times more plastic explosive than was used in Operation Bicyclette. What's it for?" he demanded.

"I don't know. Even when Fowler goaded him, 'Go play with plastics,' he didn't reveal anything. He doesn't speak openly about it, even in the Legation. Yesterday evening he took me to a party there. He told visiting Congressmen that America has clean hands and so can win the confidence of 'the Asiatics'."

"By blowing some of us up and then elevating their strong man Thé to suppress terrorism and unite the country. It's what they're doing in Korea." He took her by the shoulders. "But what you need to find out is where Thé is going to use those explosives. We've got to be ready."

"I'm trying to get it out of him. He talks enough!"

She thought of him waving books at her by York Harding, who he still believed had the answers to Vietnam's problems. "You won't understand this, Phuong, but I've studied it, studied it..." he'd said. We study too, she answered silently from behind her empty expression. Perhaps, if you read *our* books, you'll understand. But his mind was already stuffed with certainties. He'd said, "Dad's an isolationist. He came round in the end of course—saw that Hitler needed to be dealt with. We had to help the

Europeans out, even though they're colonialists. Fortunately, we're not tainted in that way." Not tainted at all, his large smug face seemed to say—sanitary, like the food his mother sent him wrapped in clear, brittle paper. "But times have changed. It's not fascism that's the threat to the free world now; it's communism. We've got to meet force with force."

She could tell Heng all this, but it got them no nearer knowing exactly what Pyle planned. "You've wasted too much time already," Heng warned her, before letting her go. She tried to go back onto the roof to speak to Tha'm again, but the hatch had been bolted from above.

One morning, she thought she saw Fowler walking along the rue Catinat, briefcase in hand, but then wasn't sure it was him, just another overly tall European stooped and shuffling his way towards the Pavilion where Fowler had drunk coffee ever since she'd known him. What would she have done if she'd been sure it was him—go up and greet him, as if he were an old friend? There was nothing more to say or hear from him. The first time they'd met in the cafe, she'd enjoyed irritating him by being late, then revelled in his frustration at her passivity. *Unsettle a settled enemy,* advised Sun-Tzu, but she knew that wasn't why she'd tormented him. To keep something back, to own a part of herself, whatever demands made on her body, a secret solace. "Sometimes," he'd said to her accusingly, "you're invisible, like peace." And then she knew that, although perfection had gone, there was still a Phuong left to protect.

That evening, as the light was dimming and she sat inhaling the soft, sweet jasmine wafting through the open window from the gardens that adorned the elegant French district, Pyle arrived home and, blushingly, told her he'd had a conversation with Fowler—or *Thomas*, as he always called him. She wondered if that name had connotations too. She measured her response. "What did you speak about?"

"Politics. And he asked about you, of course, and I told him how excited you were about coming home with me. I explained that we'd be married in Boston, properly, with my folks there. Then we'll have a real honeymoon. Just wait 'til you see Niagara Falls!"

The rushing water, the foam, she saw her first attacker again, smelt again his unwashed body suffocating her. Her first kill had left her shaken. He had, after all, been one of her own countrymen; perhaps, in another place, an ally. Pyle moved in front of the window, a dark shadow close enough to smell. "Thomas saw it had all worked out for the best. He has so little to offer you. He opened a letter from Britain while I was there. He didn't say what was in it, but if it had been anything to his advantage, he sure would have told me."

"Can't we leave Vietnam straight away?" she asked. "Is the Economic Mission so important? What are you doing that you must finish?"

"Hey, Duke!" The dog was panting beside him, and Pyle grabbed the great black ears and nuzzled into the dog's fur, then explained, "I'm halfway through something big. It's important for the sake of your country."

"Tell me. Then I will understand."

"It's not the sort of thing that would interest you. Don't worry. We'll soon be out of here. I'm glad Thomas sees all's turned out best for the three of us."

Pyle lived, it seemed, in a fog of wishes and daydreams. His political cadres had achieved a more thorough indoctrination than hers. Like the *crachin* that had descended on the north ending the war there for a season, visibility was obscured. The American's beliefs dimmed his senses and narrowed his vision, but his plan was coming together.

CHAPTER 32

A too black dog.
—Graham Greene

One morning, after Pyle had been gone a few hours, Duke barked excitedly, and she realized he was returning. She pushed *The Role of the West* back on the shelf and picked up a *Vogue*. Pyle rushed in, agitated, shoving aside the dog's drooling welcome. "Good, you're still here. I thought you might have gone to the milk bar."

"I shall go later."

He knew it was where she met Lan, thinking they met as sisters, making the most of their time together before one left for America. "Don't go there today," he said gravely.

Instinct drove her straight to the door before she could stop herself. He grabbed her. "What are you doing?"

A mistake, she'd made a terrible mistake. She should have asked—why not? The Phuong he knew would ask; his Phuong would not have understood immediately that bombs were primed. Too late, she asked "Why not?" and his grip tightened. Duke prowled around her, his black tongue flapping.

"Where were you going? Phuong? Oh my God, you already know, don't you—about the bombing?" He let go of her and turned away, as if quietly recalling words and phrases, snatches of conversation, signs he'd been trained to recognize, and missed.

When he swung back and asked, "How much do you know?" she feared it was too late to retrieve the situation. She was not deceived by the unemotional, almost formal tone he used. He was on guard now. Duke was growling by his side, immobile, watchful.

The Quiet Soldier

She tried to calculate, to think, realizing that she was not even sure of the time. How long had she got? She usually met Lan at eleven thirty. Was there time to try to find out where the bombs were placed or get out the door as soon as she could? She'd cut him down if she could, but he was three times her size and, she suspected, armed, while her knife was in the box under the bed.

He cursed. "God, I haven't got time for this! Phuong—why did you run like that? What do you know?"

"Nothing. I was frightened. I thought you were forbidding me to go out..."

"Why would you think that? Haven't I always been good to you? I've never reproached you for your past. I've told my folks I'm going to marry you! My father calls me a dumb fool. And I've introduced you to everyone at the Legation. I can just hear what Joe'll say if..."

She saw the wheels turning and took her chance. "I must have misunderstood your meaning. My English is poor."

He looked at her, brushing back his jacket. She glimpsed the bulge of a gun in a shoulder holster. "So you were just worried?" he said doubtfully.

"As you came in, you were so... loud, so aggressive, and different." She smiled. "Not my quiet American."

He glanced down at his watch without returning her smile. "I've got to go." Aggrieved, he added, "I came to *warn* you."

"Go," she said. "Go quickly, and we shall talk later." She resisted the impulse to move towards the door. He could still stop her, but he was eager to leave. He went without another word.

Then she heard the key turn in the door. He had locked her in. She heaved her shoulder against it, but it was solid. Picking up a chair and ramming it, legs first, against the frame was futile. The legs splintered and broke. Dropping its remains, she ran to the window and slid out onto the ledge, two storeys up. She shook as the traffic flowed beneath her. Slowly the ledge was letting her go, so she gripped the sill behind her as she tried to stop shaking. Looking down, she saw the top of Pyle's head as he left the building and turned in the direction of the square.

Her only chance was to jump towards the plane tree whose highest branches reached as far as the first floor. She tried to throw herself forward, towards the tree's center, but felt herself falling. All she could do was cling to a lone branch that snapped as soon as she gripped it. She fell onto the pavement on top of a girl riding a bicycle. A basket of eggs lay smashed around them as Phuong and the girl untangled themselves. The bike was twisted, the girl was hugging her shoulder and Phuong found, as she put weight on her right leg, that her ankle hurt.

Passers-by yelled as Phuong limped away with shreds of silk from her torn *ao dai* fluttering about her, but no one followed. As she turned the corner, she looked back and saw stooped figures trying to salvage egg yolks. With bloody scratches and shredded clothes, to get to the square without being stopped, she had to make her way through the gardens set in the middle of the boulevards.

"*Etes-vous bien?*" asked an old European walking his little dog as she stumbled toward the Boulevard Bonnard. The chimes from Notre-Dame Basilica sounded the half hour. Let her be late, she prayed. Let Lan be late today, or not come at all. Maybe Joe had warned all the secretaries—but some unwarned were essential—Pyle and Thé would not waste explosives on a bombing without casualties.

Even as she ran, the force of a blast blew her backwards. Fire and smoke rose up. The pavement trembled. She tried to lift herself to her feet, rubbing at her eyes to clear the dust. Chaos in the silence: children open-mouthed, dumbly screaming; blood pumping from severed limbs; and dust-covered figures moving like spirits amongst the fallen buildings.

She spat into her hands and then smeared the spittle onto her eyes to clear them. Her ears were ringing now and sounds from the shattered world outside her started to edge through. She pushed past a woman with cuts to her face and shredded *ao dai* wandering in a daze. Phuong stumbled towards the milk bar. A police car sped by, stopping abruptly by the entrance to the Place Garnier. Four policemen jumped out and started to cordon off the square. Flames flickered in the rubble. A figure—it could have been Fowler—distressed and passionate, was pleading with a policeman to let him get to the milk bar. "A friend," he seemed to be saying. "I have a friend in there." Amidst the smoke was another familiar figure—Pyle, stooping. Momentarily she thought he was bending over one of the injured, then she saw that he was trying to wipe blood from the bottom of his trousers.

She tried to reach the collapsed building but another policeman pushed her roughly back, raising his baton across her face. She strained to see what lay in the ruins. By one upturned table, she caught a glimpse of canary yellow silk enfolding a crumpled body. "My sister," she said. "My sister."

★

"He must be stopped." The words stayed tight around her, thudding in her head as she repeated herself, knowing that the committee would not be easily swayed by her appeals. Her ears still rang from the blast. She hadn't changed her clothes. Shredded and dust-ridden, her *ao dai* hung about her. A patch of blood was drying over her heart, stained when she had cradled Lan's body, after the cordon had finally been lifted. Her sister would have died instantly; her deep wounds made that clear. "He must be stopped," she insisted, as she paced the room, biting her nails. The brick dust dried her throat, so that her voice grated. No one answered her.

They sat, watching her with hard, frozen expressions. "You could have stopped him. You wasted time. This is your fault."

In the ante-room, she was the only one on her feet. Even if they offered her a chair in recognition of her loss, she wouldn't have been able to sit still. Smoke hung amongst the rafters. Three of the committee were smoking, and tea cups lay in front of all four. She struggled to find the argument that would sway them. "My sister," she began, her voice faltering as she thought of Lan as she had last seen her. "My sister was one of you. She served the cause well. She deserves..." She did not know what Lan deserved. "He killed her. Let me kill him!"

Heng snapped, "Now you want to act, when a far more valuable operative than you is dead. What will we gain now? We have bigger concerns. If we kill one meddling American, another will soon take his place." He looked to the others for agreement, and Phuong saw that her controller had lost face because of her failure. Power had slipped from him. She looked directly at the widower of an hour who was sitting at the head of the table in an ornately carved black chair. He hadn't even seen his wife's body. She wanted to cry and bury her head in Long's lap, to remind him of the happy time when he had said, "A man would be a fool to seek anything closer to perfection than that fish sauce."

But that man had disappeared years ago. If she was to persuade them that Pyle must be killed, she'd need stronger arguments. First, she must accept the blame for disobeying orders. She bowed her head and let a few of the tears she wanted to shed for Lan water her appeal for vengeance. "I was wrong to delay moving to the American," she said humbly. "My sister has paid the price of my disobedience. Let me do what I can to make amends."

"He is CIA—there'll be reprisals. And for what?" said one of the other committee members.

"Only if they can trace the assassination to us," said Phuong. "If I do it right, they won't."

Long held up his hand to stop her speaking. Chinh had entered. He whispered into Long's ear, then Long spoke softly to Heng, and her controller left the room.

Long said, as mildly as ever, "There is a season for making fire. Maybe a way of killing Alden Pyle and escaping repercussions has offered itself to us..." He was interrupted by Heng, who'd come swiftly into the room and whispered in Long's ear. Long gave the signal that they should leave quickly. Only Heng stayed behind.

Phuong followed the committee members into the attic room, which was as full of Heng's family as usual. Soup was being cooked, mah yongg played, and small children wandered amongst the battered furniture. She was baffled, for Long's signal had indicated an intruder, but no one had fled. Why had they needed to leave the ante-room so quickly? Who had arrived, and why? There was no one she could ask, since the committee members were mingling with the family, blending inconspicuously into the domestic scene, concealed in the open, like leaves on a tree. One took a ladle out of Uoc's hand and began stirring the soup. Long joined a game of mah yongg; no one remarked on those who had joined them. Phuong approached Long. "What is it? What's happening?" Mr Chou looked up from the game, with a look of disapproval for her rashness.

Long replied calmly, "Thomas Fowlair. Has come here. Heng is speaking to him."

"Fowlair, here?" Her first thought was that he'd followed her to the Quai Mytho, having realized at last that she was Vietminh.

Long moved the pieces on the board carefully, as if absorbed in the game. She smelt the oil about him and watched his stained fingers wrap themselves around the ivory. "He came here and asked for Mr Heng, having been much disturbed by the big bomb."

The Quiet Soldier

"So he *was* there! I thought I saw him when..." She was trembling again.

"Strength!" said Long, still looking at the game board. "Strength, little sister. *The skilful warrior stirs and is not stirred.* You may get what you want. Depend on Heng. He is talking to Fowlair now. If he can persuade him to become *engagé*..."

"What can Fowlair do? You mean kill Pyle?" Was it possible? She wiped her eyes with her tunic, covering her face for a moment, then let the shredded silk drop. He was an old man. Pyle was young and now carried a gun. "Fowlair is no soldier. He doesn't even own a knife," she said."He fights with words..."

Finally, Long looked up at her. "Who wields the knife is another matter, but if you kill Pyle in the open, our whole unit is in jeopardy, but if Heng can convince Fowlair to arrange a rendezvous with Pyle—somewhere remote, then we can cut the American down."

She grasped his hands, elated. She'd seen the same dogged look in his eyes when the Sûreté police pulled him from her father's house fifteen years before. "Yes, brother, yes." He did not withdraw his hands.

Only when Mr Chou noisily dropped a piece on the board did Ngo Quang Long seem to remember where he was. "Now go and clean yourself. Dress properly. If Fowlair agrees, Pyle will die this evening. Then it will be up to you."

"Tell me."

"Your duty will be to watch Fowlair. If Pyle is assassinated, the Sûreté will be forced to investigate thoroughly. They will question the Briton. Watch for signs that he implicates Heng. He knows this place and something of our organization. We must have immediate warning of any risk. If Fowlair divulges anything to the Sûreté, kill him."

Heng walked in. He crossed the room, smiling. "He's agreed," he told Long. "I said to him, sooner or later, one has to take sides. If one is to remain human. He's chosen our side." He glowed, his sharp fangs showing.

Long clapped him on the back, so forceful a gesture for him that she sensed for the first time his personal sense of loss. "Well done! Will it work, do you think?" He turned to Phuong. "Fowlair must lure Pyle for us. Will the American take the bait?"

She considered. "It is likely," she said, adding bitterly, "It's as Fowlair said—in his way, Alden Pyle is very innocent."

CHAPTER 33

Death Ground

Washed, wearing Uoc's only *ao dai*, threadbare and sombre grey, Phuong stood beside Long, as her sister, his wife, was lowered into a bleak grave. Other victims of the day's bombing were being buried elsewhere in the same municipal burial ground on the south side of the city, but she and Long were the only mourners at Lan's graveside. No more than an embrace apart, they watched the swaddled remains disappear under the black soil that was shoveled over her. There had been no time to find a propitious site following geomantic laws. They must leave her spirit far from home.

Now only a few hours of the afternoon remained, and Phuong had to hurry back to Pyle's apartment, so that when he returned, his day's work completed, work to shame the devil—devastation in Saigon's main square and a meeting with the Minister—she would be there to greet him. He had locked her in and must find her still inside, waiting. She would need the help of the women in the building to climb back through the window.

So dry was the black earth that Phuong began to cough again; the dust from the bombing still lay in her throat. It should be the red soil of Cu Chi, she thought. Lan, you were not destined to have your fine wedding. You never drew on the red robe embroidered with the imperial phoenix or balanced a *khan dong* on your head. Yet you married Ngo Quang Long, son of a mandarin from Hue. The children you should have borne him would be full-grown by now, older than I was when forced onto the road with Van. All you have is this last resting place, which is blown by the pernicious White Tiger wind in the forest of tigers.

She pushed away her tears. She was ready to participate in killing Pyle. She felt no doubt, no resistance, as she had done before. Finally, her heart was in a mission. They must strike like lightning and disappear as swiftly. She turned her back on the grave, aware that the sun was sinking and that she had to be back at Pyle's apartment before him. She felt a surge of pride in the skills of which she had so often been ashamed. CIA trained though he was, Pyle was to be lulled into carelessness. She and only she could do it! She'd smile at her sister's murderer and persuade him he was safe, that he would not pay for what he had done. She had to travel across the city back to the rue Danton, and there was no time to run, let alone walk. A trishaw would take her. The loyalist-driver would stay close, waiting below in the street, Long told her, as they walked away from Lan down the tree-lined avenue. She should signal for help if Pyle was still suspicious, as he had been that morning, and threatened her. She bowed when he said that, the first time she'd thanked him for anything since she'd become a soldier in his small army. She would not see Long again, nor, like the child she had been, search for him again. As they parted, she saw that he wished to say something to her, but it remained unsaid. Whatever Long suffered, he accepted the pain, offering it on the altar of warfare.

As the trishaw sped through the streets, she reflected that a comrade standing vigil outside the apartment was futile. Pyle could kill her with his bare hands before the driver crossed the road. Was his presence a sign of the committee's continued distrust? She remembered Fowler's account of being trapped in the watchtower with Pyle and two puppet soldiers. He'd grabbed the Sten and asked casually, "Shall I shoot them?" He could do the same to her, and the Sûreté would not bother to investigate a Vietnamese girl's death. She had no diplomatic privileges. Yes, she realized, the driver is not there to save me, but to carry the news if I fail.

When the trishaw stopped in the rue Danton, she made a show of paying the driver, controlling her expression in case she was being watched. She went into the building. The landing was heavy with the metallic smell of raw blood soup and the chatter of the women. "He locked me in this morning," she told them, wishing she'd had the time to befriend them as she'd done with the women in Fowler's building. "I must enter another apartment and climb along the ledge to re-enter." Wordlessly, they helped her into an apartment on the same floor and, breathing fast, she edged herself out onto the window ledge. That morning, she'd jumped from this height, but now the tree that had broken her fall was out of reach. She looked down, terrified of slipping. Gingerly, her hands reaching up to grab pieces of stucco, she edged towards the open window. She stopped, hearing something or someone inside. Was Pyle already back and lying in wait? Then she identified the sound: it was Duke's threatening growl as he guarded his territory from an unidentified threat. He was waiting on the other side of the window. If he didn't recognize her, he would leap as she came into view.

"Duke, good boy," she stammered, trying to recall the soft gentle phrases Pyle spoke to the animal. "Good boy. Heel, Duke, heel." Any second, Pyle might enter the apartment and find her on the ledge, or a passer-by look up and cry out at seeing her there. Duke's growl had either lessened, which meant he'd recognized her voice, or deepened, and he was ready to pounce. She took a chance, throwing herself forward off the closest remnant of ledge to the window, scorching heat in her arm as Duke's teeth bit down. He was going for her throat now, and she rolled over, trying to fight him off. His weight was heavy upon her as she was flung towards the bedroom. On her back, she struggled along the floor, trying to placate the frenzied dog, but all that came out was, "No, no!"

Momentarily, Duke drew back, giving her just enough time to leap up and slam the door shut on him. Gasping, she tore at the sleeve and looked at her arm. Blood dripped down and ran between the floorboards. The animal had ripped a chunk of her flesh down to the bone. She felt dizzy, wanted to fall onto the bed and rest, but Duke's abrupt retreat was ominous. She listened. Yes, the dog had heard his master's footsteps on the stairs. She ripped off the tunic of Uoc's *ao dai*. A babble of female voices told her that the women were trying to delay Pyle for her. She heard him replying harshly in Vietnamese—he'd given up pretending to be a cub; she had the tiger to fight.

She tore a strip off Uoc's tunic and, wincing, hastily bandaged the wound, then ran to the wash basin and sluiced her face. Her knife had fallen free with Uoc's tunic. She picked it up, wishing she'd cut the cursed dog into morsels days ago. She heard Pyle's voice again. "Let me go! I've no idea what you're all talking about." Duke, hearing him too, scratched further grooves into the apartment door. She pulled Pyle's favorite western dress from the wardrobe and threw it over her head, struggling into the sleeves. Their length was just sufficient to cover the clumsy bandage. She cried out with pain when she took her brush from the dressing table and tried to run it through her hair.

He'd reached the outer door to the apartment. She kicked the splintered remnants of the broken chair behind the table as his key turned in the lock. Duke jumped up to greet his master, and Pyle let it lick his face and eyes before he ordered, "Enough, Duke, down." The dog fell at his feet; Pyle scanned the room. She was sitting in her usual chair, reading *Paris Match*. The smile she gave him was luminous.

CHAPTER 34

When Trouble stands resolute, blocking your path, meet it head on.
Remember, if you strike, strike to kill, as I have seen you do.
—Van

"Oh!" His expression was uncertain. "You're not mad at me?" He came towards her, and she saw that he was no longer wearing the clothes he'd had on earlier in the day. He must have changed at the Legation out of the bloodied trousers he'd tried to wipe clean. She tried not to jump with pain as his hand fell heavily on her arm. She felt the blood coursing from the wound; the bandage was heavy with it and would soon seep through. He'd always been clumsy, like a monstrous child. Leaping up to free herself, she asked lightly, "Mad? Que fait ce moyen?" Duke slavered round her. She could smell him on her, as if she were half-eaten prey.

"What does it mean? Angry, annoyed as hell. I locked you in. I'm sorry. The way you rushed for the door when I said stay away from the milk bar threw me. I guess I see things too complicated sometimes. This is a hell of a place. It gets to you." She realized that his morning's suspicions were allayed but he was shaken by the carnage in the square and that might make him reluctant to meet Fowler. Some men, how strangely they needed sympathy for their callousness. His voice rose almost to a woman's pitch. "The sea's eating the land from under us, did you know that? Darn it, Phuong..." He reached for her. "I've had a terrible shock today."

She let him wrap his arms around her. When she closed her eyes, she saw the bodies in the Square. "Tu es troublé," she said, each word faltering. His nearness was suffocatingly hot, as if he'd brought the fires in the square with him.

"What? Oh, Phuong, I've seen things today that no one should have to. It's tough, you know, the sort of work I do. Now I just want to snuggle in here with you, away from everyone."

How was she to make him leave the apartment when he felt so sorry for himself? She said gently, "Your work is very important. Don't worry about today. In a week, we'll all have forgotten it." Forgotten Lan slumped against the wall, a resigned look on her face. Severed limbs, a woman covering her dead baby with her hat to conceal its mutilation, matters of great delicacy exposed by a blast designed to be blamed on her compatriots. Forgotten? For him yes, if Americans have no afterlife.

He unfolded a little, assuaged by her words, and pulled cajolingly at the bodice of her dress. "Okay, you're right. Do you want to go out tonight? That's the outfit I saw you in when I first fell in love with you."

She let his hand linger by her breastbone. A finger began to brush the swell of her left breast. She feared he would feel her heart hammering beneath his large hand. The desire to be free of him was intense. Blood, she was sure, was seeping through the sleeve of her dress. If only she could lead him straight out onto the streets and be rid of him. Would Heng be able to deal with him without Fowler as bait? No—and killing him would be easier tonight than it would ever be again.

"You do not have more work to do, because of your terrible day?"

His hand drew back. "Well, Thomas left a message for me at the Legation. I can imagine what it's about, but it won't be pleasant."

She pushed him away lightly, trying to sound indulgent. "Go to see him. Or perhaps I should go instead..."

"What? No. I don't want you near him. This doesn't involve you. I'll go to his apartment."

"I will be waiting when you return. Take Duke. He has been in all day."

"Darn it, of course he has! Sorry boy! He slapped his thigh, and the dog bounded to his side. "Don't worry, I'll be back as soon as I can."

"No!" She'd sounded too emphatic, she realized, and tried to adjust her tone. "Not for me. Stay with him as long as you wish." The next words came painfully from her lips. "I shall go to the cinema. With my sister."

As soon as he'd left the apartment, she ran to the bedroom and bundled the remains of Uoc's ao dai into the box under the bed, just in case he returned suddenly. But he'd taken her at her word, she saw, as she looked out the window, for he was standing at Duke's side as the dog defecated fulsomely on the pavement. When the dog had finished, Pyle strode away in the direction of Fowler's apartment, followed by the trishaw driver.

She paced the room, tidying the objects that had been scattered in her fight with Duke. Cushions, papers, she could not stay still. For a soldier, inactivity is more unsettling than battle. Terror accompanies combat, but waiting brings the uneasy spirits of the past. Van had told her that, when he'd instructed her on their long journey together.

Her first killing on the road to Ba Ra came back to her. She felt the fear and disgust again, tasted the bitter-sweet relief at seeing her attacker's lifeless body. She thought of the times she'd escaped by the skin of her teeth with a lie or an evasion, and then forced herself on to memories of Lan and their recent meetings in the milk bar when they'd looked like sisters but traded bitterness and disdain. The spirit of their father Co would have urged reconciliation. One day, she'd return to Cu Chi and rebuild the family shrine. She'd honor him to make up for all the missed anniversaries and tell him about Lan. She'd tell him too that they'd both striven to be worthy of him in the forest of tigers. Perhaps his spirit remained to look over her, knowing that she'd followed his advice—listen and watch, my little Phuong, listen and watch. When Lan had fled from Cu Chi, he didn't understand her cause or the Vietnam she dreamed of, but, nonetheless, he'd given a blessing: Wheresoever you go, go with all your heart. Lan had obeyed him in that, giving herself unequivocally to Long and the Struggle, which were one and the same. But until this day, she had failed to do that, never believed enough, committed herself enough. She'd tried to remain the pampered baby of the Trungs, or maybe she'd never quite woken from the cahn Heng had fed her, never accepted the present to be as real as her past.

Tired of pacing, she sunk into the armchair. She smelled of dog but was too restless to wash. To think that now their plans depended on the Briton. If only she could be with Heng as he stalked Pyle! The Dakow Bridge would be the place of reckoning, she calculated. Fowler was fond of dining at the Vieux Moulin, and that offered a clear view of both sides of the bridge. The Sûreté did not venture to the farther side after dark. She bit her nails and tried to estimate where Pyle would be now, what Heng would be doing, what Fowler would be saying. She would not be needed again until the assassination was complete or had failed. If Pyle escaped, she'd hear the dog bounding the stairs, and then they would enter, maybe Pyle knowing her part in the attempt on his life. He had the dog and a gun. She took her knife from its hiding place, breathing more easily with it at her side.

If the plan worked, if Fowler succeeded in persuading Pyle to meet him in a place where he could be abducted and killed, then she was to go to Fowler's apartment and pretend she was worried by Pyle's lateness. She knew that the Briton would conceal his part from her, though she might get him to talk after plying him with opium. They would both feign concern for Pyle. He's such a punctual man. Then the old man would beg her to sleep with him and she'd have to say yes, so that, when the Sûreté came knocking at his door, she would be there to accompany him. She picked up the discarded Paris Match that she'd so often hidden behind and began to gouge it. She'd bitten her nails so deep that thin trails of blood streaked the pieces, like the red ribbons flying high to celebrate a new moon.

CHAPTER 35

Master Sun said:
Ground where mere survival
requires
a desperate struggle,
where without
a desperate struggle
we perish,
that is
Death Ground.
—Sun-Tzu

She waited in a doorway of the rue Catinat, opposite Fowler's apartment. The heat of the day was dissipating, the grand French shops had closed their shutters after the bombing, so there were no late shoppers lingering, as they usually were in the late evening. She glanced up at the open window of Fowler's apartment. Through the gauze curtain moving faintly in the breeze, she saw him walking about, alone. Of course he couldn't settle, just as she'd been unable to sit still earlier. Only now, when she had a role to play, did she feel less agitated, though an ordeal lay ahead. To walk into the Sûreté headquarters having evaded their notice for so long was going to be like peeling off her own skin. She hated the jackals who served the colonialists. Even more, she feared their overseers, the French officers with their fine accents and careless brutality.

Duke's bite was throbbing now, the flow of blood finally staunched by the tourniquet she'd used, tearing a strip from the first silk scarf Pyle had bought her after she became his mistress. She brushed her injured arm against her side, comforting herself with the feel of her knife. Unwashed, she'd changed again into an *ao dai* so that she could conceal it securely at her waist. Her trousers were white, her tunic splashed with the vivid red of the lotus flower. Wearing it always brought Nam and the north to mind. With Lan's death, the yearning for their brother deepened to a pain more intense than the one in her arm. What she would give for a message of the kind that used to reach them in Cu Chi about Lan. *Your friends say they are well and that they love you as they love their country.* She could go on fighting in her soiled way if she knew her brother, somewhere, was fighting nobly. Long had never mentioned his old friend. Was Nam dead to him, like the past? What a heart he had to turn such losses into steel.

She drew further into the doorway as a few late workers went by. It was quiet, the city still subdued by the bombing. There was no sign of Pyle. When, past midnight, Fowler came down the stairs and approached her, it was not difficult to wear an expression of concern. He'd aged since she'd last had to look at him. His hair was whiter, thin veins traversed his face like red rivers, and the skin beneath his disconcerting sky-blue eyes was puffy, as if he'd shed tears.

He came close enough for her to smell the familiar brandy and guilt. "Phuong," he said, "he isn't here."

"I know. I saw that you were alone at the window."

"You may as well wait upstairs. He will be coming soon." The trishaw driver pedalled slowly by, giving a slight swing of the head to signal that Heng's mission was still operative. Her step faltered as she followed Fowler to the doorway, wondering whether Pyle was dead already.

She trailed after Fowler. He had to stop every few steps to wait for her and when they came to the women on the stairs, they jabbered at her. "What are they talking about?" he asked.

They were commiserating, good-naturedly enough. "Back with grandfather, little sister? So, a horse knows its old way!" Their ironic best wishes echoed through the stairwell. *"Chúc may mắn!"*

"They think I have come home," she told him. When she entered the apartment, she saw that he was more slovenly than ever. The tree she'd carried in for Tet celebrations two months before stood leafless in the corner, apricot blossoms trodden into the floor. The room smelt of unwashed clothes and stained bed sheets. She took a pile of dirty garments from a chair and sat down stiffly.

They talked of Pyle and his absence, lying to each other. "He will not be long," she said, as if reassuring him.

His replies were meant to be similarly comforting, but his manner was brittle and defensive. She could see his eyes straying towards the bed. She felt revulsion at the grey jumble of sheets. He fell on top of them, then, watching her out of half-closed eyes, began unbuttoning his trousers. She rose so quickly to light the pipes for his opium that she felt lightheaded.

As she prepared the bowl, he asked, "Is he still in love with you, Phuong?"

Rage made her hands shake, forcing her to put down the pipe. As if it meant anything, this *in love* that burnt bright in embrace but disappeared in the morning, abandoned like a stray dog. War casualties, he'd say. They died for democracy. What did she care for his being in love? She kept her eyes down, hiding her thoughts. Mad, what does that mean? She'd asked Pyle, knowing the answer. Angry, livid, beside oneself with rage, bent on vengeance—dangerous emotions that must be controlled as an archer controls his bow. She said very slowly, using the ploy of her wonderful ignorance again, "In love?"

Fowler's hands were down his trousers, rubbing, his eyes closed. Quickly, she prepared his pipe, laying it on the tray beside him. Hearing her, he opened his eyes and withdrew his hand from his flaccid *dương vật*. He reached for the pipe. She thought, he wants to forget what he has done. He knows that taking me will not help him do that.

For all his experience, he smoked like a novice, taking short pulls. She was ready with a second pipe by the time he'd inhaled the first, his head sinking back on the leather pillow. He would become garrulous soon, and sleep after four refills. As she anticipated, he began to talk. His misery at losing her, the comforts of opium, Pyle's absence, his need of her, the comforts of opium, Pyle, round and round. He quoted poetry about loving and losing. She was Vietnam to him, he told her, and she thought, yes, we are both ravaged by war. Between pulls on the pipe he spoke plaintively of his wandering spirit, as if offering an excuse to all of those he'd deserted, reminding her of Pyle's saying that if Fowler had taken her to London, sooner or later, he'd have abandoned her there in the cold.

"Are those flowers on your dress? I saw some like them growing by a canal when I traveled to Phat Diem. There was a terrible sight—a woman, with her child... How I've missed you. I wish I were Pyle."

As he said the name, there was a knock at the door.

Her hand reached for her knife. "Pyle," she said, as if it were a warning.

But it was not him. She'd opened the door, her knife sheaved: A Vietnamese Sûreté policeman stood with his feet far apart, as if prepared to withstand a blow. She stared at him. He glared insolently back. "Monsieur Fowlair," he barked. Fowler could barely raise his head from the bed as he answered. She wished he'd refuse to go. He'd sleep and she could rest, maybe risk tending her wound if he slept soundly, and they could answer questions in the morning. But if he went, she must too. The policeman gestured her out and, fearfully, she went down the stairs beside Fowler.

His trousers were still undone, she noticed, as he said belligerently, "I'm, not going to walk. You'll have to pay for a trishaw." The policeman looked along the street and beckoned one waiting close to the area devastated by Pyle's bomb. It was her comrade. Heng and Long would hear that she'd entered the Sûreté building; but if the interrogation went badly, no one could get her out.

CHAPTER 36

Mort Pour La France
—Vietnamese tombstone

The driver stopped outside the gates of the imposing building, not wanting to approach the Sûreté headquarters more closely. How beautifully the French build and how ruthlessly torture. As she and Fowler walked up the steps towards its grand white marble facade, Phuong stopped. "Wait," she said. "I must tell you something." Her arm ached, and she suspected she was developing a fever to fight infection from Duke's venomous teeth. If only she could sleep quietly, to be the peace men told her she was.

Fowler looked down at her as their police escort stood impatiently at their side. He was used to suspects' reluctance to enter. After all, few left as healthy as when they arrived. "What is it?" She struggled to keep her thoughts orderly. Why did she want to tell him that she was Vietminh? Did she hope that if he knew that he would struggle to protect her inside? But he wouldn't take kindly to the realization that he had been duped. He was as likely to betray her to the French as save her.

She shook her head, "I don't feel well."

He took her elbow, as he used to do, propelling her along. "Don't worry. I can handle these Frenchmen. *We* didn't run scared in '40."

They were escorted into an office. He recognized the officer sitting behind the desk and said malevolently, "Ah, Vigot, how's your wife?"

The man smiled wryly. He wore a green eyeshade and sweated, despite the cool air coming from the fan whirring noisily behind him. Ash fell from his cigarette as he waved his arm to indicate that Fowler should sit. With studied courtesy, Fowler held the chair for Phuong, then dragged another chair from a corner of the room and sat down heavily. The policeman pushed aside the book he'd been reading. Nam had had that very book. She

The Quiet Soldier

recalled it in his hands the year he'd studied for entry into the Sorbonne, which his father had assured him was the passport to a wonderful future in the Vietnamese civil service. Concentrate, she told herself. This man has nothing in common with Nam. He is the enemy.

As if he'd heard her thought, Vigot asked sharply, "*Combien de temps avez-vous vécu avec Monsieur Pyle?*"

She willed herself to remain quiet for a while, as if she found his words difficult to follow, and then answered slowly in English. "I live with him two months, I think."

His next question was even more insulting. He meant to disconcert her, or maybe it was Fowler he wanted to unsettle. "How much did he pay you?"

Fowler intervened. "You've no right to ask her that. She's not for sale." He was drawing Vigot's fire, but the policeman was no novice: even as he began to direct his questions to Fowler, his gaze remained on her.

Vigot uttered the name Pyle. "Please believe me it is very serious." She waited for confirmation of death, felt it would help her breathe more easily in the smoke-filled room and forget her wound. The jackal had brought in three coffees and, though the pain now reached her shoulder making it difficult for her to lift her arm, she forced her hand out to take the cup, letting it linger there to suggest that her attention was wandering.

Vigot said, with heavy emphasis, "A very quiet American." She sipped her coffee as if the words meant nothing. The policeman was waiting for one of them to speak, but she looked down, her face closed. Did Fowler take the words to mean Pyle was dead? He'd often boasted that opium made him quick-witted. He needed to be now, if both of them were to escape arrest.

"How did you meet him first?" Vigot asked, but he got no answer. She could not help thinking, though, of Pyle striding towards them as they drank in the Continental. His tone had been deferential, not like the noisy bastards Granger, Joe, and the rest. *I was wondering whether you and your lady would step across and join my table...* Well, they'd stepped across, and here they were being interrogated about his murder.

Abruptly, Fowler asked, "Is he in the mortuary?" So!

Vigot said slyly, "How did you know he was dead?"

Again, Fowler remained silent, but he slowly turned to her. She had to sit on her hands to conceal their shaking. He looked at her pityingly, and she realized that he believed in her love for Pyle. When he said, *she's not for sale*, he meant it. He put himself in the line of fire, asking, "What hours are you interested in?"

"Between six and ten."

Meticulously, Fowler accounted for his movements. She wished she could warn him not to be too precise, because it meant he'd planned his version of events, the way she used to rehearse what she told him. He gave the names of witnesses, even to his visit to the cinema. She wondered whether he recalled all the occasions she'd used that alibi. But he left out Pyle's visiting him. He said Pyle had telephoned. He was pretending he hadn't seen Pyle tonight at all, that he'd waited to have dinner with him and the American failed to turn up.

Vigot turned, the green eyeshade glinting in the lamplight. "And this girl of his? Do you know where she was?" He looked at her suspiciously. Every Vietnamese was an enemy to him, as every Frenchman was to her.

"She was waiting for him outside at midnight. She was anxious. She knows nothing. Why can't you see she's waiting for him still?"

Reluctantly, Vigot said, "Yes."

Fowler took the advantage, asserting that neither of them had a reason for killing Pyle. Pyle was going to marry Phuong, he told him. They'd been about to go to America, to settle close to Pyle's parents in Boston. "That was her dream. She'll be crushed when she realizes it's over. You know what a good marriage means to these people."

These people—one weary colonialist talking to another. He made a good case, convincing enough for her to remember how she'd had to pretend to want to marry Pyle, live near *Mom and Dad* and learn to play some game called Canasta. She risked looking up at Vigot briefly. He seemed lost in thought, but she wasn't deceived by his distracted air. Maybe he was an intellectual—she read the title of the book he'd had in his hand as they entered. It was Pascal's *Pensées*. Nam had loved that book—but a man could be a thinker and a soldier too, as her great, great grandfather had been. This Vigot could dispose of a native like her with impunity. Fowler's support was her best protection, and he was leaving the room, invited by Vigot to identify the body.

Never had she wanted his presence more. She waited, her back to the door, alert to the sound of someone coming in, willing herself to stay in

The Quiet Soldier

the hard, uncomfortable chair, concealing her nervousness. She wanted to bite her nails, to tear away the cover of the *Pensées* leaving it covered in her blood.

The door swung open. It was the jackal who'd escorted them. He stood over her for a moment and then moved to the other side of the desk. He bent to seat himself in Vigot's chair, thought better of it, and stayed standing. Licking his fingers, he leafed through the papers. She saw lists of names and crudely sketched maps of the rue Catinat and square. Would they be able to link her to Lan? If they could, they'd have their motive, but no, they'd both lived under aliases too long. Abruptly, the jackal asked, "*D'où* êtes-vous? *Je veux dire à l'origine, avant que vous soyez devenu une putain pour des* étrangers."

He lingered over the word *whore*. She answered softly in Vietnamese, "What did you say? Perhaps we should speak our own language, Uncle. Your accent is hard to follow. In Hue, when I was in school, we were taught French as it is spoken in France."

"Don't bloody call me *Uncle*, you whore!" he yelled, but in Vietnamese this time. "You say you're from Hue? That's not a Hue accent you've got. I know your type. Vietminh sympathizers every one of you. You might take in these foreigners, but you won't take me in!"

"Foreigners—like your superior officer? I don't think Inspector Vigot would like to hear how you speak of foreigners."

He banged the desk. Papers scattered and the full ashtray tumbled to the floor. She half rose from the chair as he moved towards her, then Fowler and Vigot walked in. Both were solemn, united in some shared sense of decorum. Fowler took her arm and said, "Let's go," and for once she felt relief and safety in his presence.

He kept hold of her as they walked through the corridor and out into the night. They did not speak until they were through the gates onto the deserted street. He would expect her to ask why they had been summoned to the Sûreté, so she asked, "Where is Pyle? What did they want?"

"Come home," he answered. The French quarter's street lights illuminated the rambutan plants falling luxuriantly over the walls of the villas. She saw that they were shedding their deep red fruit, the blood red splashing onto the footpath. The rains will come soon, she realized, her thoughts falling back to the gardens of Cu Chi. She had an impulse to tell this elderly Briton stooping beside her of the childhood he'd never enquired about, to say, I had a home once, when I was young. If she said to him now—Thomas, I am from Cu Chi—all the lies she had told him would unravel. Her impulse to confess to him before the interrogation had been a tactic to gain his support, but he had protected her anyway, and now she could repay him with the gift of her true self.

They stood on the corner of the boulevard. She could not tell him that, and then watch him as Long had ordered. And if she disobeyed, and Fowler betrayed Heng, then he and all his army would be endangered. No, speaking the truth was a luxury she had lost long ago. He must remain blind to who she was.

Even Pyle's apartment, dog-free, would be a refuge of sorts, but she must go with him. Would he betray Heng? If he spoke to her of their contact and of the Chous' place in the Quai Mytho, she would kill him, but with regret, for he had said that she was not for sale as if he believed it. As they walked along, she stooped to pick up a flower fallen from a bougainvillea. It was the vivid yellow of Lan's dress. She caressed the flower, walking slowly, scattering petals along the way as she followed Fowler to what he had called "home."

The echo of his heavy shoes clicking on the marble rebounded hollowly around the empty landing. Had he locked the apartment? She couldn't remember. If so, the lock had been efficiently picked, but the intruders had left their mark in the piles of folded clothes and papers stacked tidily on the desk; having searched, they had been unable to replicate Fowler's squalor. She wondered what they had expected to find. As Fowler flung off his tie and shoes, she noted that he too realized the apartment had been searched, but he said nothing. His hands were at his belt.

"Another pipe?" she offered. Though he didn't answer, she refilled the bowl and lit the lamps as she had done earlier.

He moved towards her to say gently, "*Il est mort.*"

Yes, he is dead, she thought, looking up at Fowler's apprehensive face, both of them complicit, both pretending shock—for all of my life, she thought, I have never been honest with any man. "*Tu dis?*"

"*Pyle est mort. Assassiné.*" She knelt before the low table where the pipe stood and tried to shed the tears he expected. None would flow. She thought of burying her head in her hands, but then he might notice her chewed nails and begin to guess at her fraught weeks with Pyle. No *Cheo* actress able to throw herself about in feigned grief, she stayed silent. As the silence deepened, it seemed best to rise, take up the needle again and finish heating the thickening brown liquid.

CHAPTER 37

That passion may not harm us, let us act as if we had only eight hours to live.
—Pascal

South Vietnam 1967

Commander Chot stands at an empty grave in a small clearing. The fading light obscures the vast grey roots of a banyan tree twisting their way through the red earth as if escaping from the dejected group huddled together. Phuong's comrades stand beneath the tree's tousled canopy, close to her, facing their commander who rubs at his mutilated shoulder while waiting. He is ill at ease; even in these circumstances, it is difficult for him to hand out praise, as he is required to do in his funeral oration. He glowers at Kha, whose face is shaped by anguish. Few return after a burial mass is conducted in their honor prior to their mission. Kha begged to go with her, but Chot told him he is too inexperienced, a liability. Phuong's chances of infiltrating the training center at Trung Hoa are greater without him. This is likely to be the final time he will see her.

Chot speaks too quickly, as if he can wring emotion away by tumbling words one after another. "Let us bury comrade Phuong with full honors. She has been a fighter since her childhood and injured many times. Each time, she has shrugged off her wounds and returned to the fight. She won the Military Exploit Order, second class, for her extreme bravery and determination when facing the enemy. She is a soldier of great resourcefulness, who has never hesitated to engage the enemy—when prudent to do so."

Typical Chot, thinks Phuong, turning to smile at Ngoc, who holds her baby in her arms. He can't avoid a little lecture. Even my funeral has to be a training session. Ngoc tries to return her smile, lips quivering, and

The Quiet Soldier

her expression quizzical, as if she wants to ask, how can you smile when you'll probably die before the night is done? Ngoc has her baby and a husband somewhere. Not Nam, though it is pleasant to dream of having a sister-in-law. Friends she has, but no family. Parents dead, Lan dead, Nam lost forever. She found no cousins, aunts, or uncles, when, after training in the north, she was at last sent to Cu Chi.

The Briton came into her mind, the man with the unnerving blue eyes. Fowler, who never wanted to go home. He kept his secret, never revealed his own part in the assassination of that first American, never betrayed Heng—never so much as breathed his name, so there had been no reason to kill him. And at some point, she had ceased wanting to. Her hand had been on her knife as she kissed him for the last time, but she'd never drawn it. He had remained human by choosing her side, though he never knew it was *her* side. She walked out that day, after he waved a letter in her face. "Here's your happy ending," he said, as if there was such a thing.

It was the end of wearing silk scarves, splendid *ao dai*, and eating her fill, but the beginning of fighting cleanly. She surveys her comrades as Chot lists the battles she has fought in. She tries to picture them in the fine broad boulevards of Saigon—Ngoc with milk leaking from her left breast onto her fustian tunic, Kha with odd shoes and caked dirt on his face and arms. And Chot—he least of all could cling to the pole as she did for years. He carries his revolutionary fervor openly like a peasant balancing buckets of fish from his shoulders. He talks of her battles, but she fought hardest before he ever met her, and no one gave her medals for those squalid fleshly struggles.

Her eyes are drawn to the grave over which Chot's shadow falls. It's badly dug, too close to the banyan, so that the diggers soon found themselves thwarted by the tree's pervasive roots. No matter; the hole is symbolic, a last opportunity to pay their respects to her as a fighter, since they all know that, if she dies in the American camp, her body will not return. *A soldier's death* was how the American's parents were told Pyle died. She was glad when she heard that, since it confirmed his combat role. A soldier should not be surprised the enemy kill him.

She's calmer than she's ever been before battle. She feels like a bird that has been trapped in a room. Having beaten her wings against the closed glass, suddenly a window is open, and she can fly away. Ngoc begins to sing of Cu Chi "our heroic land."

Not everyone could make it to the ceremony. Dr Tin has to operate on a severely wounded soldier, brought in with abdominal wounds and a gangrenous leg, slimy and green and bare to the bone. The surgeon, two nurses and Day, who is cycling the generator, are beneath in the tunnels. One of the nurses is the young girl who wets herself when the B52s drop their bombs. She was raised tenderly and will be a suitable wife for the surgeon, despite her frailties.

Phuong looks again at each of her comrades in turn, trying to fix her memories of her only family. Tha'm gone, never seen again after their harsh words on the roof, Heng's little army dispersed, Long still in Saigon, now in command of the whole city. She remembers the time, not far from where she stands now, when he grabbed her round the waist, scooped her up as if she weighed nothing, and sat her on his lap. He kissed her on the cheek. *Little Phuong, how lovely you are.* She draws a deep breath, inhaling the sweetness of Cu Chi. The earth, the blood-red soil, home.

SUGGESTED READING

A number of chapter epigraphs come from fine works written about the conflict in Vietnam. In particular the author would heartily recommend the following:

Appy, Christian G. *Vietnam: The Definitive Oral History Told From All Sides*, (Britain, Ebury, 2006).

Chanoff, David & Doan Van Toai. *Portrait of the Enemy*, (London, Tauris, 1986).

Herr, Michael. *Dispatches*, (New York, Vintage, 1991).

Marr, David.G. *Vietnam 1945: The Quest for Power*, (California, University of California, 1997).

Mangold, Tom & John Penycate. *The Tunnels of Cu Chi*, (Britain, Cassell, 1985).

Weist, Andrew, ed. *Rolling Thunder in a Gentle Land: the Vietnam War Revisited*, (Britain, Osprey, 2006).

Wolff, Tobias. *In Pharaoh's Army: Memories of a Lost War* (Britain: Bloomsbury, 1994).

ABOUT THE AUTHOR

Creina Mansfield was born in Bristol, England in December 1949. She was named after one of Queen Elizabeth the Queen Mother's ladies in waiting, according to her own mother who worked at Buckingham Place. She is married and has two grown up sons and a grandson. A teacher, she has degrees from Cambridge and Manchester Universities. She has published seven works of fiction for young people, some of which have been translated into French, German, Portuguese, Italian, and Danish. Her special interests are the modern novel and the theory of narrative structure. She lives in Cheshire with her husband and their dogs and cats.